IT NEEDS TO LOOK LIKE WE TRIED

IT NEEDS TO LOOK LIKE WE TRIED

A NOVEL

TODD ROBERT PETERSEN

COUNTERPOINT
Berkeley, California

It Needs to Look Like We Tried

First hardcover edition: 2018

This book is a work of fiction. Names, characters, places, and incidents are the product of the author's imagination or are used fictitiously. Any resemblance to actual events is unintended and entirely coincidental.

Library of Congress Cataloging-in-Publication Data
Names: Petersen, Todd Robert, author.
Title: It needs to look like we tried : a novel / Todd Robert Petersen.
Description: Berkeley, CA : Counterpoint Press, [2018]
Identifiers: LCCN 2017050415 | ISBN 9781640090651 (hardcover)
Subjects: LCSH: Interpersonal relations—Fiction. | Failure (Psychology)—Fiction. | Life change events—Fiction.
Classification: LCC PS3616.E84263 I85 2018 | DDC 813/.6—dc23
LC record available at https://lccn.loc.gov/2017050415

Jacket designed by Nicole Caputo
Book designed by Jordan Koluch

COUNTERPOINT
2560 Ninth Street, Suite 318
Berkeley, CA 94710
www.counterpointpress.com

Printed in the United States of America
Distributed by Publishers Group West

10 9 8 7 6 5 4 3 2 1

Für Alisa

IT NEEDS TO LOOK LIKE WE TRIED

1

The Impeccable Driver

Doyle got an early start. Nothing in that motel would make a person want to linger: loud wall-mounted AC, brittle sheets, heavy polyester blankets, and a prime view of an eastern Arizona frontage road. Behind that were undulating utility lines and a tan haze. Then, open horizon.

He left the on-ramp with a bland breakfast sandwich squatting in his belly and half a thing of purple Gatorade swirling in its bottle. Ten minutes later, Doyle was bored of his music, bored of the unchanging landscape, bored of the whole trip. He was even bored of the wedding he was driving to, a wedding that was still two days away. But the groom was his father, so there was no way out of it.

When he gassed up at a truck stop on the east side of Winslow, Doyle decided his real problem was the interstate which had all the charm of a tract home. He leaned against a white steel pipe that seemed like it was once an important part of something but now stuck out of the ground and pointed at the plain blue sky. He took out his phone and tapped, then swiped and pinched a map. A trucker in cutoff sweatpants and a Pittsburgh Steelers cap stopped alongside Doyle with a giant mug of soda in each hand and a disapproving look on his face.

"Government tracks your phone, brother," he said.

Doyle scrunched up his face subconsciously. "Excuse me," he said.

"All your locational data goes to a building in Utah. They can use it against you in court. Ain't constitutional, but nobody cares."

"Okay," Doyle said. "Thanks."

"Digital money. Digital maps. Digital porn. Brother, once you insert yourself into the grid, you don't ever come out."

"I'll be careful," Doyle said.

"You'll be dead," the trucker said, laughing.

Doyle squinted at him and wanted to run away, but he was trapped by the steel pipe.

"Seriously, though," the trucker said. "Those itty-bitty little phone maps aren't hardly accurate." He started walking. "Follow me."

Doyle stayed put, nervous to follow this guy anywhere. *What if he was a serial killer?* It was broad daylight, though, and his truck was right here in the open.

"Fear not, I promise not to eat your liver. I got a couple of paper maps I'm not using. And I don't feel good about having you drive the interstate with that thing in your hand," he said, pointing to his phone.

Doyle agreed and followed the trucker, who exposed most of his butt climbing into the cab. He rifled around the space and threw two maps down to him: one of Arizona, another of all the western states.

"Won't you need these?" Doyle asked.

"I know where I'm going. I'm not so sure about you, friend."

Doyle went back into the gas station, got a cup of ice, and unfolded the map. He looked at the route he'd planned for himself back in Texas, thought about how much he hated it all, and without trying to control things, he let his imagination drift across the paper.

AT FLAGSTAFF, AS PART OF his new plan, he left the interstate by disappearing into the ponderosas. The road took him through a narrow canyon full of trees and hairpin turns. A smile uncurled across Doyle's face. On his phone, he thumbed away from the "Dad's Wedding" playlist and hit the shuffle button. First song: Van Halen, "Panama." Next thing he knew, his Gatorade was gone, the bottle tossed in the back. The pines gave way to oaks, which gave way to the red rock amphitheaters of old cowboy matinees, which transitioned to a view of open desert.

He crossed the red mesas and ramparts of Sedona quickly, then climbed out of the valley, and wound through the old mining town of Jerome. After that, more pines, more songs, ELO, Pearl Jam, U2. He was in a flow state: not thinking about work, not thinking about his father's wedding, not thinking about being in his thirties, not even thinking about eating a whole bag of red Twizzlers Bites until it was empty, crumpled, and thrown over his shoulder.

The animal appeared and exploded against his bumper in the same instant. Doyle's car screamed to a stop. "Bullet the Blue Sky" roared in the sudden silence. He pulled the auxiliary cord out of his phone and quiet filled the air around him.

Doyle glanced behind to see if any cars were coming, then he checked the state of the car's interior: things were scattered everywhere. He yanked the parking brake, threw open his door, and scrambled out to investigate.

Thirty feet behind the car, a small, white-and-tan straight-haired dog lay perpendicular to the center line, its legs splayed in all directions. Doyle stepped closer and crouched. The dog's eyes were wide open, a small pool of blood collecting under its belly and running toward the far side of the road. Otherwise the creature was in shock.

The desert air seared Doyle's skin, sweat evaporating before it could bead up on his brow. He braced his hands against the waistband of his jeans and slowly bent over to quell the waves of nausea filling his body.

He twisted around, looking past a phone booth that stood monolithically against the sky. Beyond that, there wasn't much in his field of vision but some old forklift pallets and a cloud of dust lifting in the desert wind. The sun burned on Doyle's forehead while he paced the length of his rear bumper.

"Eighteen accident-free years on the road, and then you," he said, pointing at the dog, who tried to lift its head. The struggle was too much, so it lay back down and looked up at Doyle, who would not look back.

Doyle tried to comfort himself, thinking back to the days when his father taught him the "rules of the road." *You have to keep three things in mind when you put a vehicle on the road, son. One, the size of your rig versus the size of the road you've got it on. Two, the size of the other guy's rig versus the size of the road you're sharing with him. And three, the size of his rig versus the size of yours.*

They were fine rules in the abstract, but they had nothing to do with the unpredictability of an animal. Doyle stooped a little to see if he could understand the condition the dog was in. It stared straight into the desert now, like it couldn't bear to look at Doyle or his car. Doyle was close enough now to the dog to hear its wet, labored breathing. He squatted down, and when it didn't flinch, he put his hand out. When it didn't growl, he stroked the bridge of its nose with his thumb and forefinger.

This dog was a goner. Doyle knew it, and it seemed like the dog knew it, too. There was no scenario in which he could drive away and live with the decision. If he had a gun with him, this could just be over. But he had no gun; in this he had broken with the traditions of his family.

Before, Doyle's mind was blank; now he was thinking about everything at once. The dog, his life, this trip, his dad, and his dad's fiancée. He thought about Santa Barbara, where he'd never been before, his mother, dead now for half his life. He was thinking about how kids don't go to their parent's wedding. It's all in the wrong order. Sure the old guy was lonely. Doyle also felt like he had to get out of Texas before he went stir-crazy. Then out of nowhere he thought about how death gives people a free pass.

Doyle watched and waited for something else to happen, but nothing in the scene changed. A vastness settled over everything. He noticed an abandoned town that was pretty much the same color as everything else. He looked toward his car and walked over to see if there was any damage. There wasn't. He stared into the distance, and, as far as he could see in each direction, there was nobody coming or going.

He walked over to the dog and knelt again, cupping his hand in front of its nose. He then reached across the head and stroked the ear. This time, when he touched the animal, it started to seize. Doyle stood quickly and stepped back. The dog made rapid rasping barking noises and thrashed about. Its tags tinkled on the pavement, then its eyes rolled up, and its mouth snapped like a windup monster. After another thirty seconds of thrashing, the dog went still.

Again, the air filled with the silence of the world unspooling. Doyle

"Quit," he hollered at the crows.

The phone rang again.

"Git!" he yelled, covering the mouthpiece.

One crow hopped up onto Princess's body and started tugging at the hair on her belly. The phone rang two more times. "Go on, get away!" he shouted, then threw the tags at the birds. But when he raised his hand, they flapped off, and the tags just clinked onto the pavement. The phone rang again, then someone lifted the receiver. The crows flew up and settled back on the crossbar of the power pole.

A woman's voice said hello.

"Uh, yes, my name is Doyle, Doyle Mattson."

"What can I do for you, Mr. Mattson?" The woman had slight drawl, which reminded him of home.

"Well, I . . . uh, have bad news. Really bad news, I think."

"Excuse me," she said.

Doyle turned back over his shoulder. The crows were still up on their perch.

"Do you all have a dog named Princess? White and tan—I don't know—about two feet or so tall?"

"Where is she?"

"Well, I'm here—in . . ." Doyle looked around and saw the faded black letters CONGRESS, ARIZONA painted on a sign that had fallen to the ground. "We're here—in Congress, I think."

"Where?"

"Congress . . . Arizona."

"Oh, of course, that's right. Thank you," the woman said. "She's been gone for close to a week."

He gripped his forehead as the event replayed in his head: empty road, U2, Twizzlers, some kind of ghost town, dog, impact, brakes, seizures, rock, phone call.

"Mr. Mattson?" the woman asked.

"I'm sorry."

"Do you have the dog with you?"

"I do." He glanced out at the Nissan.

"Well, if you have her, then what's the—oh no," she said, her voice faltering.

In his peripheral vision, Doyle saw the crows land on the road and hop onto the dog.

"Hey!" he shouted, lowering the phone then immediately raising it back up. "Can you excuse me for a moment?" Doyle ran toward the crows, screaming and waving his arms. One of them was pecking at the dog's face.

"Go on! Hyah, hyah!" he yelled, kicking gravel at the birds. They flapped toward the furthest houses, cawing and crisscrossing in the air. Doyle stood over the body until he was sure they were gone. Then he grabbed the dog's collar and dragged the body across the gravel, trying not to drop his phone.

"Sorry," he said.

"You're in Congress?" she asked. "That's not really a place."

"I gathered," Doyle said.

There was a pause, then Doyle heard the woman's breathing speed up and deepen. "But you're close," she said.

"I'm sorry. She just came out of nowhere," he explained. "I didn't mean to hit her. Ma'am, usually I'm an impeccable driver."

At first it seemed reasonable to offer to bring the dog home, reasonable for about a minute. By the time he knew what he was saying, he regretted not leaving Princess to the crows. Nobody saw him; nobody would have known. Dogs get killed all the time. It's nothing strange. The world keeps turning.

But Doyle felt the pull of a deep, unexplainable code to do the right thing even when it was the most ridiculous choice. Doyle was an impeccable driver and an Eagle Scout to the core. The accident shocked him because he didn't see it at the time, but he could replay it clearly in his memory. The dog materialized in the middle of the road, hovering in front of him on an invisible pad of heat wash.

Despite it all, the hardest thing for him to admit was that he cared more about his personal driving record then he cared about the dog. Driving always exacts a price. *Every road requires a toll.* His father had said that years ago, when they'd come across a red-tailed hawk obliterated on a county road outside their home in Bushland, and Doyle wept shamefully. Power always has a cost, and the person with power is never the one who pays the fee.

So, with a sigh, Doyle offered to bring the dog home, and the woman accepted. She gave him directions to her house, which was only five miles south of this little town at the end of another mile of dirt road. He made her repeat the directions twice, then he hung up and tied Princess awkwardly to the top of the Nissan with some old twine he kept in the trunk.

As he pulled away from Congress, the sun was still high in the west. Other houses past the service station were just as run-down, but they hunkered closer together and didn't look as forlorn. Doyle adjusted his lumbar support and glanced down at the empty Gatorade bottles and hamburger bags on the floor.

On the west edge of town, he came to a four-way stop. There was still no traffic, but as he was turning off the highway, he saw someone peek over the edge of a roof. Whoever it was watched him drive through the intersection. He thought he was alone, but apparently he was wrong about that.

Doyle had no idea how he would present Princess to her owner. When Doyle's mother lost her teacup poodle, Mr. Buttons, it had been his brother's fault. He had left the sliding glass door open, though they had been formally cautioned time and time again of the consequences. Mr. Buttons weaseled his way out onto the back patio and got himself killed by a rattlesnake.

Doyle found Mr. Buttons in the backyard. The little dog was puffed up like a pool toy. A torpid snake, its jaw unhinged, was trying to swallow one of the dog's hind legs. The whole scene was pathetic, but in a certain way, he was proud that Mr. Buttons had bought the farm with some dignity. Of course, Doyle had no idea what to say to his mother. He and Kenny were just kids and couldn't know that a rattler would go for a poodle. Doyle was absolutely certain they could not use a direct approach. He also knew that it was Kenny's problem, so he behaved as if nothing had happened. But that night his old man found the dog while he was cleaning the barbecue grill. Doyle saw it happen and ran downstairs to find Kenny, who was playing video games in the family room.

All he said was, "Play dumb, man. Listen up, Kenny. You . . . don't . . . know . . . anything." When their father came downstairs with Mr. Buttons's rhinestone-studded collar in his hand, he shook it at the boys, saying, "Mr. Buttons turned up snake bait in the backyard, and it wasn't me who left the door open." Doyle and Kenny looked up, blinking their innocence. "The snake's in the freezer under some deer steaks, so your mother doesn't have to know anything about that part of it, you hear?"

Doyle and Kenny nodded.

"I buried that damn curly-haired son of a bitch out in the side yard by the rosebushes where he can earn his keep." Their old man cocked his head and eyeballed each one of them in turn. "And she doesn't need to know about that either. Y'all better come up with something good to tell your mother, because it's TV dinners until she's over this."

Kenny started crying.

"Oh look, the little sissy's bawling," their old man said, then he shifted his attention to Doyle. "See that he doesn't mess this up. I won't fix this any more than I already did."

Doyle nodded.

Kenny shuddered when the door slammed, but he immediately started sniffing and pacing, saying, "Oh, Mama, I'm sorry about Mr. Buttons," like an incantation that would get rid of the mistake. Kenny kept at it, moaning and thrashing across the room, rehearsing variations of his sorrow.

After a few minutes, he bolted out of the room.

Doyle watched from around the corner of the entryway as Kenny flailed himself like a monk and fell into his mother's arms, begging forgiveness. At first she didn't know what he was talking about, but eventually she pieced together "Buttons," "door," "Mister," "forgot," and "disappeared." But Kenny was such a mess that her maternal instinct quashed her grief, and she took to stroking Kenny out of his hysterics. It was like magic. Even that young, Kenny was the Houdini of family relations.

Doyle wondered if he could manage to bow and scrape enough like Kenny to steer away this woman's grief. Probably not. But all he needed was a quick distraction so he could make his getaway.

"Oh, ma'am," he began, turning off the music so he could practice his confession, "I'm sorry about Princess. I know she must have meant the whole world to you. I can't believe that I—she just—I don't know what to say—it was all so . . . stupid." Doyle slammed the flat of his hand against the steering wheel. "This is stupid. I am stupid," he shouted to himself. "The fleabag was probably as rabid as a preacher anyway." He kept on driving. The ground was littered with stone and yucca. Everything was washed-out: the sky white with heat, the clouds still threatening.

He slowed when he turned onto the single-lane dirt road. There was only a scattering of houses in the distance, all of which looked abandoned. He kept forging on, gripping the wheel at two and ten. He turned on the radio, but getting static, he switched it back off and stared over the steering wheel. He still had no idea what he would say, and he was oblivious to the four turkey vultures falling into position behind him.

WHEN HE PULLED UP IN front of the house, the woman was waiting for him. She sat in the shade on the top step of a rickety porch, her head wilting into her hands. She didn't look up as he crept along the driveway, but stayed slumped, her shoulders twitching.

Doyle parked the Nissan behind the woman's truck, put on his game face, and got out. The woman raised her head but didn't stand. Doyle steeled and then forced himself toward the house. The woman was not particularly old, perhaps thirty-five, maybe forty. She had Southern hair, all teased up and sprayed. Her makeup was theatrical, and she wore a denim cowboy shirt with pearly plastic snaps and half-moon cutouts right above the pockets. Her red jeans were tight through the thighs and boot cut. Doyle had seen plenty of country girls like this.

"Mr. Mattson, that's not . . ." She swallowed hard. ". . . up there, is it?" she asked, covering her mouth with one hand. Doyle nodded, then went to the back of his car and began to untie the dog. The car trip and the coagulating blood had pulled the skin on Princess's lip back into a snarl. Her fur had stiffened and separated into gills.

"Ma'am, I'll get her down right away," Doyle said, tugging at the mess of rope. The knots were tight, and he was having some trouble getting them undone. Doyle fooled with the twine for a while, then, exhausted by the process, took out his Swiss Army knife and cut the cord free. He put the knife back and took the dog by her collar and slid her off the roof with his hand under the rump. He brought Princess to the step just below the woman's feet, set the body down, and stepped over to the rail. The woman's perfume stung his throat.

Quietly, she leaned over.

"I'm so sorry, ma'am. I was just on my way to my dad's wedding in Santa Barbara, and she just came at me out of nowhere. I didn't have . . ."

The woman crouched and quietly smoothed down the dog's ear with a hand that was capped with perfectly manicured red fingernails. Doyle waited for the woman to burst out crying, but she didn't. She just kept cursing over and over while she stroked its ear.

"Ma'am," Doyle said.

She looked up. He expected mascara to be everywhere, but she looked fine.

"Ma'am. Princess ran right out in front of me. I didn't see her. If I had, it would be a different story, honest. It was just, smack, like that, and the next thing I knew, I'd hit her. I'm sorry, I'm so . . ."

The woman looked at Doyle's car, then sized him up, flipped her hair, and managed a smile. "There's a lot of sons a bitches in this world, Mr. Mattson, who would have kept on driving."

Doyle was surprised, which made him want to look away. When he eventually met her gaze, the woman was nodding and staring him right in the eyes, her lashes caked in mascara.

"Mr. Mattson," she said, "I have to say that I am proud to know you. You had every reason in the world to keep going and make it to that wedding, but you didn't."

Doyle scratched his head and looked at his feet. "Ma'am?" he asked.

"That's enough. We both know you could have drove off, but you didn't. Something blew you my way."

She looked at him like she knew something about him. Something he was just about to discover on his own.

"Since you're here," she said, smiling, "do you think you could—if it's not too much trouble—do you think you could . . . help . . . me bury Princess? Doc would want her close to . . . the house. I'm mostly alone these days. And no good with tools." She drew a deep breath and let it sigh out dramatically. "You know how it is."

Oh Lord, Doyle thought, trying not to bug his eyes out in surprise. He stared down without trying to seem like he was looking away, and he saw the woman stroking the dog's fur with the knuckle of her forefinger.

The "old inch and mile" is how his old man put it. "Never agree with a woman," he used to say. "You can do what she wants—in the long run it's less trouble for you to do it that way in the first place—but you can't agree with her, not out loud."

"Ma'am," he said before he could stop himself.

"Quit it," she said.

In his mind, he had taken himself by the shirt collar and the seat of his pants and was carrying himself toward the Nissan, but the Eagle Scout inside him said: "Show me where to take her."

The woman rose, smoothing out her jeans, pressing her painted lips together and peeling them apart. "Mr. Mattson," she said, "would you please call me CJ?" She grinned slightly and winked at him. "All this ma'aming makes me sound like somebody's mother."

"Well, you're certainly not my mother," Doyle replied.

"That is the truth in almost every way you can think about it."

"Okay then, CJ," he said, reluctantly. "Where does your dog go?"

"It's not my dog," she said.

Doyle froze, with a weird look on his face and one eyebrow cocked.

"It belonged to my husband," she said. "And now we're free—now she's free from the troubles of this world," she said, placing a hand on her stomach. "There's a shovel against the back door. I'll be out in a tick to show you where you can put that thing to rest."

THE BACKYARD WAS MOSTLY DIRT and cinders. Three or four cottonwood trees grew in a circle around the area directly behind the house, but it was not much of a place anyone in their right mind would call a yard, not the kind of place anyone with good sense would choose to live. Out where the dirt stopped, desert grass started toward the Mojave in loose tan bunches. In the distance, Doyle could see dark tongues of rain lolling here and there in the wind. To his left, an old, badly painted barn leaned west with its doors half open. Inside was the unblinking passenger's-side headlight of a broken-down International Harvester pickup and some large plastic-covered hoops dangling from the rafters.

Doyle set Princess down and wondered what CJ did with herself this far into the middle of nowhere. He knew people got stuck, and home is home no matter how ugly it is. Doyle surveyed the yard again, shaking his head. He shuddered, then his eye fell on another fly that had homed in on Princess and was buzzing around her head. *Poor dog*, he thought to himself, wondering how long before the coyotes would skulk in from the scrub and scratch her carcass out of the ground. Wasted work.

"Mr. Mattson," CJ called out.

Doyle jumped so sharply that he tripped over Princess and fell to the ground. The fly buzzed a quick lap around the three of them, then landed again on the dog's face. Doyle looked up at CJ, who was carrying a tall glass of iced tea.

"Are you okay?"

"I'm fine," Doyle said. "Sorry again, about all this."

"Nonsense, a whole lot of business got itself resolved today. You think you might want a little something," she said, wiping condensation from the glass tumbler with a folded dish towel, "what with all this thirsty work I've tricked you into." She smiled. Her teeth were so perfectly aligned that, for a second, Doyle thought she might be wearing dentures.

"I haven't really started, but a little something sounds nice," he said, climbing to his feet. He took the glass and dragged it across his forehead, then drank the sweet tea until the ice clinked against his teeth and the glass was empty. The cold made his teeth ache.

"Wow," CJ said, taking the glass from him. "I'll have to go back inside and fill this up again." When she said it, she took the glass and ran the bottom edge of it along the bare skin inside the half-moon cutouts of her cowboy blouse. Doyle watched as she continued to run the glass back and forth until the fabric darkened from the condensation. He looked away before anything else came up.

Her words from before sunk into the base of his skull as if shot from a bow: "I'm mostly alone these days. You know how it is."

"Yeah, I suppose. Where should I dig?" he asked.

She walked over to a spot away from the house and traced a rectangle with her boot heel. Then, as suddenly as she'd appeared, she spun around and sashayed back into the house. Doyle blinked for a while at the spot where CJ had been standing, then he shook his head.

Doyle's work crept along. Every third stroke Doyle would knock the shovel blade against another stone, stop, forearm another ounce of sweat from his brow, then pry the stone out by digging under it and leaning on the shovel's handle until the rock popped out of place, which he would then heft into the weeds. Then he'd start digging again. At this pace, it took him the better part of an hour to chip a hole that was just deep enough for the task. When he finished, Doyle set Princess mechanically into the grave and began shoveling the orange dirt on top of her body.

As the dirt puffed lightly on the dog's fur, Doyle felt a strange swimming in his throat, and he thought for a moment that he might have been poisoned. All he wanted was to finish and get in his car and get back on the interstate. All the cars would be headed in the same direction. There would be Shell stations and truck stops full of beer and Dr Pepper and pay phones. He could call the motel in Santa Barbara and let his father and his fiancée know he was a little bit off schedule, but not to worry. He'd make the rehearsal in time. Nothing would be ruined.

He'd get a Whopper and double the fries and soak into the soothing sameness of I-10. He'd go back to the playlist and pick up where he left off, and he'd wait for the Milky Way to materialize somewhere between Blythe and Indio. He'd be able to see it fine from behind the wheel.

But as the loose soil settled in around the dog's profile, he began to postulate about the afterlife and consider karma, his and the dog's. Could a right action correct a wrong action, or were all deeds written indelibly into the past? Did they just stack up and pass away forever, turtles all the way down? Above his head, an insect started buzzing. As he tossed in the last shovel of earth, Doyle wondered if the occasion didn't require some kind of ceremony. Then he instantly regretted the thought.

When Doyle's mother died, family flocked to Texas from as far away as West Virginia. She'd been struck with breast cancer that leached into her lungs and esophagus. The treatments were severe, and her death came quickly. Doyle was sixteen and had been a licensed driver for only a month when she passed away. As the family called with their itineraries, his father instructed him to run shuttle trips to the airport in Amarillo: seven trips that day, and three of them in the dark.

"Why, Doyle," they'd say clutching him to their breasts, "where's your daddy at?"

"At home," he'd say back to them.

"Poor man," they'd say, "too broke up to even drive into town. Maybe we should rent a cab."

"I can drive," Doyle said, holding up the car keys. "Got a ninety-three on my test. The man said I was an impeccable driver. Told me that to my face."

This made the relatives cry again, right in the terminal with passengers struggling to get past them with their luggage and squabbling children. Doyle would point and start to say something about letting people by, but they would grab him up again and crush him and call him a good boy, stroking his hair. By the seventh trip, the back of his head was slicked like a greaser's. Doyle never squirmed or complained about the treatment, because, even at sixteen, he took his family's grief like a man, without flinching.

At the funeral, Doyle sat quietly in the front row of folding chairs in the funeral home. People knew his mother was sick, and Doyle himself was glad she had passed on. He knew he'd miss her, but even then, he knew that living and dying weren't ultimately in his control. *Maybe if I leave God's business to Him*, he hoped, *He'll leave me to mine.* It never occurred to him to think otherwise.

After the pastor said his piece and Doyle's father said his, the relatives began filing past the open coffin, clutching handkerchiefs. They were all crying and snuffling. He thought their behavior was just to prove that they felt bad, but when a hand would linger on the frilled edge of the coffin lining, or when he could see one of his uncle's beer bellies tremble with grief, it would occur to Doyle that perhaps he had the wrong idea, that maybe he should be crying, too, that somehow his reservation to do so meant that he did not love his mother as much as it was possible to love. Even his brother was crying, dragging his arm across his cheek to mop up the tears, and it was real this time. But Doyle didn't feel like that. He couldn't manage it. As the line of weeping relatives swept past him, he wondered if there wasn't something monstrously wrong with him.

Finally, the line dwindled. Doyle had been hanging his head and didn't notice that the room was mostly empty until his father "pssst"ed in his ear and pushed him out of his chair toward the casket. His mother lay still, with her arms crossed over her chest just as Doyle would have expected her to be, but her lips seemed as if they were drawn too tightly together. They were thinner than normal and strange to look at, like two caterpillars stretched across the teeth. Doyle glanced back over his shoulder and his father was hugging some woman. Seeing that it was clear, Doyle carefully poked at his mother's lips. They were cold and tight, and as he tried to lift the top lip, he discovered that they were sewn shut.

He recoiled and looked back at the few relatives left in the room. They were crying on one another's shoulders. Doyle felt that there was something wrong with sewing up a dead woman's lips, so he fished in his pocket for his Swiss Army knife, folded out the scissors, and snipped the thread away. As he did, the flesh relaxed a little, and Doyle pursed the lips together by squeezing at the sides as his mother had often done to him. When he did, he noticed a gap in her teeth. Doyle stopped, wiped his hand against his suit pants and then shifted his position a little in order to hide his actions. Then, glancing briefly again over his shoulder, he thrust his forefinger into his mother's mouth, pried the jaw down, and looked into the gap. His mother's gold tooth was gone.

Doyle pulled his finger back out and closed the mouth by pressing upward on the underside of her jaw. Slowly, he turned around, and in the far corner of the room he spotted the mortician's assistant, standing pale and skinny with his back to the wall.

The relatives kept crying and hugging his dad and little brother. Doyle took three or four deep breaths to control himself while trying to think of some way to break this news to his father.

DOYLE WHAPPED THE DIRT WITH the backside of the shovel to make sure Princess at least looked like she was covered. It was five thirty, and the sun was tangled in the cottonwoods. He'd be late, but he would still have enough time to find where he was going, get some sleep and a shower before Kenny found him and the rehearsal started up. His father was marrying a motor-mouthed real estate agent from Santa Barbara who was in her late forties at best. Her name was Bonnie Jo, and she wouldn't let you call her by anything but both names.

The whole situation was upsetting, but not in an exceptional way. It was just generally upsetting. Doyle turned around and stared into the windows of the house and found nothing. It didn't seem right to just leave, so Doyle walked around to the side of the house and peered up to the front yard, finding nothing. He wondered if he should holler but decided against it and tried the other side of the house. He felt like a kid again, looking for his mother down the aisles of a supermarket. After a minute or so of searching, Doyle crossed the yard to one of the scroungy trees near the place he'd been working, and he leaned the shovel against it. Behind a clump of higher grass, Doyle spotted what seemed to be a headstone. *Good Lord*, he thought, then looking nervously over his shoulder, he stared harder, wiping his wrist along his upper lip. It was. Some person was buried out there. The dirt was loose, fresh, recently worked.

"Oh, no, she didn't," Doyle muttered, twisting back toward the house. His pulse was at full throttle. "Nope," he said out loud, and then turned back to face the headstone. "No, no, no, no, no," he said, stepping forward. The stone was waist-high and read:

ROSCOE "DOC" JASPER

1953–2016

LOVED BY MANY

REST IN PEACE

Doyle stood up quickly and fell back a few steps, then looked over at the fresh grave that held the dog's corpse. He turned to the left side of the house, and then, as if trying to come to his senses, he stopped and turned back to the grave, then stopped again, trying to choose a course of action.

"Doyle," CJ called out of nowhere.

He jumped and clutched his chest to keep his heart from squirming onto the ground.

"You look like you seen a ghost," she said.

He bent over with his hands on his knees, sucking air and shaking his head.

"Is Princess all safe and buried?" she said.

"What? No. Safe?" Doyle said, glancing back at the grave. "It's done. She's all . . . right there. Your shovel's against that tree. I've got to get—"

"Doyle, I've set you back on your schedule, haven't I?" She smiled and peeled her lips apart. "I thought that after all this work you must be starving, so I fixed you a little something—"

"No, really, I need to get to Santa Barbara." Doyle stopped trying to hide the alarm on his face. "I sidetracked myself on my big adventure, and I really need to get back on the freeway and make up for some lost time."

"Well, you need to eat, honey, and I've got all these leftovers from the wake just waiting to go bad. It's chicken and dumplings, and I can't eat it all before it spoils."

Doyle shut his mouth and surrendered with a weak, fluttering gesture of consent.

CJ HAD THE ANTIQUE OAK table decked out in linens. It was candlelit and full of food: a bowl of peas and pearl onions, steaming-hot biscuits, a cherry pie, German potato salad with dill and hard-boiled eggs, a casserole dish full of baked chicken, and more than a dozen dumplings the size of limes in a thick, tan gravy flecked with black pepper. A boat of even more gravy was on the side, bobbing with bits of heart meat and giblet. There was also a pitcher of lemonade and two glasses of rich, white whole milk that looked like cream. CJ snatched a dish towel from the counter and walked over to the casserole dish, picked it up, and waved it right underneath Doyle's nose.

"Now, I know it might be a little heavy, but Doc's family is Southern folks, and that's how they do a spread." She smiled coyly, then blinked twice.

Doyle stroked the bridge of his nose and asked if there was someplace he could wash his hands. CJ smiled and pointed him down the hall.

"Hurry up, so it doesn't get cold," she called after him.

Doyle dragged himself through the archway into the hall and to the first open door he came to. He muttered as he went inside and leaned over the sink. He turned on the faucet and splashed cold water onto his face. He checked his watch again: five fifty. "This is ridiculous," he muttered. "I'm a better driver than this." Doyle stretched the back of his legs by leaning over as far as he could while clutching the edge of the sink with both hands like he'd been struck suddenly with a fever. He tried to figure a graceful way out, and had none.

He stood and turned off the faucet, dried his face and hands, and prepared himself to survive this meal so he could head off to his old man's wedding. Kenny's company would seem almost normal after the outright insanity of this afternoon, he thought, rehanging the towel. Finally, he thought he'd have a story that would keep up with the lies his brother's army buddies would tell.

A story like this one would make him one of the boys for a few hours, not Kenny's cautious, super-lame older brother. Six hours of driving. Six hours and he'd see the coast, have all this behind him, rolling itself up into a tidy little story like something out of *The Twilight Zone*, good for a laugh, good for showing everyone that he wasn't just a kid anymore.

Doyle closed the bathroom door, mentally preparing himself to swallow the food whole and wipe his face firmly in a single pass before taking to the open road. Down the hall, he could hear CJ singing to herself, the faint din of dishes and utensils clattering in counterpoint.

Time to get this project moving, he thought, trying to fortify himself. *You just eat and dismiss yourself, Doyle. You've got manners and charm. Use 'em.*

He took one step toward the kitchen, then another, and in five strides he covered half the distance. Pausing to get himself together, he noticed a flickering—low and orange—that emanated from the dark living room.

He leaned through a pair of open pocket doors into a giant room, almost completely bare but filled with electric tea lights at every point. He crept across the room toward the far end where there were more tea lights, most set in clusters on the brick mantel in shot glasses, sat flickering. He reached out and pressed his hand across a collage of photographs that ran along the mantel. In each snapshot was a man wearing a black Snap-on tools cap, who was involved in some kind of physical or mechanical task: gutting or presenting a fish, replacing a carburetor, welding. The mantel itself was littered with knickknacks, beaded Indian change purses, an autographed baseball, two or three trophies, a pair of dark metal work spurs, bowie knives, and a fist-sized chunk of dark-gray basalt. On the brick above the mantel, a series of five leather belts with steak-sized brass buckles were mounted like run-over rattlesnakes.

Above them and between two wrought-iron sconces with oil-burning lamps hung a large, professional photographic portrait of the man against a background of aspens in their fall colors. The man's mustache was full and black, his eyebrows heavy as the creases alongside his eyes. He was staring off into the distance past Doyle's head. Doyle stepped back, flushed and disoriented, and below this strange altar he saw that the firebox was backlit somehow and full of boots, which had been arranged precisely against the back wall. A few pairs of wing tips, loafers, and brogans had been lined up in front of the boots like pawns.

The man in the photograph looked across the room exactly the same way that Doyle's old man would stare off over Doyle's head. It reminded him that he was always looking for something so far away that only he knew exactly what it was. He certainly never shared it with Doyle or his brother. There in that strange room in that strange house, Doyle understood that there could be no devotion without love. He wondered about the woman who would memorialize a man in this way. It was crazy and somehow beautiful, unrefined, and real. It showed Doyle that true love, like cheap jewelry, was available to everyone. As he considered this tawdry memorial, Doyle struggled less against the idea that his old man never loved anyone or anything and allowed himself one tiny grain of a thought. Perhaps his father could actually be devoted to this real estate agent from California, maybe even in love.

"Doyle, your supper's getting cold!" CJ called out.

Doyle looked around at the rest of the room. His eyes had adjusted to the dimness and he could see a rocking chair covered in a knit afghan. A single overhead lamp hung down from the ceiling, and the glass shade was full of black specks that looked like they had once been insects. There was no other furniture in the room, but heavy drapes covered the windows.

When CJ called again, Doyle turned and rubbed his eyes. "I'll be right there!" he called out. He went back into the kitchen and sat quietly at the table. His plate was already dished up. He stared down at the fork for a long time before he finally slid it into the dumpling and lifted it from the table. As the delicious gravy-soaked dumpling dissolved in his mouth, Doyle noticed that CJ was beginning to remove her jewelry, unscrewing her rings one at a time and setting them into a saucer next to her plate. Doyle shoveled some peas onto his fork with a slice of bread.

CJ unclasped her watch and set it in the saucer as well.

Doyle forked more potatoes into his mouth.

CJ removed her necklace.

He took up a chicken thigh with his fingers.

She removed her earrings.

A gulp of milk.

And one by one, she undid the buttons of her blouse.

Doyle always guessed that things like this never really happened, not like anyone tells it. Not like the lies Kenny's friends would one-up each other with. These stories were part of the great sham American Dream of eighties porno magazines. Everyone knew it was fake but hoped otherwise. You had to believe these things, because if you didn't, you were voting against yourself. Some very organized and normal guy goes off the beaten track, kills a dog, then buries the dog next to the dead husband. The wife throws him a feast and then starts a strip show. There couldn't be a more normal fantasy in the world. It was like flying out the window of an office building, or finding a bag of money in the snow, or swirling gold dust from a riverbed.

As everything unfolded, Doyle knew no one would believe him, not in a million years. This story would be less credible than somebody's Canadian girlfriend. But the truth is that this woman *did* come across the table at him, and together they did, in fact, push food to the floor. Not all of it, however, not the pie. They carefully set that aside for later. But it all happened.

When the impracticality of doing it on the table became obvious, they moved themselves to the linoleum, which was frigid and dotted with little black ants. When they were back on their feet, kissing with clumsy abandon, CJ pulled Doyle by the hand and guided him to a couch in the front room. After a few minutes' struggle, they left a pile of clothes on the coffee table and fled naked to the bedroom, where the whirlwind ceased as abruptly as it had started.

would not recommend a lowball offer. Annie nearly came unglued. She sat there, clenching and unclenching her jaw and fists. I leaned over to her and whispered, "Hey, he's just doing his job. Let's do ours." Annie straightened up and clicked her pen. She swallowed and nodded her head. I made the offer.

The realtor puckered his lips and lifted his eyebrows. "You're not playing around, are you?"

"Nope," I said.

"First home buyers your age don't usually have finances like this," he said.

"My husband makes blue meth," Annie said calmly but with an edge. "We've got all the money we need."

I grabbed her forearm and smiled. "She's kidding," I said. "I'm just a history teacher. Heh, heh. Not chemistry."

The realtor belly-laughed then slapped the desk. "*Breaking Bad*, right? I love that show. You're not laundering your money in real estate, are you? Ha, ha. Now I guess you'll have to kill me." His jokes didn't break the tension.

I looked at Annie. She stared at the floor and put her hands on her stomach, which domed like a mixing bowl under her sweater.

"Okay," he said. "I'll take your offer to the sellers. I'll text you when we hear back."

THE NEXT DAY, AS WE were getting ready for school, my mother called to invite us to dinner.

"I know it's late notice," she said. "I hope you and Annie can come."

"That's fine," I said. "Is everything okay? You sound weird."

"I'm not weird, Steven," she said.

"I didn't say that. I said you sounded—look, never mind. I think we can. Let me ask Annie and check the calendar. We'll come unless you hear otherwise."

"Is there anything Annie can't eat?" my mother asked.

"She isn't throwing up anymore," I said.

"Oh good. You made me throw up all the time, and I couldn't have chocolate. It was the worst," she said. When I didn't respond, she said, "Oh,

"It's okay, Doyle," CJ said, resting a hand on his chest. "Once we get some pie in you, you can try it again."

And they did try, a couple of times. By the morning, Doyle lay awake in this woman's bed, watching a spider trundle across the ceiling. He looked over at CJ, not expecting her to be awake, but she was watching him without blinking. "Take me with you," she said.

"What?"

"Take me to California."

During the night, Doyle told her everything about his mom and dad, but mostly about Kenny. She listened, with a hand on his arm. She encouraged him to keep talking, and he did. He told her that he'd never done anything like this before. She said it was okay to break the rules when you had to.

"Take me to California," she said again. "You need a date for this wedding, right?"

"They're going to kill me," he said, then lost himself in thought. "And I don't know that I *need* a date," he said. "But it probably wouldn't hurt."

"Take *me*," she said. "I am good at this kind of thing. And you need to show those people you've got a little outlaw inside you they didn't know about."

Doyle sat up and leaned forward, the morning light was cool and blue and filled the room with ghosts. He reached over and dug his phone out of his pants; it was dead.

"The thing is, I'm not an outlaw," Doyle said.

"I am," CJ said, smiling, "and I got enough to spare."

"Can you just up and leave like that?" Doyle asked.

"I'm done with this place," CJ said.

Doyle studied her. Without makeup, she was only about half as pretty as he remembered. Her eyes were the saddest ones he'd ever seen. "You got a dress?" he asked.

"I've got a dress that's so hot, I can't wear it on Sundays."

Doyle stroked his chin, and clenched his whole face.

"Don't think about it, Doyle," she said. "Don't think at all. You don't need to. You already know what you're going to do."

"I do?" Doyle asked.

CJ looked at Doyle without an expression, until he eventually said, "Okay. Let's give them something to talk about."

2

Cape Cod Fear

When I say that the events surrounding the purchase of our first house were a literal horror show, I am not misusing the term. In order to tell the story right, I must begin with mundane details that seem unimportant at first, really these moments seem ridiculous to say out loud. What I mean is that I would not believe this story if I were hearing it. I apologize for that now. It will make sense in the end. I promise.

I am a millennial, and, like most of my generation born in the eighties, I was not interested in owning a home, not at first. We had good reasons for it, mostly centered around watching our boomer parents go weird in front of our eyes. I have read the think pieces, so I know you are thinking this shows how my generation has walked away from our responsibilities to carry the torch along and take our place in the order of things. I know you think I pooh-poohed buying a home because I was broke/single/lazy/living in my parent's basement/making a statement, but that is not true. To be fair, I did spend the first summer after graduation living with my parents and working at the aquatic center, but not in the basement. And I actually had a job teaching history at a Catholic high school in Santa Barbara, my hometown. My contract did not start for three months, and my mother begged me to come home. My little brother had started a legislative internship in Sacramento, and the house was empty. She said with just my father around, the place would be too lonely.

Living at home after college was a kind of regression. I got by understanding that it was short-term and by thinking about making my mother happy. The silver lining to everything was my aquatic center, which is where I met my wife, Annie, who came laps at eleven o'clock every morning. By July, I had learned that also a teacher at St. Jude's, where I would be working in a month. tember, we both knew that this was not a temporary arrangement, many of our generation, we did not see marriage as a necessary part "together." Behind it all were the wicked questions we would never with each other: What if we were wrong about this relationship? this is just a good person I am with and not the right one? What if up unhappy like our parents?

In public we would talk about how we did not need some contr support our commitment to each other. We would talk about how we le in our anthropology classes that marriage is just more patriarchy, blah, blah. We would nosh our tapas and quaff our craft beers and agree with other in a way that sounded like arguing.

When Annie became pregnant with our first child, we started think that a little tradition and stability and legal agreement was probably okay the baby. We would need health insurance, and a better way to file our ta A couple months after the wedding, my father died of a stroke on the g course, leaving me a rather large inheritance and instructions to use it fo down payment on a house.

Why do I mention all of this? Because it sets the stage for how careful we moved forward with things. We were not casual or cavalier or slacker in any way. We were not like those young people in slasher films who sor of have it coming. We were thoughtful, methodical, and prepared. Well, we thought we were prepared.

If we were going to buy a house in Southern California as twentysomething high school teachers, then this money was our lifeline. We would be able go into any deal with 25 percent down. We found a great three-bedroom half a mile from St. Jude's. It was not showy, but Annie loved everything about it. The realtor said several people were looking at the house, so he

Stevie. Once you were born, you were fine. Your brother is a different story. I barely noticed he was there until he turned two."

"All right, then," I said. "Six thirty?"

"That will be fine, dear. Give Annie my best."

SHE PREPARED A NICE MEAL for us, which should have been a sign of what was coming. My mother is not an incompetent cook, but she is not a particularly extravagant one either, so this all came as a surprise. She set us in the dining room with the good china, not in the kitchen. Three chairs huddled at one end of the table near the window.

My wife leaned in and kissed my mother's cheek.

"Oh, Annie, you look gorgeous. Motherhood suits you." It did. Annie had the halo of a Madonna. Seeing my mother there with my expectant wife gave me a feeling for which I had no words, a feeling I have felt now and then in art museums.

Mother served chicken Kiev, green beans with slivered almonds, and roasted red potatoes. As we ate, I noticed my mother was downing two glasses of wine for every one of mine. We talked about everyday things: the yard, her book group, the presidential candidates, our students, the ultrasound, Annie's family.

We had carrot cake for dessert, and after we started in, mother set down her fork and said, "Steven, Annie, I have something a bit uncomfortable I'd like to talk about."

Annie and I tried not to look startled. "Sure, Mother," I said, "We're all ears."

My mother did not speak immediately. She was exerting a lot of energy trying to keep her composure. "It's about your inheritance."

A saline wave, like weak adrenaline, rushed through me. We had been through probate. What could possibly be wrong?

"Somehow," my mother said, "your father's concern over you and your family and his hope for you to have a home here in Santa Barbara appears to have given him a conservative approach to the way he structured your trust."

"We're very grateful, Brenda," Annie said, "Paul left us a generous gift. It's a lifeline, really."

"About that," my mother said, "Paul was conservative in structuring Steven's trust in a way that he was not with the rest of our finances." My mother picked up her fork to have another bite of cake, then set the fork back down.

"I was with the financial planner this week, and apparently your father left quite a large portion of our portfolio in funds that are still climbing out of the recession. He also didn't leave me much cash. The life insurance is helping with a few of the problems, but he'd borrowed against it for some ventures that didn't pan out. The planner says I'll recover a little as the market climbs, but for now I have some immediate concerns."

"What do you need? We can help." I looked across the table for Annie's support. She was carving away bits of her cake and letting them fall to the plate.

"It would be temporary help, Steven."

We helped my mother clean up, and because she was always with us, Annie and I did not have a chance to talk before we left. I knew that it would not be a good conversation and very probably the first of many not-very-good conversations to come. So I was glad, I guess, for another hour of détente.

The second we were in the car, Annie said, "Steven, we just made an offer."

"I know."

"This feels really fishy to me."

"I know it does."

"Should it be surprising that she didn't say anything about your brother?"

"Maybe she's already gone to him."

When she declined to answer, I admitted that she probably had not gone to him. Why would she? My brother very likely burned through whatever my father was going to leave him years ago, begging for bailouts and help starting up failed businesses. We all knew to stay away from Michael and his finances.

"I don't want to lose this house, Steven," Annie said.

"I don't want my mother to lose hers."

"That's not what I'm saying," she said, meaner than she meant.

"She said it's temporary. And really, it's her money."

"Just let me be angry," she said. "Okay. I've got to let it work all the way through."

As you can imagine, it was a house of cards mashed up with a domino effect. Without the cash for the down payment, the maximum loan amount dropped. We readjusted our offer and lost the property. Our first realtor pretty much lost interest in us when it looked like we were not going to be buying in a price range that maximized his opportunity costs. We tried another realtor on the recommendation of one my dad's golf buddies, Burt Mattson, a loudmouth Texan who was a telecom executive after coming out of the air force. His young fiancée was supposed to be a high-volume agent who worked with people like me and Annie who were just starting out.

Once we lost her dream house, Annie was reluctant to keep trying. I said, "Let's just meet the woman, okay?" She agreed, and by "agreed" I mean "conceded."

It was probably just as bad as Annie thought it would be, but worse than I imagined. The wife of my dad's buddy looked like a cross between Sarah Palin and a Pilates instructor. She introduced herself as Bonnie McKittrick, and said that Bonnie was short for Bonnie Jo, which was short for Bonnie Josephine. She spoke so quickly I nearly missed the explanation that followed: "But Josephine's not my middle name—that's Sherill—spelled with an *S*, *I*, double-*L* and not a *C*, *Y*, *L*—Josephine is a biblical name, so I guess it comes from the Hebrew—supposed to mean 'he will increase'—don't know how that got to be a girl's name—must've switched over sometime back when all those French guys were wearing wigs and high heels—but it fits me because I made top closer as of last month—hope to do it again so I can keep the parking place—but I'm planning a wedding—it's my own wedding, so who knows. Anyway, Bonnie comes from the Latin word for 'good'—my sister told me that in an email—but I looked it up on the internet last year and found out that in Scottish Bonnie means 'pretty' and/or 'charming'—I've had people tell me I'm both, but they leave out the 'or'—but that's for you to decide—anyway," she said, extending her hand, "nice to meet you two—what's your budget?"

Annie and I looked at each other. I shrugged. Annie stabbed this very cross look at me and said softly but firmly, "We're teachers."

Bonnie Jo picked up a ballpoint pen with a rubber snowman on the end and scribbled something on a notepad with her face printed on top. I was certain her garish nails would keep her from writing anything, but miraculously they were no problem at all.

She took a moment and sized us up. "Teachers are the best." Tapping on a map of town with her nail, she said, "But that's going to eliminate anything here, here, or here." She paused, making a dramatic thinking face, then continued. "Or here, here, or here." She could tell we were crestfallen, so she said, "Don't get me wrong. There's plenty of bustling cute neighborhoods full of young immigrant families. I think it would be great if we could get those houses back to single-family dwellings, if you know what I mean."

While we were deciding if we did know what she meant, Bonnie Jo's phone buzzed. She turned it over and checked the screen. "I really should take this. Getting married tomorrow, and there are a million loose ends," she said, then stepped out of the small office and started talking. Even though she was trying to hush herself, we could hear everything.

"I know the rehearsal is tonight. I wouldn't normally meet clients on this tight a schedule, but these people are friends of yours—okay, kids of a friend, same difference." Annie looked at me and shrugged. "Fine, but remember you asked me to do this." She paced back and forth a little then said, "I won't be late . . . It's on the calendar, that's why. I've got nails today and hair tomorrow . . . For crying out loud, it *will* be a waste of money if I try to sleep on it, Burt."

Bonnie Jo's heels tapped out a regular gait on the floor as we listened to her listening. "What do you mean Doyle just showed up? Do you mean just-just, or like just in the last hour? . . . I wouldn't know. He was supposed to be here yesterday, so I can't help anybody with that question." She poked her head in, and placed her phone on her shoulder. "I'll be quick," she whispered. She got back on the phone and paced back and forth a couple more times and said, "How am I supposed to know how he got blood all over his car? You'll have to ask him . . . I also have no idea how something like that would happen. Well, if he brought along some floozy, we'll *have* to redo the seating arrangements, won't we?"

Bonnie Jo didn't come right back. After a minute or so of silence in the office, Annie and I wondered if we should try to find her, but she popped back in. "Super sorry about the interruption," she said. "I wouldn't normally do it, but . . ."

"You're getting married?" Annie asked. "That's fantastic."

"He's an older gentleman with grown kids. Distinguished. Retired, you know. Used to live in Texas. Widowed. I'm not wearing white to this thing, so you'd think I'd be cool as a cucumber, but I'm not. I am all out of sorts. So, I apologize if my mind drifts in and out a little today. So, where were we?"

"You were going through all the places we couldn't afford," I said.

Bonnie Jo winced. "I'm sorry. You can't have any secrets in real estate."

"Apparently," I said.

"Why don't we look at a couple of listings, just to get a feel."

I looked at Annie, and she shrugged. I knew what a shrug from Annie meant, but even more, I knew what *that* particular shrug meant. And I was not ready to embrace it.

"We'll follow you," I said.

We walked to our car, Annie looking like some poor soul in a cartoon with a rain cloud scribbled above her head. It should have felt like a victory for her that this agent was a nonstarter, but it did not. Not in the moment or after a fruitless afternoon of finding nothing again and again and again.

Later that night, I could not find my wife. Our apartment is tiny, so it seemed strange to find her missing. I thought maybe she had gone out. I went to the window and looked down in the parking lot. The car was still there. I sent her a text, and a second or two later, I saw a blue light flash in the car. I sent a quick follow-up and waited. A second flash. I put some shoes on and went down to see what was happening.

I bent down and knocked on the window. She spooked a little and then turned away. I went around to the passenger's side, and while I was going, I heard the locks clunk. "Hey," I said. "Come on."

"I need some time," she said.

"Okay, but you can go up to the apartment. I'll go running or something."

"No," she snapped. "I don't want to be up there. And a pregnant lady can't go to a bar."

I stood there without saying anything, then I took out my phone. I typed: *I'm sorry about the house.*

The car lit up, and in a few seconds she sent: *I know I'm not being rational.*

You don't have to be rational if you're sad.

She sent: *>:(*

I sent: *0:)*

I walked around to the other side of the car and motioned that I was going back up. I waited for her approval and she looked at me like someone who knows they are being left.

The next day I told my friend Roger about the whole thing. Roger Reed is the varsity baseball coach at my school. He also teaches health and keyboarding. Besides teaching at St. Jude's, we have nothing in common. I have literally never seen him not wearing maroon wind pants and a St. Jude's Wildcats golf shirt, tucked in. He is fit, but he's balding, and his forearms look like they were built out of the bridge over the River Kwai. His voice is not just loud, it booms. And he likes to slap people on the back.

I guess you can say Roger is my best friend. Besides Annie, he really is the only person I actually talk to about anything. Sometimes that is a mistake.

"It's your money, Brougham," Roger said.

"Brougham?"

Roger's attention snapped to something happening a couple of tables down, but it did not escalate into anything worth following up on.

"Roger," I said. "She really wanted that house."

"You need a house, Stevie."

"I hate it when you call me Stevie."

Roger gave me a quick "pow" with his forefinger and thumb. "Gotcha," he said, but he said it weird, winking like somebody's pervert uncle.

I could not look at him, so I turned away and concentrated on a sophomore just as he was folding something into a freshman's mashed potatoes. I should have stopped it, but I did not.

"Renting is expensive, and if you two are bringing some offspring into the world, you need to have a place of your own. Nobody's American Dream is to be under a landlord their whole life. So, they didn't take your first offer. So what?"

"She liked that house."

"A house is a house. You turn it into what you want."

"I'll try telling that to Annie."

"Are you going with a realtor?" Roger asked.

"We've tried two already. It's depressing."

"Skip the realtors. Don't inhale. They. Will. Rob. You. Blind," he said. "The title guy handles everything that matters. And you're already paying him. You shouldn't be on the open market anyway. It's a screw job."

Roger loved saying "screw job," and he would concoct situations that would lead him to that punch line.

"You should be looking into short sales, my man. Realtors hate 'em—doesn't take an Einstein to figure that out."

"Listen, Roger. I need a house, not a seminar."

"Look. You got some stiff who got roped into a bad loan. Balloon payments hit. Wife loses her job. He wants out before the crap hits the fan, and he goes into foreclosure. Bank takes the loss, doesn't want to fill out all the loan mod paperwork. If he sells the house, he can maybe walk with clean credit. Or maybe he bought too high in the market and now he's underwater a hundred grand, can't refinance, wants out. You can profit from that. You can get that eight grand from out of Obama's welfare sack, and boom, you're in business. Jeez, man, don't just lay down in the road and let the stimulus drive back and forth across your face. You're a teacher. This country owes you, man."

"Roger, you know Annie. She's not going to be cool with any of this."

"At least come to a foreclosure auction with me, see how it works," he said. "Six percent of anything you can buy around here is twenty-five grand."

WHEN I GOT BACK TO my classroom, I sent Annie a text: *Roger's going to show me a house, then he'll bring me home.*

An hour later she wrote: *I think I found another realtor. I'll call her after school. I know Roger is your friend, but I'd rather take real estate advice from a hamster. P.S. Remember, you're making dinner. No takeout. It makes the baby crazy.*

I taught my two afternoon classes then met with the student government kids for forty-five minutes, helping them plan a service project. After that I puttered around my room, reading some Alexis de Tocqueville and waiting for Roger to show up. At quarter to five, he knocked on the window in my door with a tape measure and then motioned for me to come out. I closed my book and shuffled to the door.

"Shake a leg, Walsh. You know what they say—sloth is the Devil's mattress," Roger said, swinging a small plastic cooler.

"Who says that?"

"Old-timers," he said, then he eyed me suspiciously, turned, and shot past the office, zooming through the front doors. I followed him to the truck, and as soon as we drove off school property, he opened the cooler and offered me a beer. "Go ahead," he said, grinning. "We're gonna be house hunting. It's not right to be sober."

As we drove, Roger told me how they don't really let you see the insides of a foreclosure property. "Why not?" I asked, surreptitiously lifting the bottle to my lips and taking a dainty swig.

"Well, because a lot of the time they still have somebody living in them."

"So how do you—"

"Well, you can't really. I mean, it takes an eye, and with a little time and energy you can go down to the county courthouse, or wherever they keep records, and you can get the plans—won't tell you how well they kept up the house—but you can sort of count on them letting the place go to hell. People who default on a mortgage usually have other problems than being a flake about money. Still, I think with some binoculars and a telephoto lens you can get a pretty good idea of what's going on inside—and sometimes . . ." Roger finished off his beer, dropped it behind the seat, and switched lanes. "Moron," he shouted at the car in front of him.

"Sometimes what?" I asked.

Roger sniffed and gunned through a yellow light. "Sometimes," he said, "you can sort of sneak in the back when they step out."

"Roger!" I twisted around and craned my neck to see if we were okay.

Sliding around in the back of the truck was a stepladder and some rope he had stuffed into a five-gallon bucket. I kicked a gym bag that was on the floor, which rattled metallically. "I've got to be home by six," I sighed.

"That's where you're wrong, buddy." Roger swigged his beer. "You don't have a home. You see, that's the disease, and old Roger has the cure."

We drove for a while, drinking on the sly like we were back in high school ourselves, not teachers, but two dumb grizzlies looking for some hive to disturb. Roger constantly punched the presets on his stereo, so we never really heard any music, just a cascade of advertising and the tail ends of songs Roger used to get laid to. When I was just about to the point where I thought I would hit the roof, Roger swung his truck in an abrupt semicircle and came to a stop in front of a horrifying mission-style ranch house with its adobe flaking off in seven or eight immediately identifiable spots. Roger finished off his beer and then reached between my legs. His hand reappeared with a seventies-era pop-up Polaroid Land Camera. "Let's do her," he said, grinning.

Roger walked around whistling, but he looked about as nonchalant as a cop on roller skates. When he thought no one was looking, he brought the camera ineptly to his eye and snapped a shot, which he plucked from the front of the camera. As he continued his survey, he flapped the picture and glowered as it developed.

I rolled down the window. "You need me to do anything?" I asked. Roger shushed me wildly and continued flapping his picture. When the image came in, Roger looked at it briefly and then skulked back to the car to hand it to me. He repeated the cycle a few times until I had this poker hand of nearly indecipherable photos of a nearly uninhabitable house.

"I'm heading down," Roger said, stealing furtive glances over his shoulder. "You watch my back." Just as Roger broke for the laurel hedges, I saw a curtain in the house part, and a small wizened face peered out.

"Hey, Roger!" I called out.

He shushed me and threw himself against the bushes, and after a few seconds he crept on.

"Roger!" I called out again. I could now see the face of an old woman peering out the corner of her front window, looking right at Roger's position in the shrubbery. "You've got somebody at three o'clock," I hollered.

Roger glanced up just as the curtain dropped, then he inched forward. I saw the woman move into the kitchen and pick up her phone. "She's calling the cops, man," I shouted, and Roger came loping up the driveway, threw the camera into the truck, and we sped off.

"For crying out loud," Roger said. "I need some intel on that place."

"Well, she had your number as soon as you crossed the driveway."

"Gimme one of those beers," he said.

"Maybe we should wait until we know there won't be any cops on our tail."

Roger glanced in the rearview mirror and then forearmed a light film of sweat from his brow. "Yeah, you're probably right."

I told him to watch the traffic rules. "They're always catching the bad guys on stupid moving violations."

"We're not the bad guys," Roger said. "The people who welsh on their mortgages are the bad guys."

"Nobody wants to lose their house," I said, propping my arm against my head and the lip of the window. "I mean nobody wakes up and says, 'Today is the day I'm going default on my loan.' "

Roger looked at me with an expression that was half curiosity and half disgust. "These people have made a conscious decision to renege on an agreement most of the rest of the world seems to have no trouble keeping—they think it doesn't matter what they do, that their self-centered attitudes have no effect on others." When I grimaced, he said, "Look at it this way. Nobody's out there with a gun to their head making them be homeowners. They could rent if they wanted to—plenty of people do—they could just sell the house when they run short, pick up the equity and put it in a money market for twenty-four months, rent, and look for something to buy when the time is right—but they don't—they think someone is going to carry them. It's irresponsible. You teach social studies, Steve. You should know this. Our whole system works because when someone signs a contract, we take them at their word. If we start letting people slip out of those contracts, we're no better than a pack of hyenas."

I had to hand it to him. His logic was completely consistent. And the pitch of his voice was compelling. Once he got going, he had the air of Jonathan Edwards in his rhetoric. These mortgage defaulters were just sinners in the hands of an angry god, and if they were the sinners and the bank was God, then who was Roger? The Lord's destroying angel?

While Roger was cursing to himself about making a street approach with a whole bank of windows facing the road, the light changed and we came to a stop. Roger gestured to the right of the car and said, "When we come around this next block, take a look. A buddy of mine down in the courthouse told me a Cape Cod across from the grade school might be coming up in a couple weeks."

I AGREED TO TRY THINGS out with Annie's realtor. Third time's a charm, right? I wish now that we had gone with her. Our lives would be unmolested. It was hard to see that then because there was, of course, nothing in our budget—plenty of things just out of it—but nothing that could just slide past the underwriters. This new realtor, Evangeline Raposo, was explosive for about an hour, but then she had us pegged as people whose tastes were beyond their means. I could see her squinting off into the distance, checking her phone, hoping for greener pastures. Her commission from one of these dumps would have barely covered her expenses.

"I'm sorry, Steven," Annie whispered from the sloping room of a two-bedroom one-bath that would likely need a new roof in one to five years, depending on the drought. I ran my fingertips along a quarter-inch gap in the sheetrock that ran from floor to ceiling. As we toured the basement, I could see why the house listed like a barge: someone had cut one of the floor joists nearly in two to accommodate a "new" drain stack. The joist had since split along the grain completing the breach, each end of the joist free of the other, opening satanically, like a pair of shears.

The next house seemed a little more promising. I suppose in certain circles I'd call the neighborhood eclectic or something, but in reality it was just run-down. The cars parked along the street seemed mostly operational, and a trio of Asian girls jumped rope on the sidewalk one house up and across the street. I nudged Annie, as if to suggest our baby would fit in. Evangeline was having some trouble with the key box, and it seemed like her patience was wearing thin. I wandered around the yard, testing the dryness of the lawn with my shoe. Around the west side of the house was what looked like a small propane cylinder with a blue nozzle stashed away in the shrubs. I also noticed a couple of old jars full of a cloudy amber liquid lying in a pile of lawn clippings. As soon as we went into the house, Annie started rubbing her eyes and said she was having some trouble breathing. Evangeline opened a window and took a personal call on her cell phone. The house was clean and simple, with great leaded-glass built-ins.

"This is in our price range?" I asked.

When Annie came back into the living room from downstairs, her eyes were red-rimmed and moist. "Come down here," she said, her voice hoarse and labored. I followed her into the basement and felt dizzy, like I'd spilled gasoline all over myself. "I think people used to make drugs in this house—I can't stay down here," she said.

I followed her back upstairs and out the front door. Evangeline had turned her chair and was continuing her conversation with her head half out of the window. Annie burned a line straight through the living room without stopping. I followed. When Evangeline saw that we were leaving, she placed her phone to her chest and asked if there was anything wrong. Annie told her that she was not in the market for a crack house. I had to cover my mouth and tell her that I thought it was methamphetamines they were cooking downstairs, but Annie just stormed out of the house and made a beeline for the car.

Evangeline followed us, clearly unaccustomed to moving that fast. "Listen, guys," she said, her phone still pressed to her chest. "I'm really sorry about this—"

"Nope, that's okay," Annie said from inside the car, a tissue already in her hand. "We're probably in over our heads."

Evangeline looked miffed. "I'm sorry," she said.

"We're just—well, it's just. We thought we could afford a little more than what you've shown us."

"Oh, it's not that," Evangeline said, waving her phone. "I have to meet a client in ten minutes."

We just let her go. She waved goodbye and started up her car, put her cell phone to her ear, and drove away. I walked around the back of our car and let myself in. Annie sniffed once and dabbed at her eye. "Are you crying?" I asked. She glared back. I said, "I'm not going to say anything."

"Good."

"I could, but I'm not going to."

"Steven."

I looked at my watch. "You want to swing by that other house? The one Roger and I looked at?" I proposed. "At this point, it couldn't hurt, right?"

"I don't care," she said.

"It's a nice house."

"Fine."

"The neighborhood seems okay, too. Kind of soon-to-be-hip."

"I don't care."

"I don't want to sound like I'm gloating or anything."

"Don't worry," she said. "I'm not even thinking about you."

I put on a playlist I knew Annie liked and drove to the house. Right as we were turning onto the street, Annie lifted her head and looked out the window. As I began to slow, she scanned both sides of the street. "It's the Cape Cod right there with the great trees," I said, parking.

"You're kidding. What's a Cape Cod doing in California?"

I shrugged. "It looks just like my grandparents' house, doesn't it?"

She shrugged. "It's got trees." She was brightening.

"I told you. Want to get out?"

"No, I don't want them to see us." Annie said, scanning the property. "We can afford this?"

"I don't know. It's going up for auction so I don't know what it'll cost, but it's worth a shot, don't you think?" I watched the corner of Annie's mouth curl ever so slightly. It was good to see her smile. I thought that perhaps she was gazing into the future with more hope than she'd felt for a long time. Her face softened. She arranged her hands in her lap like she was sitting for a portrait. I did not look at the house. I just watched her watching it, until she gasped.

"What is it?" I asked.

"Some man. Steven, he's staring at us."

"Where is he?"

She lifted her hand slightly, then stopped. "By the side of the house—near the bushes."

You could vaguely see him, his head motionless, his lean body swallowed by the shadows of the shrubs. I did not want to start up the car and drive off. That would mean there was something wrong with our being parked on a public street. Still, we both felt strange, lurking about in broad daylight.

"What's he doing?" Annie asked. The man was pulling the cuffs of his sweatshirt up to the elbow. As they swung into the light, you could see that his arms were thick and corded, one of them tattooed.

"I don't know," I said. "But don't get all jerky. Be cool. We've got every right to be here on the street."

"He probably knows we're scoping out his house."

"Sure. But he's probably used to it by now. Roger says these auctions are public events. They get advertised in the newspaper. I'll bet he's had people gawking at him all day."

"So he's always already aggravated?"

"You want me to talk to him?" I asked.

"Let's just leave."

"Wait a minute. Maybe he'll just go away."

We watched him stand motionless in the bushes for the next five minutes until I said, "This is crazy. Let's get out of here."

When I started the car, the man stepped into the light, raised his arms, and pretended to slide and lock a rifle bolt. Then, he pointed his make-believe "gun" right at us, took careful aim, and make-believe shot. He pantomimed the recoil. Annie and I both jumped and felt immediately stupid afterward.

As we lurched into the once-quiet street, Annie said, "He's still looking at us, Steven. He's still looking."

Monday at school, I asked Roger if he had ever come across something like that. He just nodded and poked the last bite of a salami sandwich into his mouth. As he chewed he said, "It happens, man. These people won't stick to their deals. They act like they were asleep at the closing or something. It's like they never even snuck a peek at their mortgage papers. I tell you." Roger told me that most of the time they cave and go peacefully when they know the jig is up, but sometimes it takes the cops, and you have to file all kinds of papers and then they have to get a sheriff to go out to the house. "And once in a blue moon," Roger said, "they have to haul the poor SOBs off kicking and screaming. I hate being around for that. I mean, if you can't stand the heat, right?"

"Right," I said, less emphatically than I meant to.

Roger yelled at a couple of kids who were lollygagging.

"What you need to do is get a spine, my man. As civilized as we think we are, we still have basic needs. Everyone wants to be up at the top of that guy's pyramid about knowledge, beauty, and self-aggrandizement, but you need that stuff in the foundation. It's survival and safety—food and water and shelter, my friend. When the caveman spears a mastodon, he guts that thing and drags it home. He's got people to feed. Where does he draw the pictures of the hunt? Out on the prairies? No way, he does it at home. You can't have anything if you don't have somewhere to keep it. People aren't tumbleweeds, Stevie."

"I hate it when you call me that."

"So get off your high horse about all this. Go get yourself a home, brother. Nobody's going to walk up and hand one to you. You've got to get out and hustle for it. You've got to make it known that Iron Steve's in town and people better step off."

"Iron?" I asked.

"You are made of iron. The rest of them are feathers."

"I have no idea what you are talking about," I said, but I nodded sheepishly, then swept some crumbs off the table and into the palm of my hand.

"Auction's tomorrow," Roger said. "You want me to coach you?"

I nodded.

"You bring the *cajones*, I'll bring the donuts," Roger said. Then he shouted at the dawdling kids and told them they needed to be in class ten minutes ago.

Roger did bring the donuts, but there was no auction. About six o'clock that morning the sky opened up, and it rained all day long. They rescheduled, but there was next to nobody there to hear about it.

"You could be sitting in the fabled catbird seat," Roger said, screwing down the lid of his thermos. "When it's rain on one of these auction days, all the namby-pambies stay in their holes, and a lot of the big-time players have to get on to other things. You could pull a good deal."

I SLEPT ROTTEN THAT NIGHT. I dreamed I was a lobsterman whose leg got tangled up in one of his lobster pots, which was a strange dream to have, given the fact that I know zilch about lobstermen, but it was disturbing enough to rouse me from my sleep.

When I saw that it was only two thirty, I went to the fridge, chugged some milk from the jug, got my phone, and checked Facebook. An old college friend of mine posted a YouTube video of one of those late-night get-rich-quick real estate commercials. It was unbelievable: the guy in a cerulean blue shirt and yellow tie, smiling, surrounded by charts and mildly attractive couples, also smiling, telling about how they'd like to stay and talk but they should get down to the marina for their boat christening. From there I watched some Kimmel videos and a guy who BASE jumped from a building in Rio de Janeiro. After that, I fell asleep on the couch and awoke only when Annie came into the room and said, "It's morning."

In the shower, Roger's speech about the cavemen returned to me in a single burst. All of a sudden I went from scrubbing my armpits to thinking about how Roger's diatribe had gotten into my head. I love the guy, but I did not think he was smart enough to pull something like that off.

I thought of that strange man lurking around the Cape Cod, then wondered immediately what you call someone who has been thrown out of their own house by someone who does not even live in that house. I saw my father, whose decisions put us in this place. It chilled me, so I turned up the shower until the water was nearly scalding. In the searing heat, I washed my hair and then slumped against the tile away from the showerfall until Annie parted the curtain and told me to quit hogging all the water.

She was already naked. She stepped into the shower with me and immediately knocked the faucet back to the center. "This water is four hundred degrees," she said. "You'll hard-boil this baby, right inside me."

"I was cold," I said.

She tested the water with her hands and then cupped her arms and caught the water against her chest. "Are you ready to head down to that auction?" she asked, wetting her hair.

"You think we should be trying to help that guy? You know, instead of trying get one over on him," I said.

"Which guy?"

"Bang-Bang Gun Guy."

"You're kidding, right?" Annie said. "I mean this was your idea. You do remember that, don't you? I did not say, 'Steven, we should buy a foreclosure property,' did I? I did not say that we had no need for realtors."

"I've just been trying to figure out what we—never mind." I got out of the shower and pulled a towel from the rack. This was the point of no return for Annie and me, and for Bang-Bang Gun Guy. We were soon to be changed forever.

IT WAS OVERCAST AND THREATENING at the auction, but we were not rained out. About a half dozen people appeared on the sidewalk in front of the courthouse in a ragged semicircle. They closed in on the auctioneer, *Walking Dead*–style, with clipboards and the classifieds folded and crammed under their arms. A few nursed steaming paper cups of coffee. Roger shot some Afrin up his nose and massaged it and said, "Watch out for that guy in the Eddie Bauer cap—he's a real turd job." The guy was short and trim with a gray mustache and hip-looking rectangular glasses. He was checking something on his phone, and then he slipped a piece of nicotine gum into his mouth. "You hit enough of these things you start to recognize the regulars," Roger said. "The guy in the cap does this for fun. He made a bung-load of money as an operations and liability consultant for HMOs. He's dangerous because he doesn't have to be interested. He's got the money to buy anything that comes up—speed-dials the bank as soon as he wins an auction, and he digitally signs the disclosures on the way home. They say he can close on a property in forty-eight hours, but that's physically impossible. I call him Zorro."

"I'm not going to even ask why," I said.

Roger pointed at another guy with his chin. He was lanky and wore suit pants and a pair of ancient Air Jordans. "That's the Mole Man," Roger said. "I've seen him at every auction I've been to. He always bids once near the beginning, but he's never bought anything. I figure he's some schlep works at a grocery store and wants to get out of it. When the auction's over, he disappears."

I asked him about the guy standing next to the Mole Man. He was shaped like a package of Quaker Oats and his hair came together in a weak, gray ponytail that looked like a wad of hair you pull out of the drain.

"Never seen him. Don't know any of the rest of these amateurs," Roger said, casting his eye around the square. "Except for that broad. I've seen her at a couple storage unit auctions in the last couple of weeks."

She looked like someone who won a beauty pageant a long time ago. Her hair was dry and thatched, probably color treated, and she wore a business suit that looked like it was tailored for someone else. "What do you call her?" I asked.

Roger shrugged. "It's not like I put it all in a spreadsheet—pay attention."

A man announced that the auction was officially beginning. He gave us all a rundown of the rules and procedures, which seemed to annoy everyone but me. Zorro passed on the first two properties, one of which went to the lady and the other to someone Roger did not know. The Mole Man bid exactly as Roger said he would. When they announced the Cape Cod, a wave of electricity shot through me. It felt like my mouth was full of pennies.

Roger leaned into me and whispered, "Never let them see you sweat," at which point I began to sweat in sheets. Zorro made the starting bid, and the Mole Man followed almost immediately. Everyone else held. Roger reminded me that this was the property I was here to buy, so I gestured, and it seemed as if the entire planet had suddenly shifted its attention to me.

Zorro swung his head slowly, sized me up, then bid again. The price rose. A couple other folks bid, then astonishingly the Mole Man bid a second time. Roger nearly fainted. Zorro and the auctioneer were stunned. I had to raise my hand three times to get the auctioneer to look my way and accept my bid. After that, the Mole Man was frozen, more like Opossum Man. The lady swept in, pushing the property over two ninety, which caused Zorro to bid once more with his cell phone in hand. My belly tightened as the others bid past me. The house climbed to two ninety-five, then I snapped and bid twice in a row. Roger grabbed my arm and kept me from bidding a third time.

I looked around and everyone was scribbling on their lists. Roger said, "It's outside the margins now, man. You have to hold. They're going to start backing off." Which was dead-on. Zorro pocketed his phone and started reading his newspaper again. The Mole Man just left. There was one more bid; Roger let me counter it, and then suddenly, miraculously, the auctioneer pointed at me and said, "Sold." In my head, I heard him say, *Sold to the liberal Democrat who's no longer certain he made the right move*, and then I noticed Roger was massaging my shoulders and congratulating me. I smiled and tried to get him to stop.

There was a brief pause in the commotion, a gap in the traffic on the street behind us coupled with an intermission in the deal sealing. I noticed the suspension of things, I turned slowly away from the building and the small crowd toward the street, and leaning against the front fender of Roger's truck was that strange man from the house. He was wearing a gray jacket with what my father used to call a barracuda collar. He was staring right at me. I looked away a couple of times, but when I looked back, he lifted an obscenely large cigar to his throat and looked like he was puffing on it—he exhaled smoke, but I never saw him doing anything but planting the cigar on his neck. I grabbed Roger, and tried to show him, but when I finally got Roger's attention, the old guy was gone.

"He probably wanted to see what was going on," Roger said. "Sometimes they want to try and jam up the bidding. It never works."

I sort of shrugged it off and rode the avalanche. Within the next half hour, I signed so many papers, one right on top of the other, I thought my arm would fall off. Without Roger recapping the whole affair while we were on our way to car, I would have had no idea of what happened at all.

I texted Annie this: *We got it.*

She replied: *Squeal!!! How much?*

I wrote: *Within budget.*

She sent the house emoji with a tree.

If we only knew then what we know now, she would have followed that with the little shrieking man, like the one in the painting.

Buying the house was my contribution. From then on, it was Annie's show. Overnight she gained a set of qualities television news show pundits often call "presidential." She began by winnowing our possessions, creating piles of boxes of things we were keeping just because we had paid for them once. We were forbidden to look in these boxes, and every morning for a week we would take one or two of them with us to school and leave them at the processing dock of the Goodwill as we drove home. She priced and reserved a rental truck, called a posse, promised them pizza and beer. She scrutinized each bit of paper generated by the sale and filed them in a milk crate decked out with hanging files. For a while I was useful as a kind of errand boy, but eventually she did not need me for that.

Roger called it the nesting instinct, told me not to worry. "It's a primal thing," he said. "The caveman didn't need a nest or even want one, really. That just let his enemies know where to find him. It was the cavewoman who invented agriculture and got everyone to stop schlepping around and move in somewhere. Caveman fought that. Once he was grounded, he came back with horses and wheels and boats. He tried to show her what she was missing, but she wasn't convinced. She said, 'What I want is wallpaper. You need to go get some wallpaper or you can't have sex with me.'" Roger took a racquet ball out of his pocket and bounced it once on the cafeteria floor then repocketed it and made a beeline for some boys who were throwing sandwich crusts at a new kid.

I was dumbfounded and felt a little exposed there in the lunchroom. Roger moved in swiftly and chastised the food-throwing kids and literally pulled the boy, an eleven-year-old math genius named Darren Chin, over to the offending table in his folding chair. And while Roger was brokering the apology, I realized that his theories were completely ad hoc and almost completely contradictory. How did it come to pass that a man who buys and sells homes could think that the last thing in this world a man would want is a home? I started to lose my footing in the world. How did things get so turned around? Not owning property impinges on liberty. Owning too much has the same effect. Man does not ultimately want a home; he wants to be free, riding through New Mexico on a couple of choppers. But man is a landowner, his home is his castle. He fills it with guns and defends it. He putters around it. He mows its lawn. And now I am going to be in hock up to my elbows for something Roger says I do not want.

When he got back, I quizzed Roger on this and he said, "Au contraire, Stevie. Just because a man does not have a primal need for a home does not mean that he doesn't want one. Caveman didn't want one particular cave—a cave's a good thing, but he was fine with any cave, could be this cave, could be a different one down the road. He didn't know any better. Once the cave-woman got him to understand that sometimes all the caves are already occupied, our guy realized that when you find an empty one that meets your needs, you might as well keep dibs on it, since she's going to keep nagging you for one anyway. That's where you get your possession is nine-tenths of the law."

I told Roger I thought he was making it up as he went along. He just said, "Think about it. Once man got into the home business, he took it over. Started building castles and fortresses and garages—everything he needs. It took women thousands of years to get sewing rooms. The battle of the sexes, my friend, is the battle of the home. Man brokers the deal, then woman takes over. She gets inside, and he gets the lawn, the garage, a den, a man cave. You see: we're back to caves, baby." Roger took out his ball again and rapidly squeezed it five or six times. "Put it this way. How many women did you see at that auction?"

"One," I said.

"There you go."

"That doesn't prove anything."

"Think about it, Stevie." Roger leaned forward in an awkward and uncomfortable way that made it clear he was serious.

"You call me that to piss me off, right?"

Roger squinted at me and then smiled, slightly.

"You're probably right," I said. The bell rang and Roger started barking at the kids. Even though I was exhausted and halfway hoped that this would be the end of our struggles, I knew things were going to get worse.

The mechanics of the closing went smoothly. Everyone met at the title company and signed about seven thousand sheets of paper. The only person who was not there was that old guy who defaulted. I do not know why I expected him, but I did. I spent a bunch of time gearing up for the encounter, but of course he was not there. Some guy my age represented the bank. He wore the kind of cheap suit that made him look like he just got married.

Annie nudged me while the kid made jokes about football and people suing McDonald's because their food is fatty. But in the middle of it all, this kid slipped in a side comment about how in a market like this one they used to be able to bundle the foreclosures together and pass them on to a broker. This time, though, they didn't because they had a "weird feeling" (he actually made the quotation marks in the air) about the owner, a guy named Condit. He gave some people at the bank the impression that he might be a loose cannon.

Annie grabbed my hand when he said that, and I doodled a picture of a bull's-eye on a piece of scratch paper and then "x"ed it out. She punched me in the arm. In hindsight, that was perhaps a brash gesture.

After the closing, we were a little too excited to think much about any one thing, and we sort of forgot what that kid from the bank said about this Condit person (Bang-Bang Gun Guy) until a few days later when we were trying to defuse some of our buyer's anxiety with a trip to Home Zone.

It was going to take a couple of days for things to clear escrow, and Annie was going bats packing, so we decided to look at home things. For some reason I felt an overwhelming desire to shop for tools. Annie was hungry for swatches.

It was strangely delicious to walk through the oversized sliding doors of the Home Zone as a homeowner (or a homeowner-to-be). I'm usually the kind of person who avoids shopping, not because I don't like buying things, I just don't like the way most retail operations are designed to attract the attentions of a human called "the median man." And the pressure to be impressed by mediocre design and piped-in, hopefully-hip-but-ultimately-flaccid pop music is overwhelming. But the Home Zone, even though it is a chain and worthy of contempt for that fact alone, is above all a big box full of things you will need at some point if you own a home. There are no amenities, because you are not supposed to linger. That would be beside the point. The Home Zone shopper is not a shopper. He is a procurer. He has something else to do besides spend money. He is a setter of tile, a painter of walls, an installer of light fixtures, a builder of patios. The Home Zone says to anyone who walks through its doors, *You must change your life, and you can.*

I like that message.

Annie got a cart, and we began to wander through the aisles. I picked up a hammer and set it into the basket. "We're going to need one of these now," I said, and Annie smiled.

"You're going to have to learn how to use it," she said.

We looked at ceiling fans, chandeliers, low-voltage light strips, cabinets, hollow-core doors, brass house numbers, range tops, European-style front-loader washing machines, stainless-steel-clad refrigerators, venetian blinds, mini-blinds, and louvers. Eventually we drifted to the paint center, which was, oddly, at the center of the store, like a hearth or navel.

"We haven't even seen the inside," I said.

"Don't you want to just look?" Annie said.

"Sure."

Annie began pulling paint swatches from the rack, fanning them in her hand like a cardsharp.

Then we heard this voice. It was robotic, buzzing, guttural.

"I'D GET YOU A SMALL CAN FIRST."

Annie threw the swatches into the air and we both spun around. It was Bang-Bang Gun Guy. The old guy who defaulted. Condit. And he was standing behind us in canvas boat shoes and navy blue coveralls that were open at the neck. A small flesh-colored disk with a plastic button at the center was affixed to the loose skin of his throat, and he carried what looked like a small lightsaber in one hand. He lifted the device to his throat and spoke again.

"LIGHT CHANGES A LOT IN THAT HOUSE. WOULDN'T PAINT NOTHING WITHOUT TEST PATCHES."

Condit's neck was thin, and his head seemed fitted to it. His chin was broad and asymmetrical, a light-gray stubble foresting his jaw and cheeks. The weight of his eyebrows and the flinty determination of his eyes were anything but avuncular. He looked like the kind of man who could kill you with a picnic knife.

Annie retrieved her paint swatches and then subtly swung the cart so the long end of the basket separated Condit from her belly. I glanced into his cart and found three rolls of duct tape, two one-hundred-foot bundles of nylon cord, some iron strapping, a roll of clear plastic sheeting, and a hooked utility knife. He also had a package of dead bolts. When he saw me looking, he jerked Annie's cart and surveyed it.

"HAMMER?" he said through the device, then he nodded and lifted the hammer up violently. "SMOOTH FACE. FIBERGLASS HANDLE. YOU CAN DO A LOT OF THINGS TO . . ." Then he mumbled, ". . . WITH A HAMMER LIKE THAT." Condit dropped the hammer in the cart and leaned forward, narrowing his eyes. "SO, YOU'VE GOT PLANS," he said, then paused to let some discomfort in his face pass. "FOR MY HOUSE?"

Indignantly, Annie said, "Of course we do."

"OF COURSE YOU DO. OF COURSE YOU DO," Condit parroted, arching his brows. "BUT YOU AIN'T EVEN SEEN IT YET, EXCEPT WHEN YOU WAS PEEPING. HOW DO YOU KNOW SHE AIN'T GUSSIED UP ALREADY? OR HAUNTED. OR DRENCHED IN BLOOD AND BRAINS."

"You know what," Annie said, taking out her phone. "I'm video taping this. And then I'm sending it to the police."

Condit reached into the cart and picked up the hammer again. "I BET IT WOULD ONLY TAKE ONE SWING."

I stepped in at this point. "All right, all right. You're upset. I get it. But this is in escrow now. It's out of our hands. Getting violent won't help anything."

Condit slowly lifted the hammer to his throat, then realized his mistake and brought up the vocalizer. "LET'S RUN AN EXPERIMENT," he said, then dropped the hammer again and pocketed his device. He made as if to leave but did not.

Annie backed slowly away with the cart between us and Condit. Then she left the cart altogether and headed toward the customer service desk, leaving the two of us alone in the aisle. Condit set his basket on the floor and thrust his hands into the pockets of his coveralls. I rattled my watch and scrubbed a finger under my nose as some guy with two gallons of primer excused himself and walked slantwise between us.

"YOU'RE CARPETBAGGERS," Condit belched, this time without the gizmo. He sounded like a talking dog. "RUN ME OUT?" He croaked, brushing his thighs with the palms of his hands. "YOU GONNA RUN. ME. OUT?"

"Listen, friend," I said. "My wife and I didn't go through the trouble of buying a house just to spite you. You're not that central to our lives. We were just buying a house we could afford," I said, feeling a kind of rush as I spoke.

Condit took his talker back out and said, "HOPE THAT SCHOOL HAS GOOD INSURANCE ON YOU."

"Is that a threat?" I asked.

"SOMETIMES IT'S HARD TO KEEP UP WITH YOUR MORTGAGE IF YOU AIN'T WORKING."

"Why wouldn't I be working? Wait a minute, how do you know where I work?"

"COULD GET HURT. NEVER KNOW. ACCIDENTS HAPPEN. QUACK QUACK."

Right then Annie reappeared with somebody from the store. Condit scooped up his basket and disappeared through a break in the aisle where the paint mixing center was. "What happened?" she asked.

"Nothing. He's just bothered."

Annie turned to the fella in the orange apron. "He's an older man in a blue jumpsuit."

"How old?" the guy asked.

"I don't know, maybe sixty-five," Annie said.

The store guy looked at me with a screwy look in his face. "Sixty-five? Does he work out?" Annie glared at him so fiercely that he apologized and said, "Someone will escort him out of the store. After that, I'm sorry. You're on your own."

We made a couple more stops and went home. I kept my eyes on the rearview the whole time and did not see anything suspicious. While we were unloading the car, Annie's realtor called. "Hi," she said, "I hope everything's going okay with you guys. Sorry I couldn't do anything for you. You still looking? 'Cause I think I found a couple of really cute properties that might fit your budget. A house just listed in a really cute part of town. Quiet street full of cute little homes. It's right next to the cutest little Cape Cod that just sold to a really cute couple. Isn't that the strangest coincidence?"

"Yeah, it is," I told her, then Evangeline told me the address, and I told her we were not interested.

"Who was that?" Annie asked.

"The realtor. The house next to ours just went on the market. Looks like it's in our budget."

Annie rolled her eyes and said, "This is the weirdest thing I've ever dealt with."

When the date for us to take possession came, we got the keys from the title company and went down to the house, but they did not work. I immediately knew what had happened. "That jerk from the Home Zone," I said. "He changed the locks."

"He what?" Annie said.

"He changed the locks," I said, and then stepped back from the door.

"Well, what do we do now?" Annie asked.

Just then, one of the neighbors came over from the house next door. It was the one for sale. She was a nice woman in her early fifties holding a miniature schnauzer. "That man is crazy," she said, the dog clawing its way up the front of her sweatshirt. "He's been terrorizing us for months. Making threats. He's been building something in there, too. We can't stand it. We bought a condo up in San Luis Obispo, so we can get away from this toilet bowl of a neighborhood. We've had enough of that no-account and his episodes." Then she set the dog down and instructed it to go potty. When it did not, she picked the dog back up and returned to her house.

Annie looked over at me and very calmly said, "Let's give Roger a call," which was strange because Annie has always thought of Roger as a kind of troglodyte, and not only because he was a coach. I asked her if she was sure and she said, "If anyone knows anything about kicking people off a property, it's got to be Roger."

"No."

"Okay, then. I will."

"Fine," I said. As I was dialing I thought I saw something moving on the roof, and then Roger picked up.

"Where are you, man? You loving your new house?"

"Sort of."

"What the hell does that mean?"

"Key doesn't work."

"How does a key not work?"

After a bunch of back-and-forth, Roger said he would be right down.

Annie returned to the car and stood alongside it. One minute later, she went over to the neighbor's house and took one of the real estate flyers from the sign in the front yard. Then I saw something moving again up on the roof. I told Annie to get in the car. She refused to budge, but I made her. I did not see that movement again, but we sat in there for about five minutes until Roger showed up.

"That was fast," I said.

"I was scouting properties down in Buena Vista. So, it looks like you've got a barnacle."

"A what?" Annie said.

"A barnacle. You know, some guy you have to scrape off the boat."

Annie shook her head, even though I am certain she understood what he meant.

"Let's work up a little recon on the situation," Roger said as he leaned through his truck window and brought out a pair of binoculars. "Annie, maybe you should wait in the car, what with the baby and all."

"How about I go wait at my parents' house in Kansas City?" Annie said, but she got in the car anyway and locked the doors.

Roger scanned the place with his binoculars, spitting out bits of a report as he did. "No movement. Some evidence of fortification on the ground floor. Mostly. Looks like he hasn't moved out. You got a barnacle for sure."

I asked Roger for the binoculars and he told me where to look and what to look for. In one of the windows to the front room I could see the dull glint of plastic sheeting. It could have been anything, really, but my heart kind of sank.

"It doesn't look like he's there," Roger said. "Let take a closer look."

I told him I had seen something on the roof, and Roger said I was probably just imagining things or that maybe it was a bird or something. I agreed, mostly because I was hoping it was not Condit on the roof, that this wrinkle was not, in fact, an all-out warping of reality.

We approached the house cautiously, and when we got to the front door Roger asked for the keys. I tossed them to him and he tried them and they did not work. Roger tossed them back and began knocking about in the shrubs. "Come look at this," he said, and I went over. A trip wire ran along the ground about six inches from the foundation.

We followed it around the house and were surprised when the wire just came back to itself. "I don't think this is connected to anything," Roger said. "Watch out." He knelt and tugged the wire sharply once or twice, then stood and watched the front door. After a minute or so he said, "See what I said," and we gathered ourselves back on the front walk.

"Okay, Stevie, you got a problem. This guy is trying to make you think he's not going anywhere, which means that he's probably not planning on going anywhere."

"But how do we get him to leave?" I asked.

"Well, you need to start filling out some forms. The cops won't come without the right paperwork."

I told Roger thanks and then went up to the car and broke the news to Annie, who cupped her head in an open palm and breathed deeply for a couple of minutes before agreeing to leave. I had to fill out a thing called an unlawful detainer, which was a highly detailed complaint full of checkboxes, and when I was nearly finished with it I realized that it was the wrong form, that I had to complete a summons and then the cops could serve Condit and evict him. At that point everything got hazy. I filled out everything I needed to, spent way too much time on the phone and at city hall.

We found out through channels that Condit was no longer residing in the house (SWAT team, tear gas), and that he was also not in police custody.

The next step for us was to wait for the authorities to process the crime scene and clear us to allow our insurance people to come in and size up the situation. They said we shattered some kind of claims record. The adjuster joked that the place was broken in, so the probability of this kind of thing happening again was next to nothing.

Annie was furious. She blamed me for the mess. Actually, she blamed my mother, and my brother, Michael, and the mental health system. "We've bought a house we can't even live in. The former owner is at large. We don't know if he's booby-trapped the house or what." I told her the police didn't think the house was booby-trapped, and she just left the room. When they finally called to let us know we were cleared to enter the premises, Annie was the first to go. The cops had found a set of keys that fit the new locks, so we got in just fine. And we were completely unprepared for what we found in there.

Given the situation with Condit, you would think the house would have been a wreck: furniture heaped in front of doorways, carpet torn away from the corners, trapdoors in the bedroom, plywood over the street-facing windows, strange uretic odors omnipresent. I kept imagining something like the Iraqi bunkers they showed on television during the war, but instead we opened the door and found an impeccably arranged home, impossibly, impeccably arranged. Annie gasped. It was something to behold, really lovely.

"It's all still here," she said. "He wasn't even intending to move, was he?"

"What are we going to do with it all?" I asked.

We continued through the house like people do in science fiction movies when their ship hatch opens and they step onto the surface of a planet for the first time. All his family photos were still hanging in clusters throughout the house: parents, brothers, sisters, children. Above a recliner in the living room Condit's military honors hung. He had an Armed Forces Expeditionary medal, a Distinguished Service Cross, a Legion of Merit medal, and about thirty-five other awards, medals, and commendations.

At the center of the cluster was a framed copy of his discharge papers. He had left the military with honor. Upstairs was a sewing room, which was a little dusty but otherwise seemed like it had been untouched in years. Around the door to this room was a rim of thin wood strips nailed into the frame. In places, clear plastic serrations jutted past the strips as if the door had been covered once and someone had hacked their way through. I could go on about everything we found in that house. A list of the items we discovered would fill up a small town phone book. Condit's whole life was in there, a story you could read if you were patient enough.

He had been in Vietnam, married and widowed, he had three boys whom he did not see regularly (the pictures of them were all at least ten years old), and he was one of four kids, a brother and two sisters. The brother, it seems, was Dr. Science, the guy who does that nutty kids' science program on public television. There was a photo of Condit and Dr. Science and his sisters standing together with Big Bird from *Sesame Street*, a professional courtesy from the bird, I guess.

While I was milling around the house, wondering what we would do with everything, Annie found a phone book and ordered a thirty-yard dumpster. Right after that, she called the local Vets Administration to pick up Condit's military things. They said they had a thrift operation that could use any donation, and Annie said they could take it all.

After a week or so, Annie had arranged for nearly everything to be carried away or donated. We cleaned the entire house (checking for booby traps) and then moved in ourselves.

It was nice at first, living in this wonderful house, making decisions about rooms and where to put things, amending our choices and then amending them again. In an apartment, you feel hard-pressed to commit to an arrangement. No one leisurely moves into or out of an apartment. The purpose is to establish yourself quickly. You can rearrange an apartment, but not radically. There is usually one way things can go, maybe two. If you want radical change, you move. This is probably why I was reluctant to commit to a house. You linger in a home and take root. After years in a house, you can rise, head downstairs, and notice that a small table in the middle of the hallway should be moved to the far end, so the sunlight can climb the legs after it breaks through the window. When you are a renter, you are buying nonattachment. When you own, you are grafted in. Leaving always tears off a little something.

JUST AS WE WERE BEGINNING to feel settled, Condit began making appearances. At first he would just sit across the street in his car, smoking these mammoth cigars, one arm hanging out the window like he was dragging Main Street with a couple of his buddies. I would pull the drapes or close up the blinds and pretend nothing happened. I did not want to alarm Annie—better for me, I thought, to keep my eye on things.

During our prep hour, I told Roger about Condit, and he just shook his head. "Trying to strong-arm you, huh?" he said, then sighed. He actually sighed. "These people are no better than those Feed Our Babies commercials. They take a fundamentally good thing like having compassion for your fellow men and turn it into blackmail." Roger recapped a bottle of cran-apple juice he was carrying and then surveyed the cafeteria, squinting at the mass of blue sweaters and over-coiffed hair. "I've looked into this," he said.

"Looked into what?"

"These charity frauds. Those Feed Our Babies extortionists are based out of Oyster Bay on Long Island. Did you know that it costs something like one hundred and twenty percent of the national average to live in Long Island? I don't think you're going to find any bloated bellies in that slum."

"Isn't that where what's her name with the 'Ain't Life Sweet' lives?"

"Barbara Stein?"

"Yeah, the stupid Southern living show my wife watches."

"She ain't from the South," Roger said. "You see, you get showered with all the commercials that are supposed to make you feel bad for working hard and taking care of yourself, and what do they do but set up shop in an overpriced suburb of New York City where they shoot a richy-pants television show about deep-frying game hens. Makes me want to mow those people down with an SUV. You should just tell that Condit fella to stick it where the sun don't shine."

Over the course of the next few weeks, I kept Roger posted on Condit's strange behavior. Annie had noticed him, and because our encounters with him had already drained her vitality, she deteriorated rapidly. She started keeping the curtains drawn, the doors and windows locked. I sort of figured things would taper off after a while once Condit got with the program and realized we were not just going to turn over the house to him and keep making payments on his behalf out of the goodness of our hearts.

Over time it got worse.

One night I was up late reading and heard scratching in the yard and a dull clank. I went to the window and parted the curtains and in the backyard I saw Condit throw down a shovel and lift the body of an animal to his chest, which he spirited off into the night.

The next morning a dog collar enwreathed our front doorknob with a note attached to it written in blunt pencil on one of those old manila parcel tags. It said, DIG WHEREVER THE HELL YOU WANT TO. And in the backyard, next to some hollyhock, there was a hole about three feet deep. My shovel was stuck down in the bottom of it.

After that I began finding the parcel tags all over the house, attached to the mailbox and the shutters and the exterior light fixtures and trees and the handle of the lawnmower, on the hose rack and the license plate rim of the car. Only one of them would appear each day, each one with a cryptic message written, it seemed, with the same blunt pencil.

It began with A COWARD HAS NO SCAR. The next read, BETTER REPAIR THE GUTTER THAN THE WHOLE HOUSE. I wisely chose to hide the bulk of these from Annie, who was by then barely able to function. By the time Condit had written, IF THERE WERE ONLY SNAILS AND TORTOISE, NO HUNTER WOULD EVER FIRE HIS GUN, and THE PRICE OF LIBERTY IS ETERNAL VIGILANCE, I began to seriously consider moving. At that point we had no life. Whatever creature comforts we gained as homeowners were overshadowed by Condit's menacing. The cops just blew us off, said they could not take him in since we had no proof it was him. Annie asked them if calling out the SWAT team wasn't normally enough to land somebody in jail.

They said, "That's over. We have to move on." They told us to get a picture of him on the property. We could use it to file a restraining order. I asked them if they thought a man who would tag a house with proverbs would be worried about obeying a court order. The cop said, "One hundred percent of the people we deal with don't worry about the law, sir, but we can't arrest them before they commit a crime. It's not science fiction."

Roger said that after 9/11 they can do whatever they please and we will thank them for it. Then he said that maybe the cops cannot arrest you for thinking about socking a guy, but God has said his piece on the matter. "That's why there's a separation of church and state, right, Stevie?" Roger said, slapping me on the back. "So it looks like, in no uncertain terms, you've got an itch you can't scratch." I nodded. "You want me to scratch it for you? I know some guys who worked in Vegas who knew a guy called Scissors—"

"What are you saying?" I blurted.

"Calm down. I'm not saying anything."

"We can't have Condit killed," I said.

"Why not?" Roger said. "Just send the guy to sleep with the fishes." Roger chuckled at his own joke. When I did not laugh, he repeated the line.

"Listen, Roger. I just need this guy to stop. I gotta get my life back."

"All we need to do, Steve, is scare the guy. It's simple deterrence, nothing more or less than the stunts he's been pulling on you and Annie since you moved in. He isn't trying to hurt you. He's trying to run you off like in those *Scooby-Doo* cartoons. We just need to scare him back."

"Fine, Roger," I said. "You wear the sheet."

"Okay, you're upset. I can see that. What I'm saying is you're going to have to fight fire with fire."

The trouble with Roger is that most of the time he is right. He is right so often that when he is wrong, you still think he is right, which makes him think he is right all the time, which creates this perpetual-motion-machine/irresistible-force-meeting-an-immovable-object that pulverizes everything.

I went home with Roger's comments about scaring Condit away seared into my mind. The more I wanted to dismiss the idea, the more merit it seemed to have. Condit was not the kind of guy to fret over restraining orders—that much was clear. The cops had already told us there was nothing they could do unless we could prove that he had been on the premises, and you could tell in their faces that they believed they had more important things to do, like getting into high-speed car chases and Tasering people. But the long and short of it was that while Roger was thinking of this like *Scooby-Doo*, I kept feeling like it was *Cape Fear.*

Condit did not seem to me like one of these disgruntled old men who would be loaded into a paddy wagon in handcuffs and a blanket saying, "If it weren't for you meddling kids, I would have gotten away with it." No, Condit was the type to kill your dog and give your daughter copies of Henry Miller.

When I got home, Annie told me that Condit had come to the door dressed up like the paperboy coming to collect. I asked her what that meant and she said he had one of those newspaper bags and he was wearing a gray jumpsuit, like coveralls. Annie said he was there to collect for the papers. He had a receipt book. Annie called the *Journal* and found out that he was, in fact, the carrier for our route.

We found color photocopies of old photographs of Condit and his family in with the paper. When she opened it, they would flutter onto the kitchen table. One showed him and his wife and kid out in front, the kid on a bike with training wheels, Condit in his military uniform with his hands on his hips, his wife clutching a pocketbook, her hair impeccable. In another, Condit and his wife were in their bed with the sheets and blankets pulled up to their necks. The wife's brassiere hung from the bedpost, and a son and daughter were on either side of the bed with trays of breakfast. The next photo that came showed Condit's wife alone in the bed. She was much older, an IV threading up her forearm to a bag of fluid hanging limply from its stand. She was trying to make a good show of it, but you could see the defeat in her face: slack mouth, dark eyes, unkempt hair. The next was a headstone engraved: MARY ELIZABETH CONDIT 1956–2003.

The night we found the photograph of the headstone, I dreamed that Annie and I were vacationing on a houseboat. Our baby (I dreamed we had a girl, which we did) was older, maybe thirteen, draped over the boat rails in shorts and an Old Navy T-shirt. She was reading *Seventeen* magazine. Annie was next to her, reading *Tender Is the Night*, absently pumping a drinking straw up and down into a tall glass of iced tea. My daughter looked up at Annie, who smiled and said, "I think you're prettier than those girls."

"Mom," our daughter sighed, turning the page.

I was steering the boat. We lounged around that way for what seemed like hours. Then we anchored and ate dinner. Later, I played old Oasis and Dave Matthews songs on a nylon-string guitar. Our daughter sang harmony. Annie finally smiled and eventually joined in, and we played until it began raining. Buckets of rain. We secured everything and went inside and went to sleep with blue flashes of lightning throwing shadows at odd sudden angles. In the midst of one such flash of lightning, I saw Condit's face for an instant, rain streaming down his nose, flying from the rim of his stoma as he exhaled.

He was above us, clinging to the ceiling like Spider-Man, a pistol jammed into a belt he wore strapped around his gray coveralls. By the time I could rouse Annie, a second flash of lightning burned through the cabin and Condit was gone. Then I arose and found a large fireman's ax secured to the kitchen wall, took it down, and crept with it to the rear of the boat. As I fumbled with the catch on the sliding glass door, there was another flash of lightning and Condit materialized on the deck, holding the pistol against his stoma so the barrel pointed to one side and the chamber was flat against his throat. He began speaking in gibberish, advancing slowly toward me, his hair strewn with some sort of mucilaginous river muck, the muscles in his neck and hands wound like a winch. Another flash of lightning. More gibberish. Ax. Pistol. Lightning. Condit.

Then Annie woke me. "You were having a nightmare," she said.

I looked around the room, a gentle blue light misted the walls. The covers were heaped at the foot of the bed. It was 2:44. Annie asked me if I was okay. I said, "Yeah, I want to get some milk or something." Then I pulled the sheets back onto the bed and tucked her in and told her not to worry, but she knew better. Her face said, *Steven, I know that when you say, "Don't worry," you really mean, "If I can keep you in the dark, then I won't have to worry about you, too."* She sat upright in the bed as I left the room and descended the stairs. I did not want to think too much about what was going through her head. This need not have happened. We could have chosen a thousand different paths.

We could have, should have used a realtor. We could have worked out something else with my mother. We could have waited. I brought this on, that much was clear to me. I wanted to find a different path. I wanted to buck the system. That was all me. For whatever reason I felt like we could never make enough money to own the kind of house I felt was appropriate. My father had spent so much of his life trying to do more than simply put a roof over our heads. He wanted a home to mean something to us, to be something we would all take pride in. He did. He was always gathering people at the house, calling them home. I was the oldest, and he had worked on me the hardest, unable to help his youngest, the prodigal.

I stood at the window, looking out on the predawn blueness of the neighborhood, contemplating everything that had happened since that day I decided to go for it. The dream I had that night had nearly driven me to give up on the whole project, but Annie and the baby inside her preserved my resolve to forge on.

During my meditation, I saw movement outside near the street. Condit's outline popped into the morning sky above a line of hedges at the street. He lifted a bulky, top-heavy weapon of some kind to his shoulder. I hit the floor, hearing only a thwip outside followed by a thwap on the front window. Right after that, there came more thwips followed by more thwaps. I stood slowly, gingerly, and three huge red splatters covered the window. Condit's outline flittered against the blue morning. I went back to the kitchen and got a roll of paper toweling and some Windex. Annie called from upstairs, "What was that racket?" I told her it was my mother on the phone and that something fell against the window.

"Go back to sleep," I said. "I'm taking care of it."

After Condit paintballed the house, an old Ryder moving truck arrived with the decals peeled off and dust coating the panels. You could still make out the letters on the side—they were a shade lighter than the rest of the vehicle. It was parked in front of the neighbor's, and for three days we saw no one coming or going from either it or the house. The FOR SALE sign had been taken down while we were at work, but we did not see hide nor hair of the new neighbors. Just the truck.

One night, a day after the truck appeared, a thin strip of yellow light beamed from underneath the roll-up door. I went out to have a look and found nobody in the house or in the cab, which was tidy except for a milk crate lined with a garbage sack and filled with old fast-food wrappers and cups.

ANOTHER COUPLE OF DAYS PASSED, and there was no sight of the neighbors. I was out on the sidewalk in front of the house, pulling weeds in the median between the sidewalk and street, when the door on the truck slid up, and Condit was standing there in his pajamas with a toothbrush in his mouth. He looked at me and spat a white gob of foam onto the street, where it hit next to several dry but similarly shaped splotches. He took the small silver wand from his robe pocket and lifted it to his throat. "HOWDY NEIGHBOR," he croaked, and then drew his forearm across his mouth.

The interior of the truck had been set up like a small traveling bachelor pad: twin bed, chest of drawers, a recliner and a stack of magazines, a small table with a windup alarm clock, and a small hand crank AM/FM/shortwave radio. Two coolers were stacked one on top of the other up front, and he had a few of those inspirational posters of mountains, oceans, and golf courses taped to the walls. "WHAT A DRAG IT IS GETTING OLD," he said.

I laughed a little, despite my petrification. "Mother's Little Helper?" I asked. "My dad listened to the Stones."

Condit looked confused.

"'Kids are different today . . . I hear every mother say . . .'" I sang.

He shrugged.

"Never mind," I said. He shrugged again. I got tense, started breathing through my nose. "What the hell have you been doing to us?" I growled.

"GOING DOWN FIGHTING," he said, then he reached up and grabbed the door and pulled it down. "JUSTICE IS MINE."

I stood in the street frozen between the urge to knock on the truck door and the urge to call the cops, and then the fight left me. For no good reason at all I saw clearly that Condit was playing the game of *I'm not touching you*. You know, where one kid sitting next to another kid in the car will hover the flats of his hands over the face, arms, and legs of the other kid. I used to do it to my brother, made him scream, "Tell Steven to leave me alone!" My mother would whirl around, her finger poised, her mouth thin, compressed, and snarling. "I'm not touching him," I would say, showing how my hands were not, in fact, touching his body.

"Then stop not touching him," she would say. "Don't touch him and don't not touch him. Just keep your hands to yourself, young man."

And why did I do it? you might ask. Because it was the only power I had.

3

The Dr. Science Show

"Other materials respond weakly . . ."

I HAD WRITTEN THAT SENTENCE a dozen times in a half hour in the margins of a legal pad before I realized I wasn't even looking at the page. When I looked down, I saw that I had somehow doodled three or four drawings of the Earth's magnetic field, and a side sketch of a horseshoe magnet with a horse's head, mane, and tail coming out of the curve at the middle. The poles of my horse-magnet featured thick shoes, not horseshoes, but the kind of hobo shoes you see in a cartoon.

Elsewhere on the pad I'd written the following notes:

acts differently at a distance
1 tesla = 10,000 gauss
the force is inversely proportional to the square of the distance between objects.

There was a drawing on another page showing a line of kids stretching off toward the horizon wearing T-shirts with the horse-magnet design on them. I indicated that each child should be holding a sign that says 1, 1/4, 1/9, 1/16, and so on. Why did I do this? Because kids have a hard time with concepts like "inverse proportionality." In all reality, most adults have a hard time with science for all the reasons you've heard before.

Those few pages were all I had to take with me to the writer's meeting for my television program, *Dr. Science.* Normally I'm literally overflowing with ideas, but I took a personal day because I had recently discovered my wife was having an affair with a man you've probably heard of. His name is Chuck Vogel. He's also from television. Reality television, oxymoron that it is. Because of Vogel and my wife, I found I didn't have much to say to children about anything. My discovery of their infidelity was the beginning of the end. The worm was turning. The phoenix would rise, and fear not, for the phoenix here is me, but not yet, not while I was still dozing at my notebook.

With this story meeting on the horizon, I tried to gather myself together, but came back obsessively to the phrase "other materials respond weakly." I realized that during my reverie I'd been tracing over the letters until I had nearly cut through the sheet with my pen.

A day earlier, while I was still blessed with ignorance about my cuckoldry, I had what now seems like an ironically pathetic obsession with the phrase "opposites attract." This can be true in so many different ways. I leafed further back in my notebook and found four or five intricately drafted pages devoted to that idea. One page was a dense list of attractive contraries: ice cream and hot fudge, mouth and ear, gun and elk, man and woman, et cetera. On another page, I drew a picture of some boys huddled together and a similar group of girls a distance from them. I captioned it: *Middle School, Fall Mixer*, then drew in magnetic lines of force passing through the heads of the girls and the groins of the boys.

I thought to myself after the Chuck Vogel news that it seems I got it the wrong way around.

A ping came from my computer, and thirty seconds later my secretary called me on the phone. "Did you get my email?" she asked. I wheeled around to the computer and woke it. Her message was sitting on top of three from Merilese, my wife's personal assistant, and one from Asa Kirschbaum, my best friend.

My wife is Barbara Stein. I probably should mention that. Unless you've been in a coma for the last ten years, you know who she is. According to her marketing people, eight out of ten people have one or more of her books in their house, TiVo her shows, subscribe to her magazines, download her podcasts. I'd put even money on the fact that you've said her trademark phrase, "Ain't life sweet," at least once in your life, even if you didn't want to. Maybe you did it ironically. Most people do these days.

Everyone in this little triangle of infidelity is famous, and that adds a surreal dimension to it. Anyway, my wife is so ridiculously busy that we communicate indirectly, through one of the three or four assistants she burns through in a year. Part of me thought that it wouldn't be beneath Barb to farm off the affair to this Merilese person, the new meat. So much for wishful thinking.

The subject lines of Merilese's emails read as follows:

FW: RE: TELL HER TO GO TO HELL!!!!!!!!!!!!
RE: TELL HER TO GO TO HELL!!!!!!!!!!!!
Meet BS for Lunch at TRIBECA BISTRO?

I didn't really have the patience to reread any of these emails, so I choose the message that had come from my friend Asa instead.

Asa is a puppeteer. Strangely, he is both more and less of a celebrity than any of us. Though you wouldn't know him from a hole in the ground, you are without a doubt acquainted with his alter ego, Milo, the purple monster from the Parents' Choice Award–winning television show *Milo's Treehouse*. Asa has made millions on the licensing, which (and here's Asa in a nutshell) he used to build an avant-garde Hebrew puppet theater in the Bronx called Alef-Ayin.

The theater effectively turned Milo into Asa's day job, and the networks knew it. People in the know said the quality of *Milo's Treehouse* dropped a few years ago. I couldn't tell you if it did or didn't, but people in the know always say the quality of your show is dropping, no matter what kind of energy you're putting into it. They worry you'll end up coasting if you're not afraid.

I had a meeting scheduled later in the week with some consultants the network brought on board to help us update my program, *The Dr. Science Show*, which I had run by myself nearly as long as Captain Koala and Mr. Plaid Pants had run theirs. Technically I was an executive producer, but I'd been told it was no longer up to me to run it alone. There are no auteurs in television, they said. PBS had a lot of stakeholders, and we could no longer expect the taxpayers to treat us like Amtrak. No one who actually makes children's television ever uses a word like "stakeholder," which is why I knew my time in the business was almost up.

Asa's email had no subject line (his signature move). The message said, Wanna get a slice? I emailed him back and said, Writer's meeting until noon. I'll meet you at Ray's around twelve thirty. The millennials we all worked with were dumbfounded that we still used email. We took a certain delight in the agitation. As I sent the mail, I heard my secretary sigh into the phone and ask if I was still there. I said yeah, and she told me Merilese had been terrorizing the phones since eight. I told her to hold all my calls unless it's Asa.

"That's what you always say."

"Well, I must mean it, then," I said, and then hung up the phone.

When I arrived at the meeting, the room was already bristling. It was located in the network building on the East Side, with a view of the Queensboro Bridge. There was glass on all sides and a long, kidney-shaped table full of Danishes, coffee, and clipboards. The producer, Devin Hamblin, was at one end of the table. She was wearing the women's uniform: heap of hair, rectangular glasses, black turtleneck, gray tights, miniskirt. Pablo and Laura were kibitzing over some design magazine. The two of them were in the uniform that was in style two uniforms ago. Pablo wore his hair shaved close. He was goateed, wearing a bowling shirt with the name GLENN embroidered over the pocket in red. Laura's clothes were too tight and the color of dime-store candy. On the other side of the table, Sage and Emily were sitting in isolation, Sage reading a comic book and Emily thumb-typing into an iPhone. There was an open chair opposite Devin's—Asa would have asked, "Is this one saved for Elijah?" I tried that line once, and people just stared at me, so I said nothing, which was better for me in the long run.

"Oh, good," Devin said, "You're here . . . finally." When Devin spoke, her lips moved but her teeth remained motionless. It could have been TMJ, but I think it was more likely an affectation she picked up in college. I apologized and told the room that I was working on the magnetism show and time got away from me.

Emily stopped typing and said, "Einstein said time is affected by gravity, not magnetism. We'll need a complete unified field theory before that excuse will hold water," then she chuckled to herself without looking up. Sage lowered his comic book and looked over at Emily then shook his head and turned the page. Pablo checked his phone, which apparently had nothing new to offer, so he set it on the table.

That's how those meetings went. Ostensibly those people were the best and brightest in the field. We pulled Pablo away from *The Spongeguy* at the height of its success, lowered his salary, and told him he'd be making a difference, that *The Dr. Science Show* was one of the last things television does to keep kids out of jail. Turns out he'd been deeply influenced by our show as a kid and had erased all of his parents' cassette tapes with an electromagnet I taught him how to build in one of my first programs. He was a super-fan, which we could manipulate.

The rest of them had the job because they like living in New York, except Emily, who had taken this job to keep herself from going back to graduate school for a second PhD.

I passed my sketches to Devin, who projected them on the back wall of the meeting room.

"What's with the horses?" Pablo asked.

I shrugged. "Horseshoe-shaped magnets, I guess. I don't know. It's a metaphor."

"I don't know," Laura said, "I don't think it's actually a metaphor."

"Just tell me we're not going to dump a bunch of iron filings on a card and rub a magnet around underneath it," Devin said, flipping her pen around her thumb.

"Why not?" Sage asked without moving the comic. "That stuff is retro-cool."

"It's pretty Mr. Rogers-y if you ask me," Laura said dismissively.

Sage's eyes flared, and everyone knew at once to scoot away from him. "You leave Fred Rogers out of this. You are *nothing* compared to him. Nothing. Dust of the planet. Not stardust. Just human skin and dandruff," he growled, his comic book down, and the skin around his sideburns looking as if it might burst into flames.

"Whatever you say, but we can't do television that way anymore. He's a dinosaur," Laura said. "He's got heart but no style." At this point, Sage nearly leapt across the table, but he ended up flopping on it like a sea lion. Devin looked to me for leadership, but I just watched while Sage slunk embarrassed back to his chair. Pablo then told Laura that Mr. Rogers was dead and she'd probably better show some respect.

"We have to go into the studio on Monday," Devin said. "And we're going to need more than horse magnets. This isn't 1974. What's the hard science here, Emily?"

"Easy, except for there's really no way to tell kids where magnetism comes from without sounding like Yoda."

Sage threw his arms into the air and hissed, "What is wrong with Yoda?"

Before anyone could yell at him, I stepped in. At first it was to settle the squabbling around the table, but it fell apart quickly. "Let me tell you people a little something about magnetism. In 1600 William Gilbert published a book on lodestones. In it he lays out everything that anyone had written on the principle of magnetism since people started thinking about it. Most of what they had to say was nonsense, and Gilbert said as much. The man had a spine, the best information of the day, and style. There's a chapter in that book about magnetic coition—you know what coition is, don't you, Sage?" He shook his head. "It's what you get when you put a scheming, malcontented, borderline-OCD harpy in the same room with a blackguard know-nothing ex–drywall contractor from Coral Gables, Florida, and let the positive pole attract the negative pole. That's when you get coition, Sage. That's when they have to start hauling in the towels because the old black art of magnetism is strongest when you're right there with it, when one pole is hovering right there."

I was shaking. The room was confounded by my outburst. Devin interrupted me, which saved me from descending even more. "Max, how are we going to involve the Junior Science Corps in the magnetic coition part of the show? Could be over their heads, right? Not without the basics, first."

I looked her in the glasses and said, "They used to put magnets under the pillows of suspected adulteresses. If they were guilty, the power of the stone would drive them from their beds."

I WAS STILL SEETHING WHEN I set my slice of pizza on the counter and climbed onto the stool next to Asa. "What's wrong with you?" he asked.

"You look like you've been run over by a garbage truck." I motioned to the billboard sitting atop an electrical supply warehouse across the street. It was one of the newer ones that showed Barb in an embroidered shirt with feathered earrings. She was arranging flowers in a slender glass vase. Her hair was bright red and curly, and someone had airbrushed away most of her crow's-feet. The billboard gave the new time of her show and her tag line: CHANNEL 6 AT 9:00—AIN'T LIFE SWEET.

"Oh," Asa said. "There she is again."

"She's everywhere."

"And yet, somehow, also nowhere . . ."

I gave Asa a look, to which he said, "Every time we see a picture of Barb, it reminds us that she is somewhere else. Reproductions do that. In so many ways we have to wonder if our senses give us reality or just another reproduction of it."

I wasn't going to argue with him. Those are the kinds of things he says. He's not putting on a show for anyone, but I figured I could cut through his philosophizing with something a little more direct. "Barb has been screwing Vogel."

"Sy Vogel with the deli in Queens?"

"No, the home show guy with endorsements."

"Oh, man. I'm sorry, Max. What's his name? Chuck?"

I nodded.

"Chuck," he repeated, then he shook his head. "The rhyme is unfortunate—"

"Yeah, it is."

Asa apologized. "You catch them at it or did you find some letters or something?"

"What kind of question is that?"

Asa wiped his mouth and turned to me. "A man can't find peace by turning his head, Max."

"It doesn't matter how I know. I just know."

"How you know matters. It really does."

I looked down at my pizza and lifted it to my mouth. Outside in the street, a woman flung a shopping bag into the air. It sailed into traffic and landed on the roof of a taxi. Then she began pointing at the cab and screaming.

Asa shook his head. "You see that?" he asked.

"Yeah," I told him. The woman had run into the street and was climbing on the hood of the taxi.

"If we could see the world as God does, that woman out there would make sense to us."

"Which woman," I asked? "The one who's there or the one we might not be able to see?"

Asa didn't answer.

WHILE I WAS NEW TO my rage, I didn't want Barb to make sense to me. I wanted to invent new horrors I could unleash upon her. It was the first time I had felt truly violent, maybe ever. Those impulses kept me from being able to concentrate on any one thing for more than a couple of minutes. In public I would eat like a bird, but in private I was ravenous. I was reluctant to speak, and then suddenly I would spew forth diatribes and venomous streams of consciousness. For all of my adult life I despised Hamlet because I did not understand why he wouldn't just walk up to his uncle and run a sword through his belly.

What I did not tell Asa during lunch that day was that I had, in fact, caught them, not in bed but on the kitchen floor, with one of Barb's fancy stools knocked over and some red lentils scattered across the marble tiles.

When I came in, Vogel cursed and looked up at me with this gold cross slapping his shaggy chest. Barb was still wearing her garden clogs.

"How about some privacy," Vogel said, as he settled against my wife's body.

"Get yourself out of her," I growled.

Barb covered her face, then her breasts.

"Classy way to talk, friend," Vogel said, drying his face with his forearm.

"Friend? Nobody in here is friends," I said.

"Max," Barb said, "you're not making any sense."

"In Brazil," I said, "I could bludgeon you both to death and walk out of the courthouse a free man."

By this point I was looking away from them and up at the ceiling fan, but I couldn't make myself leave. Vogel hoisted his pants and began gathering up his clothes. Barb pulled an apron from one of the lower drawers and put it on. Her bra was on the toaster. They kept saying my name, telling me it's not what it looks like, that I've got to understand, that things got out of hand—they'd been working on a pitch for a new show that combined his world and hers. Oh, I couldn't stand it. I had nothing more to say to them, but I kept thinking of Barb's trademark, "Ain't life sweet." The more I thought of it, the more I raged, and the more I raged, the more focused I became, like an industrial laser.

"I think I should actually kill you both. It's the best choice," I said. "Yes, the best choice, definitely the best choice, but it wouldn't actually be my choice because it would be caused by your choice, which was not the best choice. No, right? Because life is so sweet. Who cares? Max is a schmuck—he didn't see this coming because he is always thinking about his fancy science projects."

This outburst left them bewildered. I know it did. It left me bewildered, too. After that, I sort of blacked out. During my blackout, Vogel left, but after a couple seconds popped back into the kitchen for his phone. Barb left the kitchen and went to our room. As she left, I saw her eyeballing the spray of lentils, so I took a step and crushed them into the tile with my shoe. I watched my wife's naked rear end, framed by the edges of the apron. It was like I'd never seen her before. She bolted from the room, and in the distance, I could hear her cursing as well. Cursing, not crying.

So, how would I tell Asa about that? How would I tell him that Merilese came over to the apartment that afternoon and hauled four of Barb's suitcases out to the Range Rover and drove her to the airport, where she flew to the Charleston house, which she set up as her new HQ? I would not have known where she was if the neighbors in Charleston hadn't called to ask when I was coming down to join her.

How could I tell him I spent three hours behind a power buffer trying to erase this memory from the tiles?

I WOULD HAVE STAYED CATATONIC like that, probably forever, if my brother hadn't called. He's ten years older than me, a Vietnam vet who smoked his larynx to smithereens. Now he talks with one of those robot voice wands.

"NO TIME FOR SMALL TALK," Boyd said. "I'M GONNA LOSE MY HOUSE."

"What is it this time?"

"YOU HEAR ME? THEY'RE GOING TO TAKE THE HOUSE . . . AWAY."

The last time I got a call like this it is was Boyd's gambling. Every time I get a call like this it's his gambling, never something else. He's gone bust three times in his life, had two wives leave him over it. The last one died of a heart attack. Asa said Boyd's addiction must have broken her spirit, right in two. That's how Asa's mother died—his father's drinking made her just up and quit living. She got too tired of worrying.

"Are you gambling again, Boyd?" I asked.

Silence.

"Dammit, Boyd," I said. "I don't have time for this anymore."

"BANK GOONS ARE OUTSIDE RIGHT NOW," he said. "GOT TO MAN THE STATIONS."

"I can't do this today, Boyd."

"THEY'RE AT THE DOOR."

"Boyd, Barb's been sleeping with—"

"I NEED TWELVE GRAND, YESTERDAY. WIRE IT. SAME ACCOUNT AS BEFORE. THEY'RE COMING. WE'RE FAMILY. FAMILY IS EVERYTHING, MAX." Next thing there was the sound of broken glass and shots. The phone hit the floor, and then there was nothing.

THEY SAY PROBLEMS COME IN threes, that the universe is fixated on that number and it wants, more than anything, to seek this trinity. Then again, three people in a photograph is bad luck. So, I gather, is three people in a marriage. Asa says that the whole thing with problems coming in flocks of three is God's way of reminding us that He does not play at dice with the universe.

"These patterns are a kindness, Max," he told me once on the phone. "Like the rainbow. He wants us to know where we stand in the world, what is within His command. The world seems random if we don't look carefully at it, or if we look without faith. God did not wait for Moses to go to the mountain before He set the burning bush aflame."

"He didn't?" I asked.

"It was always burning. Moses was the first to notice. That was his calling."

"You lost me."

"Everything is spiritual, Max. People have it mixed up. They think God despises this world for being physical, which doesn't make sense. Why would He labor to create this world only to hate it? He's not a moody painter. He is God. Our perception of His creation comes between us, keeps us from understanding where He's coming from. We separate the spiritual from the physical. That rift is our doing. If we learn to see what's really there—the burning bush, love, Higgs boson particles, gravity waves—if we learn to take note of the order with which God acts and look past the chaos that we impose on His creation, then we will come to know Him. This is why He says, 'Be still and know that I am God.'"

"I can't be still. I'm pissed off."

"You've got to release yourself from that. And you can."

"Asa, my brother has declared bankruptcy three times. If I bail him out again, he's just going to piss it away."

"He might. But your job is not justice, it's to forgive. How else will you find peace?"

"I'm not sure I want peace," I said. "I want to make Barb and Vogel pay."

At this point neither of us said anything for a very long time. It was late, and I knew Asa had to be in the studio early. He was good to put up with me. I think in some way it gave him a chance to put his faith into practice. I was a better crucible for his ideas than temple or prayer. Asa was in it already, living it, but I could be changed. I might come around and find enlightenment. But other materials respond weakly, right? I didn't want the attraction. I just wanted to hear Asa talk about these things. And maybe I was "other materials."

"God is testing your brother, Max," he said finally, "but He is also testing you."

"What if I fail?"

"You might. That's why you must be careful."

"Is God testing Barbara?"

"He's been testing Barb her whole life."

"How's she doing?"

Another long pause. "I don't really have to answer that, do I, Max?"

Over the next twenty-four hours, before the meeting and my lunch with Asa, and for the rest of the day afterward, the phone nearly rang off the hook. It was Merilese, Barb's assistant, on damage control. The poor girl was a ventriloquist's dummy. She wanted the mail, Barb's letters. She was trying to be indirect and very nonchalant about it, but it quickly degenerated into begging and threats. She must have known that I understood how Barb's mail went to her post office box, where it was handled by her squads of interns and assistants. It was fishy indeed that the mail should be of any concern to Barb, so fishy that I decided to take a look for myself.

It didn't take long, but eventually I found, in the small bundle of letters and magazines, two envelopes from her stockbroker. They were addressed to Bitya Steinberg, Barb's real name. Someone was striving to fly under the radar. A few people know Barb cleaned up her name in the eighties. She said it was to be more American. Nobody questioned it because we were in the middle of a recession and trying to wash off the stink of Desert Storm. That's how my wife turned herself into a shiksa.

I held the stockbroker's letters up to the window, and in that weak X-ray I could see the simple sheet of paper and nothing else. We were in the middle of a quarter, so it wasn't likely a statement. I set the letters down, went to the kitchen, and got a beer, but I couldn't stay there. I returned to the letters.

I know this sounds made up, but they were pulling me, or maybe it was that I was pulling myself to the letters or more accurately, in gravitational terms, that we were pulling each other. It sounds crazy, but that's how it felt—weak at first, then stronger the closer I got to them. I turned the envelopes over. One was postmarked a week ago and the other only a couple of days.

Let me be the first to say that, under other circumstances, I would have sent the mail along to Merilese, but some quiet and persistent voice enticed me to pick up the older envelope. I also need to say that I am not predisposed to acknowledge voices. I have never entertained them in the past, and I don't plan to open my thinking to them in the future. I am Dr. Science, after all, which is a secular attainment.

But this one envelope nearly leapt to my hand.

As I methodically opened it, I began to feel a confidence and clarity. The confusion of a few moments ago was gone. I withdrew the letter and opened it. It was handwritten and began with the words: *For your eyes only, destroy after reading.*

Even though it was unsigned, I could tell that it had come from Simon Barclay, Barb's broker. It was not on letterhead. It looked in no way official, no connection to the firm, unsigned, and completely independent.

Simon's message was simple.

> *SEC sniffing around your Econo-Mart divestiture.*
> *Do not—I repeat—do not sign Bullseye Emporium licensing deal, or you will go to jail!!!*

I reread the letter two or three times. This information was more shocking, more out of the blue than Barb's affair. That licensing deal with Econo-Mart brought an unseemly amount of money into our lives. That deal paid for the Charleston house, and the boat, and the apartment in Rome, and my Maserati. I tried to take my brother for a ride in that car a few years ago, after his wife died, but he refused. He said it was poison, and it would make him weak.

If Barb was planning to move money over to Bullseye Emporium, the payout would be colossal, no doubt, but it would probably leave Econo-Mart with nothing. In the last year, I've read no less than a half-dozen articles in *The Wall Street Journal* about Econo-Mart's hubris. While other retailers have diversified, Econo-Mart, out of a sense of duty or stupidity, has pushed Barb's product line almost exclusively, to the point where it seems like Barb made the deal with them and not the other way around. If she left them, they would be finished, and she'd get what she always wanted: the appearance of upward mobility, the GM model of the American Dream, the trade up.

The only thing I know for sure about corporations is that they can't stand being left with nothing, and when they get screwed like this, someone in the corporate structure will inevitably dream about or even suggest hiring an assassin, usually a classy one from Europe who has designed his own weapons. That would have solved a lot of my problems, but I could already hear Asa's position on the matter. It halted my dreaming, and I realized there was another letter in my hands. I opened it. It was in the same format as the other:

You cannot outsmart them
They want to make an example of you
Stay away from Bullseye Emp.
For the love of God, Bitya, stay away from Bullseye

As I said, it was postmarked with a later date. The "Bitya" at the end of the note caused me to notice a tickle in my brain that had been bothering me for months. Was she screwing her broker, too? The potential chain reaction of my thoughts from that point, I knew, would have led to complete mental paralysis or insanity, so I set both letters on the counter and drank the other half of my beer.

Then I called Asa.

"Hey, you sound a little crazy today, friend."

"I am a little bit crazy, Asa . . . Barb is . . ." I don't know why I couldn't tell him.

"Max?" he said. "Max, you told me already? Are you having a stroke?"

"Not a stroke. Not what I told you. Max, Barb's in real big trouble . . ." It was hard for me to tell if I was being melodramatic or if I was actually overcome. Asa waited. "Asa, Barb's in big, big, serious trouble, legal trouble. I went through her mail—"

"Max, that's a federal offense."

"Not if you're married. But listen, I'm serious. I think the SEC is looking at her for trading violations."

"Then we shouldn't be talking on the phone," Asa said, alarmed. "Hang up."

"I guess you're right," I said, looking at the receiver to see if it looked like somebody had tampered with it. "So what do we do now. I mean, if they're listening?"

"Hang up. I'm going to hang up."

"Okay, but won't that be suspicious? If we just hang up, I mean, then it'll be obvious."

"What'll be obvious?"

"I don't know—that we had a conversation. Don't you think it'll seem like we're *having a conversation*?"

"We are having a conversation. If we're cooked, we're cooked."

"Couldn't we claim privilege? I saw a *Law & Order* once where they couldn't use this guy's confession because he gave it to his rabbi."

"Max, I'm not a rabbi. I'm a puppeteer."

"Well, you talk like a rabbi," I said, ashamed now for what must have surely seemed like hysteria to Asa.

"Let's talk about this later, my friend. You going to the office tomorrow?"

"Yes."

"Then let's get a slice."

"That'll be good. Probably no bugs at Ray's."

Asa rage-sighed. "There will be."

"They don't know which Ray's is our Ray's."

"Max, it's time for you to shut up. And if you've got a sleeping pill or something, you should take it. Get a good night's sleep and we'll talk tomorrow, okay?"

"Okay."

"And don't *do* anything. Please."

I DIDN'T TAKE THE SLEEPING pill. Instead I scoured the place for files, paperwork, spreadsheets. I couldn't find anything, nothing suspicious in our records. I wanted to call Barb but didn't. Without a doubt, they were tapped in to her phones. While I was on the computer, I checked my email. Aside from the crap there was one message from Devin. The subject line was:

IMPORTANT: Network Consultants Tomorrow A.M.

The message read:

> Okay, everybody . . . this is the moment we've been dreading. As you know, the network has scheduled an 8 a.m. meeting for us with some consultants, which means only one thing. Ratings are down, and they are trying to decide whether to redesign the show or drop us. Come ready to wow them with our cutting-edge ideas for children's educational programming and be ready to run with any idea they give us. Even if we hate it. Do not, I repeat, DO NOT, take umbrage with anything they suggest, or we'll all be auditioning for the next season of *The Apprentice*. I'm not kidding.

Don't do anything rash. That's what Asa said. Take a pill and don't do anything rash. Of course, it's very easy for Asa to hand out that kind of advice. He has not had to deal with this kind of indignity: being second-guessed. His show shot into the stratosphere like a Soyuz rocket. He never had time to adjust to the new world of becoming rich and famous. He hasn't even gotten himself a new apartment, just channels all the money to the puppet theater or stashes it in the bank. Plus, he is spiritually grounded, and I am adrift.

Before I knew it, I'd finished off all six of the beers in my fridge. I was calmer but still agitated. I needed something else to drink. As I reached for a highball glass, I saw the stately rows of long-stemmed, ridiculously expensive wineglasses. My hand floated toward them. It felt drawn toward them. I took the wineglass and fumbled in a drawer in the bar for a corkscrew and went into the wine cellar, which we still called a cellar despite being twenty floors up.

The door hissed slightly when I opened it, and the lights came on serially like the ones in a bank vault. Every space in the racks was full, and a few cartons of wine bottles sat, stacked here and there, not randomly, but in the haphazard, art-directed way that everything in Barb's empire was arranged. What I wanted was the most expensive bottle here. My motivation was absolute pettiness. I wanted Barb to see that empty bottle on the counter, sitting on top of Egg McMuffin wrappers, or maybe in the sink alongside a bag of bite-size Butterfingers.

The problem was that there was too much wine and no way for me to tell the value. So, being a good scientist, I gathered data. I headed back upstairs with a list of twenty-five names and vintages and got on the internet. In about ten minutes I had isolated the 1998 Cheval Blanc, a Cabernet Franc and Merlot with a dash of Malbec and Cabernet Sauvignon thrown in to give it a stunning nose with a cashew nut and dark fruit character with rounded mineral notes, a wine I knew would absolutely lend its terroir to milk chocolate and peanut butter crunch. And it went for two hundred and fifty a bottle. Maybe I'd haul out two of them.

I drank the wine, which saved me the need for sleeping pills and got me drunk fast enough so I didn't have to mope around in agony over my wife's infidelities to me and the laws of the United States of America. I slipped into delicious sleep, and I awoke to the chirping of my cell phone.

"Hello?"

"Oh my God, Max, where are you?"

It was Devin.

"I'm at home, why?"

"It's eight thirty. The network consultan—"

"Oh, sugar," I said.

"Sugar? Who says that?"

"Can you send me a car?"

"I already did?"

"Can you take them to breakfast?" I asked. "I could meet you there."

"Max, they don't want breakfast, besides there are Danishes in the conference room. It'll seem like a ploy."

"It is a ploy."

"Listen—you get here as soon as you can."

I shaved in the elevator and went to meet the car in the street. The doorman said good morning, and I stopped. I got out my wallet and took out a hundred-dollar bill. "You ever see my wife with Chuck Vogel, that guy from *Revive Your Dive*?"

His eyes sliced around the foyer and he tipped back the brim of his green cap. "You mean the house-fixing show?"

I nodded. He folded the bill in half and stuffed it in his pocket. "He's been around."

"A lot?"

His lower lip gathered slightly and he nodded, his eyes on the street.

"How about a weaselly-looking guy, shorter than her, with red hair. Looks like a cross between Robert Redford and Conan O'Brien?"

"You mean Mr. Barclay?"

"Yeah, that weasel."

The guy dropped his shoulders a little and scrunched up one eye. "He used to come around a lot, but I haven't seen him in months."

A car outside honked aggressively.

I gestured to the cash in his pocket and said, "You tell me if my wife or any of these jokers come around. You call me on the phone." I grabbed a pen and wrote my number. "You call me if you see any of them, all right?" Another set of honks. "You will be paid. Tell the guy on the second shift. Tell him to watch out. Tell him there's money in this, for everyone."

I left the building and got in the car. The driver—couldn't have been more than twenty-five years old—adjusted his mirror and said, "Hey, it's Dr. Science. Man, I grew up on your show. You know, I actually built a replica of Mount Vesuvius in the fifth grade."

"With lava?"

"Oh yeah, baby. When we put the Mentos in there it was, like, red gore all over the room. You know what I'm saying? My mother had a heart attack. Science is so freaking awesome." He bro-shook my hand in a way I couldn't follow.

"Thanks," I said. I wish I could just bring him into the meeting with me, let him sell the show. He ran his mouth the whole way, said how he was going to be a scientist, study physics maybe or geology. But his grades were crap and college was a lot of money for his family. I asked him for some aspirin and he said he had something better, handed me a bottle of pills and told me to take one. The bottle said, HYDROCODONE/APAP. "It's generic Lortabs, man. Swiss guy left them in my cab last night." I shook one out into my hand. It had the number M358 stamped into it. You can check the numbers on the internet. I palmed one and handed him the bottle.

"Thanks," I said.

He let me off in front of the building and told me he'd been inspired. He was going to call City College on his break and see about some classes. I told him thanks for the pill and then said, "Science is the art of understanding the world." The kid smiled and said he hadn't heard that line in a long time. I got coffee in the lobby and debated taking the pill. I'd have about a forty-five-minute window, then I'd be in Palookaville for the afternoon. Probably a good thing. Because I'm a lightweight, I settled on half the pill, swallowed it with a swig of coffee, and rode the elevator upstairs. When the doors opened, Devin was ready to pounce. She appeared to be composed, but her eyes were crazy.

"Max, this is it. This is make-or-break. They're looking for a reason to cut the show. The burden of proof is ours. We have to make them want the show. Pablo's been pitching ideas for the last twenty minutes, and they're not biting. If we don't get in there right away, Sage is going to start talking."

"Maybe he should."

"Sage? If it were up to Sage, we'd just fill the show with lightsabers."

"That would probably sell."

"Max," she shrieked.

"I'm going to take care of things," I said, then redirected my attention to the receptionist. "What's your name?" I asked. She looked like she was twenty-three, her hair in a bun with a pencil stabbed through it.

"Elaine," she said.

"Two things," I said. "First, what do you think of my show?"

She looked down and then to the far corner of her desk.

"Max," Devin said, "we don't have time for this."

I hushed her. "It's okay, Elaine, I've taken opiates this morning. I'm bulletproof. You can say whatever you want."

She lifted her eyes, and her face flexed apologetically. "I'm sorry, sir. I don't really watch television."

"So, you're not an actress," I said.

She shook her head no. "I want to work in publishing. I like history." She looked small and ashamed when she said it.

"That's good, Elaine. That's good. Do you think people like history? In general, I mean? Do you think history is marketable?" Devin hissed at me again.

Elaine took in a deep breath and let it out slowly through her nostrils. "I think people don't know what they want, Mr. Condit. People don't think they can like things on their own. They make their choices because they think it will help them fit in. Or maybe that it will keep them from standing out. I don't know if that's the same thing, but I think it is, or close anyway. I think people want to be told what to want and what to like. That way they won't pick the wrong thing." Her eyebrows knit together suddenly. "Is that what you want me to say?" she asked. "Because I don't know what I'm really talking about."

"It's perfect," I told her. "No, you are perfect. Thank you."

"Max," Devin said. "We have got to go in there."

Elaine kept looking at me like there was one more thing she dare not say. I smiled at her and told her that she should finish her thought.

"I don't know. It's just that, well . . . telling people what to like, that's what your wife does. And I don't think she's making the world any better, just more the same."

"I thought you didn't watch TV," I said.

"She publishes magazines, too, you know. And cookbooks."

"That's true," I said. Then I smiled and hoped it wasn't creepy. "You have no idea what you have just done for me, Elaine. Really, you have no idea. Okay—second thing. I have an idea. I want Asa and Elaine to listen in."

"How? This isn't *Mission: Impossible*," Devin complained.

"We can do it with our phones," I said. "We'll call Asa. He'll send his comments straight to Devin as texts, and he can serve as our moral compass. Right now, Elaine, you call Mr. Kirschbaum and tell him everything you just said to me, then tell him I wanted him to hear you say it."

"Max," Devin said, "we can't keep those people waiting. You are not that important."

"I am calling in the reinforcements. Devin, do you have your phone?" I asked.

"Yeah. Why?"

"Asa is going to text you our instructions. I am all nonsense. You are too angry. Asa and Elaine will be the puppeteers."

"He's going to do this by texting?" Devin asked.

"Yes, indeed. We'll use the enemy's weapons against them."

Devin asked Elaine if she had any idea what I was talking about. She shook her head, and when she saw me looking, she smiled.

"Call Asa," I said. "Devin, let's go in there and kick some butts."

We walked into the conference room, me in front, Devin in the rear. I was emboldened by my encounter with the receptionist and the taxi driver and with the still-surging throbs of adrenaline coursing through my bloodstream. The consultants were sitting at the far end of the conference room with Sage, who was hunched over the table, sketching madly with one hand and gesturing with the other. The consultants shared a look that was one-third amusement and two-thirds confusion. "And those are the people of the Numericon Guild of Erdös, who forge the mathematical operations in their workshops and bring them above ground to—"

"Sorry to keep you waiting," I said. "I was just wrapping up a couple of focus groups this morning. I like to keep a clear sense of what people are saying about *The Dr. Science Show.*" As I went to shake their hands, the phone rang. I pressed the speaker phone and said, "Please hold the calls." But I didn't hang up. That was our connection to Elaine, who would relay to Asa. I extended my hand again, "Max Condit—pleased to meet you." We shook hands and exchanged names.

Sage tried to interrupt. "Hey, Max, the phone—"

"So you've met Sage? He's our out-of-the-box thinker, a real envelope pusher," I said. "How about Pablo and Laura?"

"Laura's not here," Sage said.

Sure enough she was not.

"Laura is spending a little time with some of the science educators at NASA," Devin said, and then she checked her phone.

I pulled out a chair and sat grandly. I gestured for Devin and Pablo to sit as well. Pablo seemed to be fuming. His brow was furrowed and his eyes were so small you almost couldn't see them through his little rectangular glasses.

"So," I said, "you have some ideas about my show."

The consultants glanced at each other, and the one on the left opened her leather notebook. "As you know," she began, "the growth of streaming media has increased the struggle for audience share in all markets, but this competition has been particularly stiff for the producers of educational content. Direct-to-school networks, DVDs, and other media have taken away public broadcasting's privileged position regarding this kind of content."

The second consultant chimed in. "Which means broadcasters have had to get more aggressive. The PBS board has brought us in to analyze each offering in the children's educational lineup, which we have done. Now we're meeting with the producers to offer our suggestions for meeting the competition head-on."

"Very interesting," I said. "Tell me, who are your other clients?" The consultants looked at each other with some confusion. "What other shows and networks have you been working on? I mean surely you weren't brought on because you were the low bidder. What I mean is, I have a PhD in physics from Stanford and I've produced the second-longest-running children's program in the history of children's television. What are your credentials?" I grabbed a Danish and sat back in my chair. The consultants whispered to each other, and the one without a pad said, "Well, Amy has an MBA from SUNY Albany."

I told him I thought Albany was pretty good for a public school.

Amy glowered at me for a microsecond then said, "We've worked with *Bob the Builder*, *Dora the Explorer*, *Carmen Sandiego*—"

"Our competition," I said. "How's that supposed to work? If you're telling all of us what to do to be more effective, isn't that a little like you running around a poker table telling people what everybody else is holding? I don't think that's the kind of help we need, quite frankly."

Devin looked down calmly at her lap and firmed her lips. "I think . . ." she said hesitantly, "we should hear some of . . . their ideas . . . um, for the show." Then she looked at me and raised her little phone slightly and set it back in her lap.

Amy smiled and said that she and her associate, his name was Parker, recognized the history of the show and its long run. "But kids want to be empowered to become independent learners," she said. "They don't need or want to rely on adult authority figures for the answers. They want to work it out on their own. We need to help them learn to face unscripted problems."

"It's television. There's always a script."

"Yes, but with technology," Parker interjected, "kids don't have to rely on adults. It's a much more democratic educational process."

With her eyes back in her lap, Devin said, "You're not really taking the adults away, with the computers. You're just hiding them, because kids don't build . . . or program the computers. They're certainly not producing or editing the content of the shows either."

There you go, Asa, I thought.

"That's right," Parker continued. "But you need to give them a modicum of control, a sense that they are behind the learning. They don't know what they want, but they know that they don't want to have to go to adults to get it."

Then Amy added, "We'd like to recommend that you reconfigure the show to focus on your Junior Science Corps group. Have them be the centerpiece of the program. Cast these roles permanently and have them work out the solution to scientific problems together, through a consensus-based group process. We've tested the idea, and kids like it."

"Where does that leave old Dr. Science?" I chuckled. The question flew from my lips before I could contain it. Nevertheless, I had the sinking feeling that I was playing right into their hands. Parker lifted the lid of his laptop and clicked a button on a palm-sized remote, bringing an image to life on the screen.

"We wouldn't suggest losing Dr. Science altogether. Parents have a lot of attachment to the brand, which brings viewers to the show, but we'd like to use the new configuration to hold them there," Parker said. He clicked another button and a cartoon image of an owl in a space suit came on the screen. "That's the new Dr. Science. He's a cyber-owl."

"A what?" I said.

"A cyber-owl," Amy answered. "A kind of STEM muse for the kids. The cyber-owl lives in a computer. The kids can access him and ask him questions when they get stuck. He can send them on quests. We'd use your voice, of course, but the owl would be CGI."

"Cool," Sage said from his seat. "Maybe his programmer could be an old wizard from a thousand years in the future."

"Shut up, Sage," Pablo said through his teeth. "That's probably the worst idea I've ever heard."

"Why not a puppet?" Devin asked, then she glanced at her gizmo. "Computer animation is still pretty . . . expensive, isn't it? A puppet would be cheaper, and you could keep the human quality. We can't sacrifice the humanity of our work."

Parker answered decisively, "Puppets are dead."

Amy followed up, "Kids don't buy into puppets anymore. Ever since

Toy Story they've had insatiable appetites for CGI. Puppets are the new eight-track."

Emily, who had been quiet for the whole meeting, pushed her glasses up and said, "You can cuddle with a puppet—I mean, kids could cuddle with one."

"Puppets are dodos, carrier pigeons," Parker said. "Time marches on, folks. Cuddle factor doesn't sell anymore, look at *Milo's Treehouse*. Licensing revenues have been down for six quarters."

"Time marches on," Asa growled, and then paid for his slice. "Puppets are dead? Are you kidding me?"

"That's what they said," I told him. But he knew. He'd been listening.

"And the network is actually listening to these people?"

"They said they're going to be meeting with all the producers in the network."

"We have a meeting with them early next month," Asa said.

"You're a goner, then," I said.

We took our food and sat at the window facing the billboard of Barb. Asa asked if I wanted to sit somewhere else, and I told him I wasn't going to let her win even the smallest victory. Besides, I was going to need to learn to ignore her smug face raining down on me. "She's everywhere," I said. "There's no escape. I'm going to have to work on tuning her out."

Asa nodded and took small bites of his pizza, chewing them carefully, arranging his napkin every little while. It looked like he was formulating a plan or comment or something, but he just kept eating. He was wisdomless.

Across the street, a cop was frisking a kid in a stocking cap and a huge winter coat. I still felt a little loopy from the pill, but mostly numb. Coming down off the adrenaline was worse. My mouth was dry; the rims of my eyes hurt.

"Everything's upside down," I said. I told him about Barb and the stock situation.

"You are having a terrible week," Asa said. "Are you tied up in any of this? Do you know where the cash is?"

I shrugged. "I don't know. I mean I'm sure she's got money stashed all over the place."

"You should start liquidating before they freeze her accounts."

"I'll have to," I said.

We ate for a while in silence, then Asa set down his pizza and said, "You ever been to Israel?"

Asa wasn't really asking a question but delivering the preamble to a proposition. In the course of reconnecting to his Jewish faith, he had fallen in with some Zionists, people who planted in his head the idea that he would be happiest if he could leave the world of television and reconnect with the land, with physical labor, and perhaps experience direct contact with children through teaching or athletics. Their suggestion was that he could do this best by moving to a settlement in the West Bank, where the borders of Israel were imperiled.

Asa told me he'd been considering this option for a long time, praying every day for insight. Then, he said, this divine call came from our phone puppetry gambit. Once he had the chance to hear the network's plan to strike down everything we'd all been dedicating our lives to, he'd had enough. God had spoken with a clarity that he felt did not require repeating. Asa suggested we both go to Israel. There, in a single stroke, I could escape Barb and my demotion to cyber-owl sidekick.

"Besides," he said, "we don't want what America is turning into, Max."

He was right. I wanted out, out of every last part of it.

Asa had arranged to buy land that was part of a moshav located in the Golan Heights. He showed me beautiful pictures, said the moshavim are collectives, but your place belongs to you and you put your crops in with everyone else's. He said the work can be difficult for some people, but the freedom it could bring would be worth it.

What he said made a lot of sense to me. If Barb was going to be swallowed up by an investigation and media frenzy, I would not be immune here. My money would be frozen as well, my movements suspect. I had very little in my name. Over the next few days Asa continued his pitch. He explained that most people farm in that area, but Asa was planning to open a school, a bilingual school, and who, he asked, would be a better teacher in the beautiful orchards of Mount Hebron than the world-famous Dr. Science?

I was still sitting on the fence until I stumbled upon some bank information I didn't recognize. Deep in one of Barb's files, I found a note card with an internet address, a log-in, and password. It was online access for a bank account in the Cayman Islands in the name of none other than Bitya Steinberg. The balance: fifteen-and-a-half million dollars. I was furious at first, but I came out of it quickly and saw this for the revelation it was.

You should know how difficult it is for me to use a word like that. As Dr. Science, I have lived a secular life, built on scientific training. This religious world of Asa's has been a curiosity for me, something I would call psychology rather than spirituality. The events of the last few weeks make me second-guess that approach. Science doesn't explain my rage at, or disgust with, my wife. In evolutionary terms, what purpose does cuckoldry serve? Wouldn't the organisms who show a predisposition to ignore it be the ones most likely to survive and reproduce? Wouldn't the moody, sad monkeys, the ones crushed by their mate's affection for other monkeys, be the ones to mope themselves into a childless oblivion? How do creatures who can be hurt so deeply by the caprices of other creatures rise up on two legs and become the kings of all they survey? In purely evolutionary terms, we lack the emotional strength of the pit viper or barracuda, and that's a strength we need sometimes.

So, as I stared at Barb's secret account, a pathway for settling the score opened before me, and I moved the mouse without reservation. I searched the internet for another offshore bank. This one in Barbados. I opened an account. When the account was established, I transferred a third of the money into it. Cleaning her out would not give me the closure I wanted. My plan was this: leave most of the money in that account and then leak the information to the authorities, let them follow the money and seize the account. Barb's stash would become a weapon against her in a very real way. I wouldn't just be robbing her, I'd be sending her to prison. And I can't tell you how the thought of that raced through my body like a house on fire.

When the money cleared, I called my brother, Boyd, with the number he left me. It was a motel in Ventura. Even with his talk box, he sounded surprised to hear from me.

"You still need money for your house?" I asked.

"UP YOURS," he answered.

"I'm serious, Boyd. I have some money, and I think I might be able to help you."

"IT'S TOO LATE. I'M OUT FOR GOOD. THEY'VE GOT A FAMILY IN THERE NOW. YUPPIES. I'M HUMAN GARBAGE."

"You're not human garbage," I said.

"YOU'RE NOT HERE. YOU DON'T KNOW."

"What if I told you I had the money to get you a house, free and clear?"

"WHAT DO YOU MEAN, FREE AND CLEAR?"

"I mean I have enough money right now to buy you a house pretty much wherever you want one."

"I WANT THE ONE THEY TOOK."

"Well, that's up to you. Do you still have a bank account, or have they closed it?"

"I GOT THE CHECKING ACCOUNT. THERE'S NOTHING IN IT. MAYBE A COUPLE OF BUCKS."

I had him get a check and read me the account and routing number. Boyd was worried that I would use the numbers to steal from him. I assured him that I would only use them to make deposits. "Go to the bank tomorrow and check your balance. I think you'll be surprised. And Boyd, I'm probably going away for a while, maybe forever."

"TO PRISON?" he asked. "WHAT FOR? SCIENCE CRIMES?"

"No," I said. "There's no such thing as science crimes."

"WHAT ABOUT THE NAZIS?"

"Except for the Nazis. You got me."

"WHAT'S WRONG WITH YOU? ARE YOU DYING?"

"No, nothing like that. I'm quitting the show and moving out of New York. I'll drop you a line when I've figured it out."

"YOU GETTING RID OF THAT SO-CALLED WIFE? SHE'S ON THE TV ALL THE TIME."

I told him that we would not be staying together. Boyd said he was glad about that, told me that Barb used to make his wife cry. Once while they were preparing Thanksgiving dinner, she saw Barb dump one of her pies into the garbage and then walk over and set the tin on the dog's bed. I told him I'd been hearing a lot of stories like that lately.

"Boyd," I said. "Go check the bank, okay? And don't . . ."

"DON'T WHAT, MAX?"

"Well, I want you to— Please just get a house with it. Promise me you'll get a house."

"I'M GOING TO GET WAY MORE THAN A HOUSE, MAXIE," he said. "I'M GETTING JUSTICE."

It was clear to me that Max thought he was going to get justice, but justice might not be the safety net he thought it would be. After I wired him the money, I also took a spare set of keys to the New York apartment and put them in an envelope with a note:

Boyd,

If you need to get away from California, you're welcome to stay at my apartment in New York as long as you like. I've kept a bunch of Mom's things there. It could be a good place to get centered. The alarm code is 1961, the year I was born.

Love,
Max

From this point on, things started moving really fast. I forwarded Barclay's letters to Barb and began to sort through my things. I didn't want much. Almost everything in the place was Barb's. I wanted a laptop, my clothes, the camera, a box of photographs, a few books (Gleick's biography of Richard Feynman, some essays by Albert Einstein, *Gulliver's Travels*). It didn't seem like I could start over with a truck full of my old stuff. Plus, the effect of my leaving would have more weight, I imagined, if I seemed to have vanished into thin air. Asa and I got our passports and visas in order and discussed the possibilities of our school, what we would teach, how we would meet with the parents. It felt energizing to imagine the change.

I was invulnerable to anything the network could do or say to me. During our preparations, Devin and Emily were fired. Pablo left before they could "get their claws into him." He got a job at the Cartoon Network working on a program about the children of superheroes. They kept Sage and Laura and brought in a new producer.

Sage came to me and said, "Hey, dude, it was going to be epic, but you can stop working on the magnetism show."

"Why?" I asked. I thought somehow he knew about my plans to leave.

"They don't want it." He reached into his back pocket and took out a piece of paper that had been folded into quarters. "They gave me a list."

"Who is 'they'?"

"I don't know. Them. The network. Here's the list."

The memo Sage unfolded said the show would need a conservation angle. They wanted programs on the rain forest, recycling, wind power, hybrid automobiles, and lots of STEM. I set the paper on my desk and told Sage to sit down.

"Sage, don't worry about what's going on around here," I told him. "You should just go finish your screenplay."

"Which one?" he said.

"The autobiographical one about the wizard who can see into the future."

Sage wouldn't look at me. "That one's not autobiographical," he said without much conviction.

"Your name is Sage, right?"

He nodded.

"Sage. Wizard. I guess your parents were thinking about the herb."

Sage grinned uncomfortably. I told him I knew the days of Dr. Science were numbered. "Listen," I said. "The future is always in motion. You've got to go catch it."

Sage grinned. "Okay, that's cool," he said, "But you got it wrong."

"What?"

"The Yoda line you just said. In the movie it went, 'Always in motion is the future.' You know, because he's got sensei grammar."

I made a face that encouraged him to think I'd never seen *The Empire Strikes Back*. "Sorry," I said.

"You're okay, Dr. Science." Doing the voice again, he said, "Luminous beings are we, not this crude matter."

"More Yoda?" I asked.

He nodded and walked to the door. "You never once made me feel dumb."

"May the Force be with you," I said.

"No, dude, may the Force be with *you*. You're going to need it, bad."

BEFORE WE LEFT, BARB CALLED me herself. I don't think she even had Merilese place the call. Caller ID showed her personal cell number. I let it ring for a long time before I picked up. She was distraught, and I took pleasure in that.

"Max," she said. "We've both been working too hard, with our shows. It's been a hard year, Max."

"Yes, it has."

"You know this thing with Chuck doesn't mean anything."

"Yes, it does. It means you're a terrible person."

"Max, why would you say something like that?"

"Because no one else will. I assume you got those letters from Simon Barclay."

She didn't answer right away. During the silence, I doodled a pillow and a horseshoe magnet and thought about magnetic coition.

"You read them, I presume?" she asked, eventually.

"Of course I did. Does Simon know about this thing with Chuck? I wonder how he'd feel about that. Doesn't seem like you'd want him to be—what's the right word here—discontented with you right now? A man with the knowledge he has might not like hearing that you've decided to cheat on your husband with someone other than himself."

"I wasn't sleeping with Simon."

"Oh, what tangled webs we weave, Bitya."

"Don't call me that."

"Simon does."

"Simon is a fool."

"Simon has the goods on you. I wouldn't tick him off right now—do you think your phone is tapped?"

"How would I know?"

"Yeah, how would you? Anyway, Barb, I'm filing for divorce. Unless you want your books opened up to the courts, I'd suggest you sign the papers. It'll be easier on everyone."

At that point she hung up. I knew she would. The divorce was simple, I wanted the apartment, and that was it. I didn't even want the Maserati. I only wanted something that would make it through whatever the SEC was going to put her through. It would also cut her to the quick. That apartment was her prestige, the way she bought herself out of her immigrant past. I also wanted someplace to come back to if this collective farming project fell through.

On the day before we were set to leave, Asa called. "I don't have the shows," he said. He was nearly hysterical. I asked him to calm down. "I don't have the shows, Max. They screwed me with the contract."

Asa's contract, it seemed, gave him rights to control and distribute the image of Milo but not the *Milo's Treehouse* program or the secondary characters. It hadn't mattered, because the licensing money was so good. Asa didn't think about it. But when Asa tried to arrange to take copies of his shows, he was told they were all being digitally remastered. The old videotape masters were being erased to make room in the archive for more digital servers.

"Anyway," he said, "I can't take Milo with me. They're holding him hostage."

I MET ASA FOR ONE last slice in town before we left. We sat at the window, eating in silence, our bodies filled with electricity. Asa got a second slice and refilled his Coke and sat back at the window and said, "If we were still in high school, I'd say we should do something to that sign of Barb across the street."

I couldn't bring myself to look at it.

"This girl from high school named Charlene Stavros—she was ridiculously hot," Asa said. "Well, she once dumped a buddy of mine for a guy on the student senate, she told him it was nothing personal, but she wanted to run for student government and thought he could help her. My buddy was crushed, but he decided to get even. He had this photograph of Charlene from an old middle school yearbook. Man, it was terrible: braces, feathered hair, huge Coke-bottle glasses, cowl-neck sweater. He took that picture and photocopied it and made like two hundred posters that said: STAVROS FOR STUDENT SENATE. I USED TO BE A BIG GEEK, SO I KNOW WHAT GEEKS LIKE YOU NEED. He plastered those things everywhere."

"She lose the race?"

"Completely. There was basically a geek riot. The physics club made a pneumatic catapult and shot a dummy dressed in a cowl-neck sweater across the football field. This kid named Marshall won her seat. She never knew what hit her." Asa stared off into the distance, then said, "What if we did something to that sign before we leave?"

"*Revenge of the Nerds*–style?"

"That's right."

"I could get into that," I said.

THAT AFTERNOON WE HATCHED TWO plans, one to avenge me and the other to avenge Asa. I was a little surprised that he would agree to something like this, since he was working so hard to become a man of peace. He said he needed something to help him break from New York psychologically. He wanted something that would make it hard or impossible for him to come back. He didn't want to see the inside of a television studio again, but he knew he was weak.

"So you want to burn your bridges," I asked him.

"That's exactly what I want to do," he said.

I'm not proud of what we did, but it was necessary, and it allowed me to return to the magnetism show I would never finish. It brought me back, in a way, to the beginning. During his interview Pablo told us how he had erased his parents' videocassettes with an electromagnet he learned how to build from one of my first shows, a show in which we did move iron filings around on a card.

I'd go out the way I came in. It felt dizzy and delicious.

Asa, believing he had been robbed of his creation, wanted to make Milo unavailable to the network, which he knew was impossible—copies of the programs were surely vaulted away somewhere in Brooklyn or the Library of Congress—but he wanted to cause a little bit of what he called the "right kind of trouble." He wanted their decision to have consequences they didn't expect. So he suggested we try to erase the digital archive (without damaging the servers permanently, of course—Asa didn't own the servers, but he felt like he owned the shows). The shows wouldn't be gone, of course, but this plan meant the network would have to go back to the beginning of the digitization project. Asa wanted someone at the corporate office to be pissed off.

I wanted to rat out my wife in some public way, and I wanted it to hit suddenly with news coverage. I was entranced by Asa's story of this Stavros girl and her public trouncing in the high school election, so I proposed this: we spray-paint Barb's offshore account information on the billboard across the street from our lunch spot. Asa thought that would be a good idea, but we needed something catchy, not just the numbers. A signature, he called it. Something that would enrage Barb in public. The problem was, we couldn't think of anything, and we needed to leave.

During lunch on our last day of work, we went down to the hardware store and bought a few simple items: a spool of copper wire, two wire nuts, and a lamp timer. The project was simple. We'd carry the wire in on a spool, hang it between two of the servers, pull enough of the wire to make it to an outlet, strip the ends, jam them in the timer, set it to go off later, and then walk out. The current running through the spool would, well, you've seen my show.

It would certainly rile all the people we wanted riled.

We set our magnet bomb at three in the morning on the day of our departure. With our luggage in the car, we left the network, the timer ticking, and we headed to the billboard across from Ray's Pizzeria. We were working on what kind of stinging barb we could leave behind, and we were also nervous because our plane would be leaving in three hours. Asa suggested something like. "My husband is leaving me for a *balebatisheh yiden*."

I shrugged.

"Respectable Jew," Asa said.

"First off, no one in this part of town will get it. Second, let's not let her know where I'm going," I said.

"But it is funny, right?" Asa said.

"It's *shpasik*."

"You're learning," Asa said.

We pulled up to the billboard and parked, got out, and looked for a way onto the roof. Asa went to a dumpster and flipped the lid back against the wall and used it like a ladder to get onto the low roof. I threw our bag of spray cans up and followed. It was remarkably easy. We took a look at the street below. From that height we could see a number of blocks in each direction. We were completely clear. I gave one of the account numbers to Asa and kept one for myself. We mounted the sign and began rattling our cans, laughing, looking at our watches, waiting for the timer to click. We had another ten minutes for that mayhem to begin, so we painted away.

Asa wanted to be sure his numbers were big enough, so he suggested we make them as big as ourselves. Writing at that scale, stopping to shake the cans, was intoxicating (I'm sure it also had something to do with the butyrolactone or other volatiles in the paint). Just as I was finishing my part of the job, a spotlight clicked on us, and we heard an amplified voice saying, "HOLD IT RIGHT THERE, YOU MORONS!" It sounded like my brother, but the flashing blue and red lights told me it wasn't. We both turned and put our hands up before they even asked us to. "WHAT DO YOU THINK YOU'RE DOING UP THERE?"

Asa turned his head to me and said, "The truth will set you free. Maybe."

"It could keep us from getting on that airplane," I said.

"SHUT UP. I SAID, 'WHAT. DO. YOU. THINK. YOU'RE DOING UP THERE?'"

"I'm serious," Asa said. "Tell him the truth." He glanced at his watch. "Three minutes and counting," he said.

I told the cop that it wasn't what it looked like. "We're not in a gang or anything. I'm Max Condit. I have a show called *Dr. Science*."

"*Dr. Science*? No way!" the cop said without amplification. "I love that show. I used to watch it with my kids." The other cop seemed to agree.

"Thanks," I shouted. "This is Asa Kirschbaum. He's the man behind the puppet Milo."

"FROM *MILO'S TREEHOUSE*?" the cop asked through the megaphone.

Asa shouted, "Yes."

"HOW'D YOU GET ROBERT DE NIRO TO GO ON?"

Asa told him that De Niro called him.

I told the police that I recently discovered my wife, Barbara Stein, was having an affair with Chuck Vogel, and that the numbers we'd just painted on the sign would embarrass her immensely. The cop said that my wife's shows and magazines had turned his wife into a certifiable nutcase. When we told him we couldn't really hear, he went back to the megaphone. "SHE CAN'T JUST PUT FOOD ON THE TABLE ANYMORE. SHE'S GOT TO ARRANGE IT. WHEN I GET ON HER ABOUT IT, SHE KEEPS SAYING, 'AIN'T LIFE SWEET, TONY.' I JUST WANT MY CHICKEN SO I CAN WATCH THE KNICKS. THAT'S SWEET, HONEY. JUST GIVE ME MY DINNER AND SCULPT THE NAPKINS ON THANKSGIVING."

I said, "Can you imagine living with her?"

The cop said he'd felt sorry for me. The second cop grabbed the megaphone from his partner and said, "THAT VOGEL HAS DESTROYED MY WEEKENDS. MY WIFE'S ALWAYS GOT ME TILING BATHROOMS AND PUTTING IN NEW FIXTURES. I'M READY TO PULL THE CABLE OUT OF THE WALL SO I CAN CATCH A BREAK."

"That's my whole life," I said. The second cop told me I should be glad, said those two deserved each other. Of course the cops didn't arrest us. They thought our project had wide-reaching importance. One of them even compared it to the Boston Tea Party, at least as far as he and a million other project-laden husbands were concerned. It was a strike against the tyranny of lifestyle porn.

They even suggested the icing on the cake, a simple grace note for the whole project. We crossed out "sweet" and added something crude.

Once we were done and down, they drove us to the airport and wished us well. It was easy to see that they were already savoring the story they'd be able to tell one day about the celebrities they helped jump from the tabloids to the mainstream news. Asa and I would hear only ricochets and echoing aftereffects.

THE MAGNET BOMB WORKED POORLY as a weapon of mass destruction. Everything was backed up in a separate server array on a different floor, and the bomb drew too much power and tripped the breaker. All the better, I'm sure, for our karma, or whatever it is called in Hebrew. Our message to the people of New York worked better. Barb is under indictment, and Vogel has been implicated. Simon Barclay turned state's evidence, which likely carried more weight in court than our graffiti.

On the first leg of our flight to the Holy Land, Asa turned to me, removing his earbuds carefully. "Max, I think I know why God says that vengeance belongs to Him."

"What brings this up?"

"You know, our escapades last night didn't seem particularly holy."

"But they felt good."

"That's what I'm saying. I think God wants us to keep away from vengeance because it's addictive. For the last hour, I've been thinking of all the people who could use a little taste of spray paint or electromagnetism—you know, or people I think deserve it."

"You thought about that for an hour?"

"Pretty much without stopping."

The FASTEN SEATBELT sign came on, and the pilot announced some turbulence. The plane bucked almost imperceptibly. "How did it make you feel?" I asked.

"I don't know," Asa said. "A little lost."

I gestured to the overhead video console that showed our plane's parabolic arc over the Atlantic. In the lower right-hand corner, I could read our latitude and longitude. The thought came to me that I'd never been so certain of where I was in my life. I was about to tell that to Asa, when I saw him wiping a tear from his cheek with the back of his wrist, and I understood exactly how much the both of us were leaving behind.

4

Unscripted

The Jessup house in Anadarko, Oklahoma, was the last location on our shooting schedule. The house in front of us didn't match the one in the production file. Could have been the wrong address, but Margot, our producer, was there when they shot the original episode, so the look of horror on her face confirmed two things: we were in the right place and something was very wrong.

The lawn was dead, and the yard was strewn with junked cars. An orange freight container blocked the turnaround so you couldn't actually drive all the way through. Next to that, a galvanized trash can sprouted rebar and fluorescent light bulbs. A blue tarp had been nailed to the side of the garage and staked into the ground, making a shelter for an odd assortment of cardboard boxes. Junk was everywhere: an extension ladder leaning against the eaves, half a trampoline rising from the tall grass, a pink wading pool full of plastic bottles, a garden hose hanging inexplicably from an upstairs bedroom window. You could zoom in on any part of this house and another universe of garbage would emerge.

Our camera guy, Bill, said, "You've got to be kidding me," then he grabbed the file and started flipping through pictures that showed the house we'd built for this family five years ago. It looked like all the homes we do for our show, *Revive Your Dive.* I grabbed the photos back from Bill and held them up for comparison. It was the same basic size and shape. The roofline was the same. A front entry stood to the right, big windows ran all the way across the ground floor, and dormers with more windows punctuated the upper story.

"I don't want to start unloading if this isn't the place," Bill said.

"Hey, Margot," somebody yelled. "Where are you going?"

I turned and saw her on foot, heading down the driveway toward the street. I got out of the van and jogged after her. When she heard me coming, she sped up without looking back. I like Margot. She and I are as different as two people can be, but we get along. If you were in a scrap, you'd want this lady on your side. She's in charge. I'm just the driver.

"Would you quit?" I said. "You're gonna give me a heart attack."

She slowed, and I eventually caught up to her and turned her around. She shook my hand off and said, "I needed a moment."

I held up the photos and pointed at the monstrosity behind us. "That house is this one?" I asked.

Margot looked away.

"Margot," I said, lifting my voice. "We can't shoot a follow-up segment here if *that* house is *this one*."

"I know that, *Darryl*."

"What's Vogel going to say?" I asked.

"He's going to detonate when he sees this place."

"At this point there's probably no way around it," I said.

"Yeah, there is. We leave."

"Running off doesn't build confidence," I said.

"I know," she said.

"How come you didn't tell us what we were getting into?"

"I didn't know they were going to do this again," she said.

What did she mean *again*? I thought about asking, but Margot looked agitated, so I dropped it. "Doesn't matter what happened before," I said. "We have to figure out our next steps."

"I don't know," she said.

"Do we unload?"

She shook her head.

"Vogel's supposed to be here tomorrow. If we're gone, he's going to split open and melt."

"I know," she said.

"What do I say when they start asking what's up?"

"Tell them it's the wrong place," Margot said, and then she fell to thinking. I turned around and gave her some space.

Back at the house, two teenage girls and their father came out. The father didn't look 100 percent happy about things.

"Too late," I said to Margot. "Cat's out of the bag."

Margot turned and saw them, too. "We have to stop this," she said. "Where is June?"

The crew gathered on the porch to meet the family. It looked strained and uncomfortable.

"June?" I asked.

"The mom? Did you see her?"

"No," I said. "That guy and the daughters is it. Don't get mad, but you need to get it together."

"I've been down this road before," she said, hustling back to the house. "We just have to get out of here before anyone talks to . . . her."

The mom came to the door, a short woman in turquoise pants and a pink sweatshirt. She set her hands on her waist like Superman and looked around. It was obvious that she did not like what she saw.

When I caught up to Margot, she said, "That's June Jessup. She's in charge. This mess is her thing."

"Pack rat?" I said.

"Something like that."

Margot opened her mouth to say more, but June spotted her and pointed and said, "I recognize you. You was here before."

Margot tried to bolt, but I held on to her. "Be cool," I said.

Margot hissed at me, then she straightened up, caught her attitude, and walked through everyone, smiling like Michelle Obama. "Hello, June," she said, "Of course I remember you." She stuck out her hand, which June would not shake. She turned to the husband and tried to greet him. He looked for his wife's approval, which he did not get. The girls stayed back and waved, which appeared to be too much for June.

"I hope you got our letters," Margot said.

"Probably in the stack," June said, motioning toward the house with her thumb.

Margot looked like she was going to fire a comment right back at June, but she didn't. "Okay, well, then it's time for introductions. This is the crew who's here to shoot the 'Has It Really Been Five Years?' segment," Margot said, smiling. "Bill will be doing the camera work. Gavin is the sound guy. He'll have the boom. Karin is our art director, and she also does a little hair and makeup. Farm handles the electrical. And Darryl is our driver and road manager."

"Oh yeah," June said. "If we knew you was coming, we'd have baked a cake."

Margot drew in a breath and then exhaled. She didn't take the bait.

"And let's see if I have it right. We have June and Hoot. Jaymee is the older daughter—probably a senior, right? And Lexi. You were nine when I was here before, so that makes you fourteen."

"Fifteen," she said. "I'm a sophomore."

The Jessups didn't show a lot of interest in the introductions, but they did clearly say they weren't ready for us. Margot said we'd come back tomorrow with Mr. Vogel. June called Vogel a pig and said she didn't want him inside her house.

Margot said, "I'm afraid it's not your house just yet."

Before it turned into a brawl, she hustled us all back into the van, and we got out of there.

Everyone wanted answers, and Margot said she'd tell us what she could, but she wanted a shower and a meal first. So, we all checked in and went to our rooms to clean up. The plan was to meet back in the lobby at six and go to dinner at a Mexican place we'd seen on the way in.

"Mexican food?" Bill said, and stuck out his tongue like a five-year-old.

Margot burned him with a look and said, "There's no Fuddruckers around here. You'll have to get by."

Margot said nothing about the Jessups until after we ordered. We were all aching to know what was going on, and she knew it. "You're probably all wondering what happened this afternoon and why I didn't say anything about it before now."

"Correct," Karin said.

"When we left before, they seemed happy with the house. Glad it was over, but it seemed like we'd been able to do something good. We helped them, and they helped us. Our first season was rough. Ratings were in a nosedive. The market was saturated, with shows like this one everywhere, but this family was built for reality television. Viewers drank these people up. This was all before *Duck Dynasty*. It happened in a time when people made their own clips and shared them on the internet. The Jessup family was what convinced the network to put our own clips of the show on online. Have any of you seen the videos?" Margot looked around. Nobody had.

"Really?" she asked.

Farm raised his hand.

"Only one of you has? Weird."

"To be fair," Farm said. "I saw the videos a long time ago, but I didn't remember it was them until you said it."

"It doesn't matter," Margot said. "Vogel was about to lose the show until these guys came on. They were crazy and hilarious and heartbreaking. Hoot lost his hearing in an industrial accident and was on disability. His kids learned sign language to talk to him. June was television's first official hoarder. Who knew there was a market for that. As weird as they are, their community got behind them. Their church, too. It gave you faith in people. The shoot was perfect, too, until we started loading all of June's junk out of the house. Apparently nobody told June that we couldn't renovate the house unless it was empty."

"I can see where this is going," Karin said.

"We had all these Boy Scouts in gas masks they made themselves out of water bottles and damp rags. They marched out all these disgusting sacks of old stuff. Apparently, it was helping them get some kind of disaster merit badge. They began tossing her junk into the dumpster, June noticed, and started flipping out. 'That's my stuff,' she screams. 'My treasures. I'm gonna sell that on eBay.'"

"Sell it?" Farm asked.

Margot shrugged, "That's what she said. But she came completely unglued, grabbing stuff from the boys, taking it back inside, screaming at them to stop."

"Someone got this on tape, I hope," Bill asked.

"We were rolling the whole time," Margot said.

"Nice," Bill said. "That's how you do unscripted television."

"Actually, it was so awful we wanted to stop, but Vogel wouldn't let us. He said if we did, we'd never work again."

"Being a jerk doesn't make him wrong," Bill said.

Margot ignored him. "June was out there knocking over thirteen-year-old kids. The daughters were crying. Hoot, who can't hear a thing, is in a chaise lounge with a newspaper over his face. Vogel starts swearing at June, then he storms off saying stuff like 'Did any of these rednecks even read the contract?' By the end of the day, June has chained herself to the blade of the bulldozer, screams when anyone comes near, says she won't talk to anyone but Vogel, but Vogel has taken off. Nobody could find him for, like, an hour. When he came back, he had a set of bolt cutters."

"Really?" Farm said.

"Bolt cutters. He sent all of us away, and then spoke with her for a half hour, maybe. When he got back, he threw the chain on the ground with the lock still on it. 'Somebody order a shipping container and have it delivered. Don't rent one. Buy it,' he said. 'We're putting her crap into it. Also, they're all going to Six Flags. I don't want them around for the next part.' Nobody knew how he pulled it off, but we were impressed. We still hated him, but, you know, props to the little guy for that."

Farm was in the corner, looking at his phone, laughing a little and shaking his head. "I'm watching some of that episode," he said. "You aren't doing it justice."

"It gets worse. We send these people off and started figuring out what to do with all of this stuff. It wasn't all going to fit into the container. We knew that much. Sending them to Six Flags bought us a little time, so we all hit the sack. That night, at like two in the morning, the house exploded."

"Shut up," Gavin said.

"It was supposedly a gas leak. Everybody said it was a miracle nobody was in the house. June's sister said it was surely the hand of our Lord, Jesus Christ."

“Vogel did it,” Karin said.

Margot agreed. “That’s my theory.”

“He totally did it,” Gavin echoed.

“That’s what I would have done,” Bill said. “Make it look like an accident. Get some insurance money as well, right? There wasn’t any tape of the explosion was there?”

Margot nodded. “That’s how we knew it wasn’t 100 percent an accident. Vogel had a GoPro mounted to the excavator. He told the police he keeps one on site for security.”

“Does he?” Farm asked.

Margot shook her head. “He does not.”

“Son of a gun,” Bill said.

“What did June do?” Karin asked.

“It put her in the hospital. She thought it was her heart, but it was panic attacks. Vogel must have bribed somebody, because he had the crime scene cleared out and the excavators back to work a week later.”

“They’re doing a whole show about hoarders now,” Farm said. “I have a buddy doing postproduction. I just texted him. He said to stay away from hoarders. It takes all kinds of training.”

“That episode changed the whole show. Starting in season two, no more renovations. We started fresh each time. It saved us so much money, and people loved the demolition. But look, we’ve got a contract to shoot these locations. I don’t need to tell you what will happen if we don’t wrap the season.”

“I can’t shoot in that dump,” Bill said.

“Agreed,” said Farm. “If I run power into a place like that, we’ll all wish I didn’t.”

“Vogel gets here when?” Gavin asked.

“His plane lands tomorrow at two,” I said.

The waitress brought our food, warned us about the plates, and left. But nobody started eating. We all just sat there looking at each other. You could see that each one of us had a clear picture of how bad it was going to get.

“They don’t really want us around, so I’m not sure how we make it work,” Karin said.

“Understatement of the year,” Bill said, unwrapping his fork and knife.

"Maybe Vogel can do that thing he did five years ago," Farm said.

"You mean blow the place up?" Bill said.

"I mean be the redneck whisperer," Farm said. "Seems like he got her off that bulldozer."

In the end, we all agreed to keep to business as usual. We'd go to the location, plan our shots, schedule the interviews, keep the production moving forward so the completion bond company wouldn't get their pants all bunched up. This gave everyone enough of a breather to start eating. Nobody talked for about five minutes, which gave Margot time to order a second blue margarita.

The crew got up early to make use of the golden hour. Bill and Karin agreed that good light would take the edge off our B-roll. Right before we turned into the Jessups' driveway, Farm pointed out a crazy orange Honda with a big, stupid spoiler on the back. "It's trippy how stuff that would be normal in LA looks so crazy everywhere else," he mused.

We parked next to the house, and everyone sat in place, drinking coffee and checking phones until Margot got us started.

"Until we hear otherwise, we just follow the shot list, pick up Vogel, and get him here for the interviews. Bill," Margot said, "can you make it pretty?"

"There's not enough lipstick in the world—"

"Don't say pig," Karin interrupted.

Bill scowled.

"It needs to look like we tried," Margot said.

"It hardly matters. We're doomed," Gavin said.

Each of us fell to our lackluster work. I sat in the van, logging miles from the trip down here from Michigan, when I heard noises on the roof. As I looked up, somebody spilled out of an upstairs window and ran along the roof like a cat burglar. A second or two later Hoot Jessup busted through the front door with a shotgun. He was watching the guy above him as he cocked the gun, pointed it into the air, and fired a warning shot. One of the daughters appeared upstairs in the next window over, looked down at her dad, then turned to watch this escape artist flee. He was tall and strapping, but he looked like he was still in high school.

Hoot followed the kid on the roof with the barrel of his gun and shot again. I ducked out of reflex and then lost track of the guy until I heard a great boom above me on the roof of the van. Hoot reloaded, swung the shotgun in my direction, and fired. I dove behind the dashboard again, expecting to be covered in safety glass, but there was only a skittering sound on the windshield. I only knew the window was intact because the kid rolled down it, bumped across the hood, and dropped cartoonishly out of sight.

Hoot looked pleased with himself and howled in victory.

The kid popped up with his hands on the front of the van and his back towards Hoot. He was unbelievably handsome, like a fashion model, his eyes wide with fear. I thought of what Farm had said a few minutes ago about things that seem wrong here but that would fit in fine in LA. This kid looked like every head-shot waiter I'd ever seen in Hollywood. We locked eyes and I screamed "Run!" and waved at him frantically. When he turned, I saw two giant hearing aids clipped into his hair. All I could think was, *How very strange.*

Above us, the Jessup girl opened her window and began screaming obscenities at her father. The kid looked up, blew her a kiss, and sprinted down the driveway unscathed.

Bill popped up from the floor of the van. I had no idea he was even there.

"What was that?" he gasped.

"You get any tape of that?" I asked.

"Not without combat pay," Bill sneered. "I was on the ground."

I climbed out of the van and looked around. The windows upstairs were empty. My people were getting up and dusting themselves off. Hoot stood in the entryway, watching the empty turnaround. His shotgun breech was open, and he pulled out the spent shells, replacing them with new ones capped in yellow wax. He loaded the second shell and snapped the shotgun shut, turned, and headed back to the house.

"What the hell were you thinking, man?" I yelled.

"He can't hear you," Margot said, pointing to one ear. "Remember, he's deaf."

The rest of the crew didn't discuss it, they just started loading stuff back into the van.

"I think he's shooting rock salt loads," I said. "I wouldn't worry."

"Does it matter?" Karin asked. "I'm not sticking around to find out if it's safe."

She looked rattled. I've seen that look on folks before. "It's pretty hard to kill somebody with salt," I said.

"Well, I don't want to be anywhere near him or his salt."

"Me neither, man," Farm said.

The rest of them said pretty much the same thing. It was a complaint without a plan, so while we were coming up with something we could actually do, a police car pulled up the driveway and two cops got out. The one driving was tall and young and wore iridescent sunglasses that made him look like a mercenary. The one riding was about twice his age, short, with some gut over his gun belt. He opened a big, thick leather notepad.

Skinny said, "Somebody call 911? We got a report about gunfire."

Chubby said, "Dispatch gave us a name, Bill Drummond. Which one of you is Bill?"

I jabbed my thumb in Bill's direction.

Skinny turned to Bill. "Who was shooting?" He still had his sunglasses on.

"The deaf guy who lives here. He went back inside."

"Hoot?" Chubby asked.

"I guess," Bill answered.

"He use a shotgun or something else?"

I told them it looked like a 12-gauge break action, probably a Remington.

Skinny finally took off his shades, and the two of them nodded at each other. "Sounds about right," the other cop said. "He point it any anybody?"

"Some kid came out of the upstairs window," I said.

"But was the gun pointing at the kid?" Chubby asked.

We all shrugged. "Sort of?" I said. "We all ducked, so it's hard to tell."

Both cops chuckled, and Skinny spat on the ground.

"He shoots that thing off two, maybe three times a month," Chubby said. "It's not real ammo. It's salt. I tell him he's going to ruin that firearm, but he doesn't listen.

Margot jumped in. "I'll guess shooting off a gun around here doesn't get a person jail time."

"Well, that's a bit of a gray zone. Incorporated Anadarko ends *somewhere* around here. There's maps at the county, but for day-to-day thinking we just let it be fuzzy," Chubby said.

The driver put his shades back on. "If you don't mind me asking, can you describe the juvenile who came out of the window?" he asked.

"Tall, muscular, handsome kid with huge hearing aids," I said.

The cops looked at each other and raised their eyebrows.

"What does that mean?" Margot asked.

"Oh, that kid has been shot at six ways to Sunday," Chubby said. "Didn't know he was fooling around with a Jessup girl to boot."

Margot was disgusted; Karin, too. Bill was chuckling. Gavin and Farm just stared at the ground. Above us all, the sisters had gathered in one window. June was in the next window over, all of them staring down at us like a line of birds.

Chubby hoisted his belt and tried to strike a pose of authority. "Y'all probably know, but if somebody calls 911, we're obligated to drive out here and check it out. But since this is a yes-gun/no-bullets situation, we aren't going to arrest anybody."

Skinny interrupted. "What are y'all doing in Anadarko anyway, all the way from"—he leaned around to see the license plate on our vehicle—"California?"

Margot stepped up for this. She had the script memorized: "We're from the TV show *Revive Your Dive*, and we're shooting a follow-up segment—"

"Oh," Chubby said, "you're the guys who blew up the first house."

Margot raised one finger in protest. "On accident. That was a gas leak, officers. Total accident."

The two cops shared a quick wordless exchange. Chubby closed his notepad and slid it into his back pocket. "We appreciate y'all's due diligence, but we'll manage on our own," he said.

"Have a good day," Skinny said, touching a finger to his shades. They both got in the car, backed up, and drove off.

Margot looked at us and we looked back. It was clear from the body language alone that nobody wanted to stick around. Everyone also understood that leaving would be complicated. Before anyone had the chance to lodge a complaint, Margot said, "You know . . . I'm going to talk to him. Darryl, will you come along? Be my muscle?"

"Me?" I said.

Everybody else thought this was a great idea, and they piled into the van while Margot and I went to the door. She rang the doorbell about a half dozen times, and after a very long while, Hoot came to the door wearing purple sweatpants and a black T-shirt with an American flag and a bald eagle on it. He didn't mask his displeasure. She tried to talk to him, but that just frustrated them both. Hoot eventually went into the house and returned with a whiteboard and a marker. He gave it to Margot and gestured for her to write. *We need to go over your contract*, she wrote. When Hoot read it, he frowned and grudgingly invited us to come inside.

There was nowhere at all to walk unless you just decided to step on things: newspapers, bulging black garbage bags, piles of magazines tied in bundles with twine, things stacked with sheets of newspaper in between. The junk wasn't scattered randomly, there were zones of it, like sections of a department store. In one place there was a collection of materials for craft projects. In another, there was a grouping of things stuffed into plastic grocery sacks. Near the kitchen was a zone for dirty dishes. I'm not sure what was in the kitchen, and I wasn't eager to find out. Near the bathroom was a weird archipelago of car parts and jugs of fluid, and, of course, an accumulation of litter boxes. Mostly, you didn't see any one thing, because it all became a texture, like the fuzz when a TV goes out. Same went for the smell. It wasn't like discovering something dead, but it was enough to make you switch from your nose to your mouth.

It took some doing, but we came to a spot with an already reclined recliner. Hoot handed the whiteboard to Margot and pointed to a couch opposite the chair. He gestured for us to sit, then plopped himself down. He pulled a second whiteboard from the side of his chair and got a marker from a cup of them sitting next to the lamp.

I tried to let the good part of myself do the thinking, and I tried to feel bad for these people instead of disgusted. Hoot looked up at us with these thick glasses that were coated in a fine spray of white paint. The quarter inch of gray stubble that covered his face and neck made him look like a homeless person. Nobody was sure who would start, and small talk is pretty much impossible with a whiteboard.

Margot uncapped her pen and wrote: *We have to shoot some interviews with you and your family and get footage of the house. We need to clean up to get it done.*

Hoot said back, "What for?"

Margot wrote for a long time: *The contract you signed five years ago said you agreed to keep this house as your primary residence for five years and that you'd allow us back to do this follow-up. You also agreed not to make major changes. Once we're done, Chuck Vogel will sign over the deed, and the house will be yours, forever.*

Hoot couldn't read it from his chair, because the writing was too small, so he gestured for Margot to bring it over. Once he read it, he handed it back.

"House was ours before you got your hands on it."

Margot stiffened and tried to get ahold of her breath. She wiped the board clean with her hand. *That's true.* She scrubbed it again and wrote: *But your old house is gone.*

Hoot laughed out loud. "Duh."

All this is beyond my control, Mr. Jessup. It's Vogel and the network, she wrote.

Hoot's eyes crept back and forth between us while the wheels were turning in his head. "Never seen anyone pass a buck like you, honey." Hoot was furious, and watching him boil over in silence was unbearable. I can see why Margot wanted me in here. Hoot interlaced his fingers and set them on his belly. "You should run for president," he said. His eyes were like concentric circles.

Margot was just about on her feet when I put my hand out and said, "Don't let him get under your skin. He's trying to work you up."

"I feel weird having this conversation with him right there," Margot said.

"He gets what he gets," I told her.

"What do I tell him?" she asked.

"Tell him he can take it up with Vogel when he gets here."

She wrote that on her board and showed it to him.

"I aim to. Him and everybody else," he said. "When Vogel blew it all up, something broke inside my wife couldn't nobody fix. Move her stuff again, and I don't want to see what happens."

Margot stopped looking tough for just a second, and then immediately recomposed herself. She stood and scrubbed her whiteboard clean. She wrote: *Tomorrow morning you get thirty minutes to tell America all about it.* Then she tossed the whiteboard in Hoot's lap.

"We'll let ourselves out," she said.

Once the front door was closed and we were a few steps from the house, I asked Margot what she had planned. She gave me a dismissive "What," and turned to stare at the least junky part of the yard, a spot where the trees were thick so there was nowhere for anything to sit. Everyone in the van turned to watch us.

Karin rolled down her window and said, "Nobody wants to stay. Not with that gun-crazy guy."

Margot called a huddle. As we gathered, I had a sense that the Jessups were watching us from behind those windows. The sun was coming up and all the glass was covered in glare.

"If you leave, it'll throw off the schedule," Margot said.

"We know," Gavin said.

"It means we have to stay longer to wrap this up," Margot said.

"We have factored that in," Farm said.

"So, we take you back to the motel while Darryl and I go to the airport to get Chuck?"

"It's safer," Karin said.

"What if we all just went to the airport together," Margot said, making a gathering motion with both arms.

"It's like two-hour trip," Farm complained.

"If you're here and we're there, we don't get a chance to talk," Margot said. "Plus, I'd kind of like to have you with me when I tell Chuck what's going down. Maybe it'll keep him in check."

"Maybe it'll keep you out of the hospital," Karin said.

They all agreed to ride along. Even so, we didn't talk much for the first half hour. After a bathroom break at a truck stop, we reconvened in the van, and drove on. Once we were under way, Margot broke the silence. "Did you know Vogel's been sleeping with Barbara Stein?"

"The Barbara Stein? The 'Ain't life sweet' Barbara Stein?" Bill asked.

"Whoa, back up," Karin said. "Stein is married to Dr. Science, right?" Karin looked around and everybody else in the van was quiet. "Right? Married to Dr. Science, who is cool?"

"Stein and Vogel are totally a thing," Margot said. "I have friends who work on her show who told me about it, like, a year ago."

"I guess I don't pay attention," Karin said.

"It's better to ignore everything that man does," I said.

What they did was ignore me and spend the rest of trip talking about how much they hated Vogel and Stein. They talked about how Stein apparently isn't even from the South, and the way Vogel recently did a bunch of ad spots for the NRA. It got their minds off the trouble ahead.

AT THE AIRPORT, I WENT to pick up Vogel at baggage claim. He'd be expecting everyone to be on location, and we didn't want to freak him out, especially since the rest of the situation was going to do that for us.

I went into the terminal and checked the board. His flight was on time to land in ten minutes. I went to the bathroom, checked email on my phone. I found a place to sit where I could see the board. The flight status changed to LANDED. After a few minutes, I got up and went to the baggage carousel. People came, and all the luggage spilled out. People took their bags and left. Then the belt was clear, and no Vogel.

I texted Margot: *No Vogel.*

WTF? she texted back.

The place is empty and he's not here, I wrote.

The information from his flight rotated off the board. I looked up and down the concourse at the couple of airport employees who were sweeping up and moving bags from behind one door to another; otherwise the place was empty.

I tried calling Vogel but it went right to voice mail.

"Mr. Vogel," I said. "This is Darryl Hines. I'm here at Will Rogers Airport in Oklahoma City, and I didn't see you. I hope everything is okay." When I hung up, Margot was standing right behind me.

"What do you mean he's not here?" she said.

"All the escalators lead right to where we're standing. There's no place he *could* go."

Margot called some people in the production offices, who said they hadn't heard from Vogel in more than a week. They checked his purchasing card and said he hadn't used it since the first of the month. They told her they were starting to get unsettled about it all.

While Margot dialed somebody else, I had my eye on a bank of big TVs just in time to catch a CNN report on Barbara Stein. She was in trouble for some kind of financial crimes. The video feed showed her surrounded by lawyers and security coming out of the federal courthouse in Manhattan. She was vexed and defiant and alone. No Dr. Science, no Chuck. Just her lawyers. I tried to get Margot's attention with a short whistle. She was annoyed by the interruption, but when she saw what I was pointing to, she came over, telling her people she'd call them back.

"Is it just Stein?" Margot asked.

"Looks like. Maybe it is. I don't know."

"They don't know anything, and this certainly isn't on their radar," she said gesturing to the screen. "You don't think he's part of it, do you?"

I shrugged. "I don't really know the man, but how could he not be?"

We rushed back to brief the crew, but we found them standing in a circle, with their phones out, briefing themselves.

"Stein's totally busted," Farm said.

"We know," Margot and I said at the same time.

"Her husband moved to Israel a couple of weeks ago. Filed for divorce," Karin said.

"She had a prenup, so I guess Dr. Science is hosed." Farm didn't sound happy about the idea.

Bill said, "I'll bet it's the only thing saving him."

"A friend of mine who does makeup for Stein says Vogel was on set about ten days ago and they were screaming at each other," Gavin said, shrugging.

"He is *so* in the middle of this," Farm said.

Margot was exasperated. "Well, he wasn't on the plane."

"What?" Karin said. "Do you think he's in jail?"

"Nobody knows where he is," Margot said, folding her arms and toeing the floor. "But if he was in jail, I think we would have heard by now."

Farm laughed. "I'll bet he's on the no-fly list, and now he's on the lam."

"Who cares. Do we stay or go?" Bill asked.

"I vote go," Karin said.

"The network will make that call," Margot said.

"I vote home," Gavin said.

Everyone else voted home but Bill, who said he didn't need a black mark on his résumé."

"You know, if we leave, the Jessups won't get the house," Margot said. This possibility stopped us in our tracks.

Margot took a moment and stepped away to make a call. She was gone longer than we thought she'd be, and when she came back we could tell it wasn't good news. The network wasn't going to let us off the hook. Margot put her phone away and said, "I'm going back to see this through, but no one should feel obligated to join this mission in any way. This is a decision I have made for myself. If it turns out that there aren't enough people to crew the shoot, I'll do it myself. Somehow. Everyone who is staying, thank you. If you're going home, no hard feelings. We'll cover for you. Don't volunteer to stay because you think I want you to. Don't do it for the money either." It seemed like she was going to say something else but didn't. She just looked at the sky and tightened her lips to keep from crying.

Everybody looked around, but nobody wanted to be the first to move or speak.

"Really, you don't have to . . ." Margot said.

Karin said, "We're not going to let you do this by yourself."

So, WE WERE BACK TO plan A. Go to the house, clean it up, and shoot interviews. The production office said they'd find Vogel and make sure he got there. Worst-case scenario, they said, he'd come in later and do his part with voice-overs.

"We're not named, like individually, in the bond, are we?" Bill asked. "It's just Vogel, right? Just the producers."

"Bill, fish or cut bait," Karin said.

Before Bill could jump down her throat, Margot said, "It's okay, Karin," then she looked at each one of us with the kindest possible expression on her face. "We're already in the middle of it. Every Friday I email in production reports and expense sheets, which means if we don't wrap the shoot this week, we'll have two days before a red flag pops up in the books. The insurance company will figure it out by Tuesday at the absolute latest and call in the bond. Nobody wants to be in that shock wave. If Vogel is mixed up in this SEC business—and there's no way he's not—then we're all going to need a job because *Revive Your Dive* is over."

"How do we make sure the Jessups keep the house?" Karin asked.

"Vogel needs to sign the title papers," Margot said.

"And you have them?" Karin asked.

"Well," she said, looking at the ground, "Vogel does."

"Margot, tell us this will work," Farm pleaded. When she didn't answer, he said, "At least tell us it's worth a shot."

"After tomorrow," she said, "Vogel is going to be on his own."

The trip back was uneventful. Bill leveraged his way to lunch at Fuddruckers, and we all ate too much. The food was heavy and made us tired, and it was too late in the day to do much of anything without Vogel, so we hit the motel, divided up, and agreed to do dinner on our own. We'd head over in the morning and try to salvage what we could of the trip.

In the morning, everyone zombied through breakfast and the short drive to the Jessup house. Margot had been talking to the network people, who said to get the video and they'd "add in Vogel" in post somehow.

The plan was to divide and conquer. Margot, Karin, and Bill identified two spots in the house and one outside that could be cleared away. My job was to check the storage container in front and see if we could move anything in there. Nobody wanted to set June off again, and at this point the concern was genuine. We also wanted them to get the house free and clear.

The container had double doors with locking bars, no padlock. The door swung open with less noise than I expected. It was dark inside, but I could already tell that the container was a different story than the house. Two long plastic-topped tables, like the ones you see at a church potluck, ran against the walls toward the far end of the container.

I took a few steps farther and found a string hanging down from the shadows. A quick pull switched on two, then five, seizing fluorescent shop lights. This place was the opposite of the house. Everything in here had its own space. Once my eyes adjusted to the jittery blue light, I saw I was in the strangest possible museum. Everything was in clear plastic bins. Bins of buttons still on the display cards, and bins of hair clips similarly untouched. There was a bin of phone charging cords of all colors and configurations. A bin of car air fresheners, grouped by scent. I filed through the little trees like they were records in a shop: morning fresh, summer linen, new car, copper canyon, pine, vanilla, cinnamon apple, ocean mist, autumn, pumpkin spice, lavender, and a dozen more. There was a bin of a hundred or more gift cards for Chili's, Applebee's, and places like that. Also a bin of animal slippers still connected by that thin plastic barb.

An extension cord with a rotary switch was draped over one of the tables. I turned it on, just to see what would happen, and it lit up a glass-windowed curio cabinet full of figurines in the back corner. Inside was a complete menagerie of porcelain horses, unicorns with blue eyes, pink manes, and golden horns. All of this was interspersed with a host of sweet, little child angels, some carrying kittens or pails of water, some with their palms pressed together and their eyes closed.

My grandmother kept versions of these tchotchkes close by her chair. I remember playing with them once as a child and having her slap my hand and sit me down. "These are Nana's treasures," she said. "We don't play with them. They are too special for that." I asked her what they were for, and she said, "Darryl, this world can be so ugly. It's easy to lose heart." She didn't explain herself any further, she just looked at them and then at me with a sweet smile. Her eyes were so clouded with cataracts, I'm sure she was mostly seeing all of it in her memory.

"Whoa, man. What's this?" Gavin said. I jumped and turned around. His arms were laden with boxes.

I shushed him, but I don't know why. "Leave that stuff and get in here," I whispered.

"Does all this stuff belong to that crazy lady?" He asked.

"It might not belong to her, but I think she's responsible for it."

"Looks like a serial killer's house." He started rifling through the buttons. "There's—I don't know—maybe a thousand different kinds of buttons in here. They aren't even cool. They're like for sweaters and baby clothes."

Margot came in next. "What are you guys doing?" she said.

"Come here," Gavin said. "It's nuts." He was trying to take pictures with his phone.

I noticed a single folding chair in the container on one side between two tables. There was a handmade seat cushion tied to it.

Margot went through all the bins of barrettes and hair ties, and then said, "We gotta get out of here." Gavin complained, but she insisted. "She can't know we were in here." They left. I pulled the string and shut the door.

"We'll find somewhere else to put this stuff," Margot said, looking around the yard. "Under that tarp. Not in here."

"That's some kind of crazy," Gavin said.

"We're in enough trouble as it is," she said. "It's time for us to leave."

They set their boxes under the blue tarp, then went about their business. My phone buzzed. It was a text from Vogel saying he was in town. I must have looked alarmed because Margot asked, "Is it him?" and I nodded.

She braced her hands against her hips and stared straight up at the sky like a woman in a dust bowl photograph. As she gathered herself, her breathing grew deep and slow. I've seen her center herself like this probably a hundred times. After a couple of minutes, she woke from her meditation and said, "Okay. When's he coming?"

I shrugged. "All I know is he's in town."

"I will need updates," she said. "I'm going inside to help Bill and Gavin get everything set up."

In the army there's the stereotype of the drill sergeant screaming into the side of your face. You expect it, so it doesn't surprise you, or get you down, really. It just is. None of us signed on to work for a narcissistic shrimp who yells at you just to yell. In the army you can at least get yourself to believe your sergeant might be trying to keep you alive. With Vogel there were no such guarantees.

My phone buzzed with a text message from Vogel: *Apparently, all the motels here smell like vomit.* He followed two seconds later with: *Where are you staying?*

Vogel's people made his reservations, so he didn't always stay where we did, which was fine with us. I wanted to know how many motels Vogel had already checked into. More to the point, how many clerks and maids had he already demeaned and humiliated? Would they know he was with us? I found myself wondering if I should lie and tell him some other place, but that would never, ever work. Was he trying to catch me in a lie? Why would this be his strategy? My pulse skyrocketed, and my palms were getting sweaty. I tried to breathe like Margot, but it didn't work. I bit the bullet and typed the truth: *America's Best Value Inn and Suites.*

Not the Knight's Inn? he wrote back.

Was he at the Knight's Inn? Or did he think we were supposed to be at the Knight's Inn? Did he think we were trying to ditch him? Vogel was in my head with three texts.

Correct. America's Best, I wrote.

Almost immediately he sent: *Well, I'm at the Knight's Inn.*

I felt like I needed to run all of this by Margot, but I didn't want to go back into that house unless it was completely necessary. The longer I waited to answer, the more Vogel would think something was weird. I was just about to ask him if he wanted us to move to where he was, when he wrote: *I got the last room.*

Again, I wasn't sure what to say. I went with the most rational: *You need a ride over?"*

Send me the GPS.

Off the hook again.

I'll be there in 1 hour.

Well, this was actionable intelligence, and it really is the devil you know.

I let myself into the house and worked my way back to the space they were setting up for the interviews. The dining room had a table and chairs in it, but they were covered in boxes. All the junk settled into the bottom four feet of each room, which made it seem like the house was flooding. I found myself getting angry because I couldn't assume a regular gait. The path was interrupted at irregular distances by things I had to step over or crush. As I came into the room where they were setting up the shot, my foot snagged on a cord, and I fell to the ground, bringing a light stand down with me. Gavin was there and caught it before anything broke.

"Sorry, man. You gotta watch it in this place," he said.

"Vogel's here," I said from the floor.

"How long do we have?"

"He says an hour."

ABOUT AN HOUR AND A half after he texted me, Vogel drove up in a brown Maserati with plates that said DR·SCI. I stood on the porch texting Margot, while he sat in the car yelling at somebody on the phone. Margot came out and stood next to me, watching him rage on, oblivious to us and the world around him.

"You think he even notices the condition of this place?" I asked her.

She shrugged. "A person like him doesn't usually notice anything that isn't part of . . ." She paused to choose her next word with care. During that moment, Vogel pounded on the steering wheel and glared at the phone while screaming at it. "Well, a person like him doesn't really notice anything."

The call went on for a few more minutes, then he suddenly ended it and sat motionless in the car for so long Margot thought we should check things out. As we started to walk over, the door flew open, and he got out dressed in his show costume: jeans, Red Wing boots, and a flannel shirt with rolled-up sleeves. His hair was a mess, and he hadn't dyed the gray to match the rest. His cheeks were glossy, and his weird eyes looked a little bit infected.

Margot pointed at his face. "You have something—some french fry, maybe—in your beard."

"Can we get this done tonight?" he asked, grabbing at the wrong part of his face.

"Well, it depends," she said. "And you missed it. It's on the other side." He brushed all over, missing the food each time. You could tell Margot wanted to just pluck it out, but she also didn't want to touch him. Who would?

"Maybe you should get some rest," she suggested.

"I don't need any rest. Has the studio said anything?" Vogel asked.

"About what?"

"About me." The way he said "me" was deeply disturbing.

"They said you weren't on the airplane," she said with care.

"What else did they say?"

"Well, nothing, Chuck. They said they had no idea where you were and they wanted to know when we heard from you so they could get the insurance company off their backs."

"Don't tell those sycophants anything."

"Sycophants?" I blurted, a little bit amazed that I didn't keep quiet.

Vogel zeroed in on me. "I have a master's, and a vocabulary, you piece of crap."

"It's cool," I said. "I didn't mean nothing by it."

Vogel rubbed his face, and refocused on Margot. "Don't tell them anything. I have a—" he began. "I need to talk to them myself."

"Whatever you want, Chuck."

"I don't want you in the middle of it, okay, Margot?"

"In the middle of what?" Margot said, lifting an eyebrow to make it obvious she wanted us to play dumb.

Vogel stared at us for a long time, without blinking, like a dog on a chain, then he grinned, sort of. It was a dark, celebratory expression. "You haven't heard *anything* about me?"

"We've been out here in the middle of rural nowhere, hauling around boxes of garbage. How could we have *heard* anything?"

"Good," Vogel said. "Good, good, good." He started patting around for his phone, then realized he'd left it inside the car. He rooted around in the car for a long time before he found it.

"Whose car is this?" Margot asked when he was back.

Vogel immediately became evasive. "I want to interview the hoarder first. While I'm fresh."

"Well, there's a problem. She's not here right now. It's just the guy, Hoot."

"What about the daughters?"

"Upstairs."

"So, why exactly did I drive halfway across the country in two days if there's nobody to interview?"

"Nobody knows, Chuck. You had a plane ticket."

Vogel looked like he was going to take a bite out of Margot's face for saying that, but remarkably, he took control of himself by baring his teeth (it wasn't a smile), shaking a finger at her, and nodding his head. "You're right. You're right. You're right," he gibbered. "I did have a ticket." As he was thinking about what to say next, he looked around, and you could see the situation of this house dawn on him all at once. "What have these rednecks done to this place?"

"Looks like June didn't get better," Margot said.

"June," he said, letting his face lift like a madman's. "I remember that nasty woman. She chained herself to the bulldozer. Cost us thousands. Maybe it was a bad move to blow that house up after all."

Margot's eyes went wide, and she looked right at me. "I thought it was a gas leak."

"When gas comes out of a pipe it's called a leak, right?" Vogel said. "Boom. Five years later, we're the number four reality show in the country. God bless America."

"Don't you feel anything?" Margot said.

"I *feel* like the tree in that idiotic book my kids made me read when they were little. Tree gives everything it has to some gimme-gimme freeloader who skips town without a thank-you, goes broke, then all he wants is to sit and rest for a while. When I look at this pit, I feel like that stump, like I've been shaken down by a bunch of con artists. Let's pause for a moment while I have a good cry and write it down in my journal."

Vogel charged past her and pushed through the front door.

Margot followed him, but stopped for just a second and took me by the shoulders. "You heard that, right?"

I nodded.

"All of it?"

"He said he felt like a stump."

Margot snorted through her nose. "Good. For the last couple of days, I've been having trouble figuring out what's real and what isn't."

"The Giving Tree is a lady," I said.

Margot considered that for a moment. "You're right."

"Just seems like somebody needed to point that out."

Margot touched my shoulder. "Indeed," she said, and then she followed Vogel inside.

I LIKE TO BE ON hand when they're shooting. It's not part of my contract but it helps a small crew get things done. Because of Vogel, Margot asked me to be on hand for all kinds of contingencies. I followed Margot into the spot they cleared, and it was amazing how they'd been able to create the illusion of a place that wasn't a disaster. They had a chair with a bookshelf behind it. Everything was lit aggressively, and the shadows hid a lot of what was dingy and broken down. Vogel sat in his chair across from the one for the person being interviewed. He already had two sheets of paper towel in the collar of his shirt so Karin could do something to salvage his face and hair for the shoot. While she powdered his forehead, Vogel shook two pills from a bottle and swallowed them dry.

They started with Hoot. His deafness posed some technical challenges. We knew he could talk well enough but they kept the older daughter, Jaymee, in Hoot's field of vision to translate. Whiteboards would be too slow. The problem was, Hoot kept wanting to look halfway between Vogel and Jaymee, which made it seem like he wasn't paying attention to anyone. Bill set up a second camera and ran a feed of Jaymee signing Vogel's questions through a laptop just underneath the camera recording Hoot.

Once tape started rolling, it was amazing to see the crew in action. It always takes a few questions to loosen up the subject. This took a lot longer with Hoot. No matter what the question was, he kept coming back to his own questions about our contract with him, about the house. He wanted to be clear on the details. "Do y'all sign over the house once we're done, or do we have to wait until the show goes on the TV?" he'd ask. His words came in bursts, loud and without inflection. These questions would piss off Vogel, and he'd make Margot answer them. Jaymee would translate Margot's answers. Hoot apparently thought Jaymee was making things up because he couldn't see Vogel's mouth moving. After they got through a few rounds of this, the interview lurched forward.

The questions were broad and general. Vogel asked them in a way that suggested their own answers. It wasn't long before Hoot started editorializing. "A big house is more work, Chuck," he said. "The old one wasn't any trouble. This one has more ways to break. Who needs a digital faucet? Power goes out and what? You'll just have pee hands."

Vogel moved on to questions about individual rooms. He tried to stick to the script, but after a few minutes, he just gave in. "The place has seen better days," he said, which didn't seem to flap Hoot in the least.

"It's true. The place ain't tidy," Hoot said.

Vogel couldn't sense that he was getting messed with. I think he thought Hoot was an idiot, which didn't work well for anybody. Vogel said one of the great American ideals is the pride of individual ownership, which he didn't see playing out around him. "In fact, it's the opposite with you people."

Hoot leaned back in his chair and crossed his legs at the knee. "The thing about freedom is you don't get to tell me what to do with mine. Y'all's show is called *Revive Your Dive.* Doesn't say nothing about any strings attached. Nobody in this family asked for a new house, did they? Nobody came begging. You basically shoved this house up our butts."

At this point, I didn't know what to feel. Hoot was fantastic for TV. He seemed born to be on camera. He told Vogel things we always wished we could say. His daughters couldn't believe what he was saying, and neither could the rest of us. Vogel bristled with rage, and it was clear he was one step away from flying completely off the handle. But he got it together and said, "All this garbage stacked up around here doesn't seem to be the work of you or your daughters, which kind of puts your wife in charge."

Hoot's face got real serious as his daughter signed to him. When she was done, he asked her to sign it again. I could see Hoot getting more and more deeply frustrated as she went on, until he interrupted her and said, "I vowed to have that woman and to hold her, for better or worse, rich or poor, healthy or sick until death do us part. Nothing in any of that gives me leave to back out because of how she keeps house. How is it you don't know that?"

Margot's hands were tented over her mouth. Vogel told Bill to cut, and Margot shook her head. She rotated her index finger to make sure he kept rolling. Vogel looked disgusted and started walking out of the room, through the teetering stacks toward the front door, when June stormed in.

"What have you done?" she bellowed, coming at Vogel with her head down like a five-foot offensive lineman. "What have you people done to my things?"

Vogel put up both hands and said, "Look, there's no way to shoot inside of this landfill, which doesn't actually belong to you people yet."

"Not here, there," she screamed. "Out there in my storage." She kept coming at Vogel, red-faced and huffing. She pointed right in Vogel's face, the charms on her bracelet glimmering.

Gavin looked at me. I looked at Margot. We all shrugged and somehow all understood that we should just keep quiet.

"My storage is my things. My things ain't anyone's business but mine." She pointed at Vogel again. "You told me that's how it would go when you got me off that tractor. You told me my storage would be off-limits, forever."

"Look, lady. Why would I want to go in there? Why would *anyone* want to go in there?"

She kept coming at Vogel, who backed up until his heels hit the same cord I'd tripped over. He went down hard, and the light fell in an arc, clipping June in the side of the head, which sent her reeling into a stack of milk crates that knocked down the fill lights. All of that brought June the rest of the way down in a tangled, squalling heap.

In the middle of all that was the sound of a breaking bulb. Farm darted to the power distribution box and flipped the switch, throwing the room into darkness. Vogel was cursing and so was June. Hoot jumped up and started pulling things off his wife. Vogel started yelling at the top of his lungs. I guess somebody was standing on his fingers.

Soon enough everyone was up and screaming. Hoot was trying to soothe his wife, but she pulled free of him and screamed about her rights and the Constitution and how she was going to search everyone for her treasures and her precious little angels.

"Leave me alone," she screamed, and ran out of the house, crashing into everything on the way out.

When June was gone, Vogel spat on the floor and walked out, saying, "All you freaks need now is a midget and some Siamese twins."

Margot said, "Let's take a break and reset."

"There's glass everywhere," Farm said. "It's going to take a while."

Margot sent me to get June in place for her interview while the rest of the crew cleaned up and reset everything. The second I got out the door, June zoomed past in her car. I texted Margot: *She's gone. Drove off.*

A couple seconds later Margot came out the front door. "How long is she going to be gone?" she asked.

"Get those kids to call her and find out," I said.

Margot was mad, but not at me. We were all at a point where you could just rage at the universe and nobody would call you on it. She told me to wait here and get June in front of the camera the minute she got back. They were going to get tape of the daughters and some B-roll.

"The only way out of this is through, Margot," I said.

She told me I was a good man, which wasn't true, but I didn't protest.

Truth be told, I didn't want to know what was going on inside the house. Vogel was almost certainly making a mess of it. Those people were smart and decent and looking to defend themselves. Vogel was crazed and careless and meaner than a snake. It wasn't comfortable to sit in the van, but there was nowhere outside for anyone to be, so I opened the back, got a book, and lay down with my feet hanging over the bumper. A lot of being a teamster on a crew like this involves sitting with the vehicle, so I kept stuff around to make it work: a foam pad, cooler, snacks, and books.

I got out the novel I was reading, trying not to let myself dwell on this craziness. As I read, I felt myself drifting. Every time a car went by on the street, I'd bolt awake and wait to see if it would come down the driveway.

After an hour, I got up, put my book down, and went over to the storage unit. The curio cabinet light was still on. Against my better judgment, I went back inside with the idea that I'd turn off the light as a gesture of goodwill, and maybe an apology. I was also worried she would know someone went back inside, and a trespass would have consequences. As I deliberated, I realized this was her collection. She treated it like a tiny secret wing of the Smithsonian. These rows and bundles of things had their place, like books in a library or records in some nerd's apartment. The house was a dumping ground. They were two completely different kinds of problem.

Right behind me somebody said, "What are you doing in here?" I jumped right out of my skin, turned around, and there was the youngest Jessup, Lexi.

"My mother is going to freak if she finds out you were back in here," she said. The girl was maybe fifteen years old, with pink and blue swirled through her beige hair. She wore thick black eyeliner and dark lipstick, and she stared at me without blinking. The light from outside haloed her, so I couldn't see much beyond that.

"I thought maybe I had left on the light," I said. "You know, from before. I didn't mean any disrespect."

"Whatever," she said. "You should get out of here. For reals."

I went down to the far end of the container and switched off the lights, then came back.

"Now, for sure she'll know you were here," the girl said. "I know y'all're judging us, but my mom is sick." She pointed at all the things in the container. "We had a room like this in our old house."

"I didn't know that," I said. "Please understand. None of us is happy about how this is going down."

"My family made your stupid boss famous. That's what's so dumb about all this."

"I've heard."

"I'm supposed to talk to him next," she said. "Do I have to?"

"It's not up to me. I'm the driver."

"You're the only person not doing something right now, so I thought you'd be a good person to ask."

"I think it's part of the deal," I said.

She thought about that for a minute, and then her eyes narrowed. "You haven't seen my room, have you?" she asked.

I shook my head no.

"It's the worst. Your lame contract says I have to keep my room like it is for five years."

"Tomorrow you can paint it black."

"Red," she said. "I want the whole thing red."

"That'll be intense," I said. "I'll guess that's what you're shooting for."

"When y'all were here before, your creep boss put a blindfold on me and took me up there with all the lights and cameras. He talked to me, right in my ear, about the special room he made just for me. When we got to the room, he pulled off the blindfold, and there I was, surrounded by ponies. A rainbow of ponies across the walls. There was even a pony *bed* with four carved pony heads at each corner. They had real-hair manes and plastic eyes. I was ten, but nobody even asked if I liked ponies."

"Did you?"

"Ponies are lame," she said "But it gets worse. He started yelling at me. 'You distinctly said ponies,' he shouted. 'She said ponies in the interview, right? Somebody remind this kid she said ponies.' Then he stomped and swore at me and everyone else. 'Why would I make up ponies?' he screamed. 'I am not into ponies.' Then he told everyone that he didn't just pull a pony room out of his ass.'"

I laughed but didn't mean to. "Our boss is a monster. We all know it."

"He put the blindfold back on me and made me walk up the stairs and into the room over and over for an hour until I loved it the way he wanted me to."

Lexi wasn't crying, but her eyeliner was starting to get bleary.

"I'm so sorry," I said.

"That's why I can't talk to him. I mean, unless you want me to claw his eyes out."

She stepped behind me, nudged me out of the container, and pulled the door shut. "You really shouldn't go inside of there again."

Lexi went into the house, and I texted Margot: *Still no sign of June.*

Margot wrote back and told me they were finishing the older daughter's interview, and based on the cruel things Vogel had said about her body and face, the girl could hire any bad lawyer in the country and sue Vogel for everything he was worth.

I fell asleep in the van and woke up to the sound of crunching gravel. Spit was running out of one corner of my mouth, and I rolled over on my book, crushing about a hundred pages. I came around the van looking for June's car and instead saw a police cruiser, the same one from before. The chubby cop was letting June out of the back. June shook her head and protested. Chubby said something to her and handed her some Kleenex the skinny cop had passed along.

She's back, I texted. I wasn't sure how to say the next part so it would signal the right amount of alarm, so I went plain: *In a cop car.* She was back, in a cop car.

Margot burst out of the door first, followed by the daughters. When she saw them, June tried to shut the cruiser's door, but Chubby stood in the way. Skinny pulled the older daughter aside and said, "She was shoplifting again, Jaymee. Manager said they've had enough, and they're through with her."

The girl stared at the driveway and ground her teeth. "You know she can't help it," she said.

"Walmart doesn't care," Skinny said. "She's banned. And they're going to prosecute."

"Where's the car?" Jaymee asked.

"You'll have to get it from impound."

The next one out of the house was Bill, with a camera on his shoulder. Vogel came next, talking on his phone and at the same time pointing and telling Bill if he stopped taping he'd have his head. Margot told Bill to cut. The two of them went back and forth. Bill kept shooting because even though he was a putz, he had the instincts to get it down. He'd reflect on the ethics once he shot the tape. Gavin, Farm, and Karin came out last.

The girls swarmed their mother. Margot pushed in as close as she could, but it was clear this discussion was for the family.

Skinny gathered all of us together. "Y'all probably feel like you have a right to be here on the property. But given the situation, I think the respectful thing to do here is clear out for a while."

"What happened?" Margot asked.

The cop pointed at Bill. "He needs to turn that off."

"I have the right to film this, officer," Bill said.

"I'm not talking about your rights, mister. I'm talking about you being a decent human being."

"Bill?" Margot said.

"You're calling cut?" Bill asked.

"I'm calling cut."

Bill unshouldered the camera, but he didn't turn it off. By the angle of it in his hand, I could tell that he was still trying to frame a shot. Neither of the cops seemed to notice. Skinny told us June was in some trouble. "She's embarrassed and tired and doesn't want to go back in the house with y'all still being here."

Margo asked what she'd done and Skinny said, "Well, that's none of your business, lady."

In the window upstairs, where I'd first seen the two daughters a couple of days before, I spotted Hoot again, staring down on us as the girls got their mother out of the police car. I followed the invisible lines of his gaze and found they led to June, who stood there in the middle of everything, looking back at Hoot. A message moved across the distance. It was impossibly sad to watch them this way. June shook her head. Hoot put his hands on the window, which pulled the shadows away from his face. And June shook her head again. The police said something nobody heard, then got in their car and drove off.

Hoot disappeared from the window and a minute or so later burst out of the front door with his shotgun. Vogel and Bill were away from the house getting video of the police car. Hoot was breathing like he'd been sprinting. His face was twisted and crazed. "Where is that shrimp?" Hoot howled.

The daughters ran up to him, screaming, but he ignored them. He pointed the shotgun skyward and fired. Everyone crouched.

Margot screamed, "Not again!"

Vogel ran to his car and popped the trunk.

His two daughters were smart enough about guns to stay back, but screamed, "Daddy, don't!"

Hoot came through us fast, pumping the shotgun and fanning out to the side to get a clear shot, then he fired once above Vogel's head, making him duck.

Time slowed. That's the one thing movies get right. Karin and I grabbed people and got them down, covered their bodies with our own. Vogel dodged behind the Maserati. Hoot bellowed, broke open the shotgun, and reloaded. Vogel reappeared with a pistol he must have kept in his bag. Without a second of hesitation he fired two shots into Hoot. The first made him drop his shotgun. The second turned him sideways before he crumpled to the ground. Bill had the camera back on his shoulder. When Vogel saw that Hoot was down, he advanced and continued shooting into Hoot's fallen body until his weapon was empty.

Even when you've been under fire before, it's easy to lose clarity, but with training you can overcome it. In the silence that followed Vogel's last shot, Karin ran straight at him. In two blindingly quick moves, she first disarmed him then incapacitated him with a hand thrust to the throat. Suddenly he was upside down on the ground with his gun hand pointing straight in the air and Karin standing over him. Vogel was coughing and cursing at her, his hand and wrist cranked almost backward. Karin threw the pistol behind her. Vogel kicked, but he wasn't going anywhere.

I ran over to Hoot, rolled him over, and tried to find a pulse. Blood surged once or twice out of his mouth. His eyes were open, but it was over. I'd seen this plenty of times. There was no life in him. Sounds came back one by one. The girls were crying. June was on the other side of me, kneeling, with her head all the way down on her husband's chest.

Next thing I knew those cops were back. Skinny was questioning Vogel. Chubby got down on his knees and looked like he was about to start CPR. I put my hand out to stop him. "I was a special ops combat medic in Afghanistan, brother. He's done."

Chubby didn't respond, he just ducked his head toward the mic of his radio and called it in. "I need an ambulance here, stat."

Everyone was sitting around with bottles of water, giving statements. At first it didn't look like they were going to arrest Vogel. I mean, they didn't treat him any different than the rest of us. They took his driver's license and concealed carry permit and checked him out. After a few minutes, once they had sized things up, they came back with handcuffs, and their attitudes had changed 180 degrees. They pushed him around, and their voices were louder, more clipped.

Vogel protested. "Hey, I'm the good guy here. We're all lucky I came prepared. That idiot came out shooting at us. I just returned fire."

Skinny said, "Shut up, Han Solo, it doesn't matter who shot first. You're named in a federal indictment for some kind of Wall Street fraud. There's a warrant out for you and Barbara Stein. Then there's everything you did here. Charles Simone Vogel, you are about as under arrest as a person can get."

"Simone?" Chubby asked.

"Shut up," Vogel snapped.

They read Vogel his rights and took him to the car.

During the rest of the day there were more sirens. The ambulance came and went. Then there were more cars, neighbors, social workers, and reporters. It was a very long day. Everybody was still taking care of business in front of the house because nobody could get inside. June and the girls sat in some ratty old lawn chairs, and a social worker with a clipboard was telling them somebody would come in the next day or so to walk them through funeral arrangements. She asked June if Hoot was a veteran, and she nodded her head.

While this was happening, I noticed the police assembling around the door end of the storage unit. One of them had a bin of hair ties and clips. They were all shaking their heads and a couple were laughing. I went over to them quick and said, "Hey, look. Don't let her see you went in there."

One of the cops said, "The jerk with the camera told us to have a look."

The short cop from before resumed their conversation and said, "It's just like the stuff we picked her up for. There's tons of it inside, just like this. What do we do?"

"What about a search warrant?" another cop asked.

"Not necesary when it's an active crime scene," Chubby countered.

At this point, June noticed people were gathering. "You don't have permission," she said. When they didn't hear her, she shouted it again. "You don't have permission!" When she saw that they had already been inside, she closed her eyes and trembled until she got it together enough to turn and run inside, slamming the door behind her.

The daughters slumped forward in their chairs. The older girl cradled her head in both hands, and the younger one pulled her legs up and curled into a ball behind them.

There was a flash of light from one of the windows on the ground floor where we'd been shooting the interviews. The nature of that flash didn't process for any of us while we tried to figure out what we'd done. A few minutes later we all saw June move frenetically from window to window across the upstairs.

Margot gathered us up and said we should pack our gear and get back to LA. She said she'd briefed the studio, and they seemed relieved to hear Vogel was in jail. I got the sense that Chuck Vogel was the loosest of loose cannons, and despite the trouble of having to clean up this mess and despite how much PR work for this would be, the studio was thinking of this as a simple way out of a contract.

Gavin and Farm asked if I would help them load out, and as we went back into the house, we could smell smoke.

"It's the lights," Farm said, once at a whisper, then again, screaming. We ran out of the house to get the fire trucks, which were gone now. It was just the police and the social worker.

Gavin ran to tell the cops, but by then, flames were licking their way across three of the ground-floor windows.

Skinny was on his radio. "Negative," he said. "Send everything you got. There's a woman trapped on the second floor." He looked up at the top story and you could see his shoulders sag. "Affirmative. There's no way to go through the house."

There was nothing any of us could do. The Jessup girls were screaming at the police to do something. June came to the open window and placed her hands on the screen. Black smoke boiled out of the soffits and you could already hear the roar of the flames. Everyone was encouraging June to climb out the window and jump. Smoke filled the upstairs windows, and as we heard the approaching sirens, June closed the window and fell away from our sight. We didn't see her again. We were watching for something: a hand or maybe for the window to open.

The fire was so intense it pretty much had to burn itself out. Bill shot all kinds of video, and everybody was too tired to tell him to leave it alone. Eventually somebody came for the girls so they could be taken to stay with relatives. By the time we left, it was dark, and the orange flames shot sparks a hundred feet into the air.

When I came back in the morning, the whole place was as flat and black as a skillet. I don't know why I came back, but I felt like I needed to see it. Nobody else wanted to come, so I was out by myself. On the way back to the motel, I stopped for something to eat, but I didn't have the appetite.

Instead, I called my sister to tell her what happened, and all she could say was "Darryl, that's horrible" and "What will those poor girls do?" The conversation didn't go the way I'd hoped, so eventually I told her I was sorry but I had to hang up.

When people ask about that day, I tell them yes, Chuck Vogel shot that man, and yes, it was on purpose. I tell them yes, he thought he was defending himself, and no, he was not actually in danger. I tell them that it doesn't matter if there was rock salt in the shotgun. I tell them about trying to drive in Iraq, where everything—baby carriages, backpacks, a crate of cantaloupes, a lady in an abaya, any of it could be a bomb. It stops mattering what it is, and it only matters what it looks like it is. That is the legacy of this world. Appearance trumps reality. I tell them that the real tragedy had nothing to do with Vogel. It was the rest of us who killed June Jessup.

The police kept us there a couple more days, lawyers deposed us, said that since there were plenty of local witnesses, they would let us know what they needed from us. They wanted Bill's tape. He protested, and Margot said they could have it. We could go home, but they'd probably want us back for the trial.

It was obvious, though, that Vogel was also going to stand trial back in New York on the federal charges. With a manslaughter charge on top of it all. Vogel's life was done, really. He'll get some of what's coming to him. Some of it. The bigger they are, the harder they fall. Folks in the middle, like us, we neither suffer nor prosper. Those Jessup kids are orphans now, and homeless. They aren't babies, and they have their wits, so they've probably got a chance if they don't end up in the system.

Once the police and the lawyers released us, the crew came to me and asked if it would be cool if they just flew home. None of them felt like driving for two or three more days. Truth be told I wanted to be alone for a while, too, maybe take a detour and see the Grand Canyon. No amount of talking was going to make any of this feel better, and it had every chance of making me feel worse. I told them I'd deliver them to the airport and take the van and gear back to LA.

I thought about trying to find those Jessup girls so I could offer my condolences, but I didn't believe it would change anything. Sometimes you have to walk away from trouble or you make it worse.

From the airport, I found my way onto the interstate heading west. It was a very long, straight, and uneventful road, but the skies over the panhandle had gone weird, full of heavy-bellied, green clouds, and way off in the distance thin, blue-white bolts of lightning lit up the horizon.

I turned on the satellite radio and drove. Normally I am an audiobook man, but there was no story I could imagine that would take my mind off the last week. Silence seemed like an even worse threat. I picked the 80s on 8 station because it seemed like the best way to shut off my brain, but I should have known, from repeated experience, that the radio or shuffle mode has a way of dropping a song in my lap that makes me seriously doubt that anything in the world is actually random.

After Bob Seger's "Old Time Rock and Roll" ended, the Talking Heads' "Burning Down the House" came on. I knew the song by the simple guitar intro. I also knew that I'd done more than my part keeping it together while everything was falling apart. As the drums came in, I moved lane by lane to the right and crossed the rumble strip. As the opening lines hit—"Watch out. You might get what you're after"—I clicked on the hazard lights and let the song do its thing.

Everything at that point was more than I could handle.

5

Providence

FRANCIS BUGG EMERGED FROM HIS trailer into the shellac of morning light, stretched his arms and lower back, then descended the plank steps. Bugg was a tall, thin man with a compact white mustache, crew cut, massive hands. He carefully unlooped the garden hose and watered the two half barrels of flowers that hid the wheels of his trailer.

Despite the general ramshackle condition of the trailer park, Bugg's place was modest, tidy, and organized. A white Ford F-250 with new tires was parked in front, but off to one side, leaving room for a bright orange Honda Civic with a massive chrome spoiler mounted on back.

Bugg dragged the hose deliberately along a gray gravel path so he could water a few shrubs that accented each end of the trailer. This ritual took a few minutes, and Bugg seemed to delight in completing this one simple task with focus and precision. When he was done, Bugg coiled the hose and took note of the sky, which was darkening. The clouds were faintly drooping underneath, which Bugg knew meant trouble. He made a mental note to check the Weather Channel when he went inside.

As he continued to scan the sky, his ear caught the bickering of three tiny finches quarreling with each other around the bird feeder. One finch, with a seed in its beak, was twisting its head wildly, eyeing the others, who lunged in fearlessly. Bugg watched for a moment longer, then went over to the bird feeder and shook a little seed into the palm of his hand, which sent the birds in all directions. He took a couple of steps to neutral ground and made a bubbling call through his teeth that sounded exactly like the finches. The birds flew past him and watched him extend his hand and repeat the call.

Gingerly, one bird swooped in and landed on Bugg's hand, where he began picking at the seed. Neither of the other two would venture in, so Bugg gently tipped some seed into his other hand and made the call again. A second finch came forth and began to peck.

The third finch, seeing the others being fed, dropped the sunflower seed in its mouth and tried to push in, first on the bird in Bugg's left hand, then on the bird in his right. Bugg turned his head to avoid the flutter of flapping wings and tiny claws. After a few seconds of pandemonium, Bugg clapped his hands together, scattering the seed and sending each bird in a different direction.

Bugg shook his head and turned to find his son staring down at him with a smile on his face.

"Didn't think that one through," Bugg said, almost shouting. The boy shook his head and pointed to his ears. Bugg nodded and then signed, *Good idea. Bad ending.*

His son, Eric, signed back, *Birds. I thought you would smash them.* He spoke the sentence, too, but it was difficult to make sense of it. Eric stood above Francis on the porch laughing, wearing nothing but a pair of orange Oklahoma State basketball shorts. He was an Adonis, always able to make Francis stop in his tracks. He was naturally strong and thin. His hair swept effortlessly back and his jaw was angled heroically away from his chin.

Lately, the boy had been in trouble at school and with the police, couldn't keep a job. Each one a small thing on its own, but all of them led in a direction Francis could line up with a ruler, pointing to the kind of trouble Francis had seen waxing strong in the world for the last forty years.

Francis cleared his throat, furrowed his eyebrows, and signed, *You're not dressed for a funeral. They are your girlfriend's parents, son. You need to dress like a man today.*

The boy's face fell. After Bugg passed through the door, Eric followed him inside. He was so angry he yelled incoherently at his father from behind.

Bugg turned. *Get your implants. I'm too tired to sign right now.*

The boy stormed off, and while he was gone, Bugg poured himself a cup of coffee and drank it unadorned in small sips. Eric returned with the massive microphones clipped to his hair, and the wires looped around his ears.

"Just so I'm understood. Every person born into this world deserves to be recognized when they leave it. Even the Jessups, maybe especially children of God like them. Jesus was plain on the matter."

"Yes, sir," Eric said.

"You mourn with those that mourn."

"Yes, sir."

"I bought you a good suit, didn't I?"

Eric nodded.

"Well, okay. You know what to do."

By the time the funeral started, the air had grown still, and the clouds had become thick.

Before they could leave for the funeral, Francis made him stop to watch the Weather Channel. The crawl at the bottom of the screen put their county on Storm Watch, but when the Local on the Eights segment came on, the Doppler showed nothing severe in the area.

"Look at that, over by Amarillo," his father said.

In the lower left-hand corner, the picture was a thick, orange-and-red crosshatch of severe thunderstorms.

That's bad, Eric signed.

"We'll be back before it hits," Francis said. "All kinds of hail going to be in that."

Eric went to his car, but Francis stopped and got into his line of sight. *Not in that orange monster,* he signed, then he motioned the boy over to his pickup.

They drove to the funeral in silence, with both windows down, each of them wearing the same suit in different sizes. Eric's tie was orange. His father's was yellow with gray stripes. They arrived a few minutes early, his dad parked, and when Eric started to get out, he signed, *We'll sit here.*

Why? the boy asked.

Because we're not family.

Through the cemetery, Eric could see a small gathering of people under an awning. The grave itself was obscured by the row of headstones. Way past everyone sat a tiny little excavator, curled up and parked. Eric looked over at his father to point out the stupid little tractor and saw that his father was looking out his window, across the street, with his hand on the bouquet of flowers that was sitting on the seat.

Eric was good at wringing meaning out of people's expressions, but with his father's head turned away, he couldn't gauge his mood correctly. The way he rubbed his middle finger across the base of his lip made Eric uneasy. His father didn't say much, but he was easy to read, and that finger going back and forth was like a weather map.

While they were waiting, Eric's phone buzzed. It was Jaymee saying they were at the cemetery. Eric texted her back, writing, *Waiting on my dad. Be there soon.*

Eric tapped his dad's shoulder. "Dad," he said in his raw voice. When he didn't respond, Eric said, "I'm going," and he got out of the truck without looking back. His father followed at a distance. When Eric arrived, Jaymee signed, *I'm glad you're here.*

Me, too, he signed back.

Jaymee pointed over Eric's shoulder. *Why did your dad come? Did he know my parents?* she asked.

Eric shrugged.

Weird, she said, then she grabbed Eric's arm and led him over to where her family was sitting. After they sat, she signed, *You look nice. An Oklahoma State tie and everything.*

Eric smiled. She pointed out who everyone was at the funeral: Lexi, of course; her Aunt Kathy and Uncle Mel and her cousin Izzy; three or four people she didn't know who seemed underdressed; Pastor Rick from church; some church ladies who go to all the funerals; the funeral director and his son, who was in training; and some lady in her thirties Jaymee thought was from the newspaper.

Francis sat directly behind them, and set his hand on Eric's shoulder. Jaymee turned and stacked her hand on top of his and said, "Thank you for coming, Mr. Bugg."

He set his hand on top of hers, which started to weigh down Eric's shoulder. "You have had a good effect on my boy," he said. "Your parents' deaths were a tragedy. I wanted you to know the Bugg family mourns your loss."

Eric rotated his shoulder to let people know he'd had enough.

Pastor Rick went to the front of the small rectangle of chairs and welcomed everyone in a strange mixture of solemnity and Will Rogers-y charm. He spoke of the Jessup family, who had been no strangers to tragedy. "As it says in the book of Psalms, many are the afflictions of the righteous, but the Lord rescues them from them all. Hoot Jessup was a man of many turns, who was taken from us suddenly, senselessly. It is true he fired the first shot, but it was just salt. Salt of the earth, brothers and sisters. We all know what happens when salt loses its savor. Wherewith shall it be salted? It becomes good for nothing and is cast out to be trodden under foot of men."

At this point in Pastor Rick's speech, people began looking at each other, squinting, trying not to seem confused.

"A moment of loss like this one makes us all look to our own mortality and wonder if our candles might be more difficult to snuff out if we put them under a bushel basket. I say to you, brothers and sisters, the Lord would not have it so. This moment is our opportunity to throw back our shoulders and spit at the Devil and rebuke the devourer and remember that when the righteous cry for help, the Lord hears, and rescues us from all our troubles. The Lord is near to the brokenhearted, and saves the crushed in spirit. None of those who take refuge in Him will be condemned."

Pastor Rick checked his note cards and clasped his hands behind his back. "Now Hoot's daughter, Lexi, will perform a song in honor of her beloved parents."

Lexi rose from her seat and took her place at the front where Pastor Rick had been standing just a moment before. She was wearing dark black eyeliner and a black shawl that appeared to be shredded in places on purpose. Her hair was dyed red at the tips and hung in front her face. She wore a black scoop-necked T-shirt and a black skirt over black leggings that stopped mid-calf. The soles of her shoes were tall in front and back, and there were rings on most of her fingers. She took a few moments to compose herself, and when it seemed like she might not sing or say anything, Pastor Rick encouraged her to go ahead.

"I read on the internet that the band on the Titanic played this song as it sank. It was in the movie, so it must be true." Lexi took out her phone and touched the screen. The small sound of a violin playing the opening strains of "Nearer, My God, to Thee" came out of the tiny speakers. Lexi joined in as the verse came around. Her voice was tentative but clear. Her song moved everyone, including the woman from the newspaper. When she was done, she forgot to stop the song. A slow techno beat started, and she was most of the way back to her seat before she had it turned off.

Pastor Rick came back to the front and wiped his eyes on the sleeve of his suit. "Lexi Jessup, we have to get you into the choir."

June's sister Kathy rose before Pastor Rick had a chance to introduce her, so he did it as she walked up. She was wearing a plain black dress, hose, shoes. Her head was draped in a black cloth that looked like it came out of a kitchen drawer. She squared herself and lifted her head. As she did, her face looked enraged. People knew why, but the intensity of it came as a surprise. Though her face was motionless, her expression shifted from anger to stillness, and she looked at each person in turn. She lifted her face to the sky, and her countenance became anguished, in the sudden but imperceptible way that light changes.

"Damn it all to hell," she said.

"Kathy?" Pastor Rick gasped.

"Damn this town, and everyone in it." She lifted a finger and pointed it at the mourners. "Damn the television and the cops and Chuck Vogel and my ungrateful nieces." She looked ready to continue, but she burst into tears. "Damn the Bible and your words and—" Kathy threw her arms wide, the kitchen shawl falling to the ground unceremoniously, like the wing of a crow.

Pastor Rick crept toward her and offered his arm. She observed him from the corner of her eye, and after a tense moment, she took his arm, and lowered her head again. "Let's get you a chair," Pastor Rick said. "Take mine."

Kathy allowed him to guide her and help her settle into the chair. People were ready for another outburst, but one never came.

Eric glanced over his shoulder at his father, who raised his eyebrows and signed, *She gets to.* Eric nodded and looked forward, and then back at his dad, then down and forward again.

Pastor Rick took his place again at the front. He breathed in a pattern that looked like one for which he'd trained himself, then he asked if anyone had anything they'd like to say.

"Please," he added. "Maybe someone could . . ." He scanned the group more than once. "Okay, then. Time for the procession."

The pallbearers brought the Jessup caskets to the grave sites, which were tidy and surrounded by chrome diamond plate. A man in a kilt with a set of bagpipes appeared out of nowhere and played "Shall We Gather at the River." At this point, no one thought to question the choice of hymn. The pallbearers set their loads onto ornate chrome rigs that held the caskets aloft until the funeral director's son tripped two small chrome levers that silently delivered the caskets into the graves with mechanical precision.

The mourners moved past the graves, slowly throwing in their dirt or setting flowers alongside them. Francis was last, and when he emerged from the other side of line, he still had the flowers in his hand.

"We can take those," the funeral director said, reaching for the bouquet.

Francis jerked them away, then politely said, "No, thank you."

Eric and Jaymee stood together off to the side, signing to each other, as Lexi and her family clustered together and wept. Francis went straight to Eric and got his attention. He put the flowers under his arm and signed, *When this is done, meet me over there, and we'll go see your mother together.* He pointed to an eight-foot gravestone with twin Confederate flags on the plinth. *Bring her with you.*

Dad, no, Eric signed.

Don't "no" me. It's been months. Have you taken the girl to meet her yet? Francis asked.

Taken me to meet who? she signed, speaking along.

Dad, Eric pleaded. *Come on.*

I see, Francis signed.

Eric, what is he talking about? Jaymee asked. She studied the two of them, their expressions, postures, the flowers under Francis's arm, the ring on his finger. *Oh,* she signed. *I see. I didn't know she was here.*

She's not, Eric said, then turned so his father couldn't see him sign. *She died when I was eleven. I think about her all the time. I don't care about that gravestone.*

But he does, Jaymee signed.

Today is about your family, Eric said. *He should have thought about that. We don't have to double up.*

Eric, my parents are gone. A funeral is for the living.

Jaymee turned back to Francis and excused them both.

I can go with you, she signed.

Eric looked at her with an expression that began with anger but softened quickly into an emotion that didn't sort itself into any state of mind with a name. *It will be okay,* she signed, and Eric nodded.

She took a few short steps toward Francis, to close the gap. "Eric was planning to bring me here, but everything went crazy with the TV people and my family and the house," she said.

"He was?" Francis asked, looking past Jaymee at Eric, whose hands were shoved deep into his pockets.

"Yes. He said it was important to him that I meet her."

"Good," Francis said. "It is important to remember. Once the grass has grown in, it's better—easier, I mean. The grass shows you're healing." He threw his thumb toward the open grave. "That is like coming out of surgery."

"What a sweet thing to say, Mr. Bugg. Today is a big day for goodbyes." She walked over to Eric, signing, *This is a small investment.*

As the three of them left the service together, Jaymee heard someone yell, "Hey!" Francis stopped, but Jaymee ushered them on. "Hey," the voice yelled again. Jaymee could tell it was her Aunt Kathy's husband, Kevin. "Where the heck do you think you're going?"

Jaymee stopped and gathered her energy before turning around.

"Your parents are over here, Jaymee," he yelled. Kathy, Lexi, and everyone else fell in behind him.

Eric asked what they were saying. His father said never mind. Jaymee took another breath and turned. "In the hole?" she called. "You think my folks are down there, in the hole?"

Her Aunt Kathy peeked around her husband and said, "Is it any wonder you and your—" she started, then she said, "Never mind."

"Is it any wonder what?" Jaymee said.

"Never mind," Kathy said.

"That is the third time in the last thirty seconds I've heard someone say that word. If I hear it again, I'm going to Hulk-out and destroy this place." She took Eric and his father by their hands and led them away, hoping she was leading them in the right direction.

Francis asked if now was a good time to do this after all. Eric couldn't hear or he would have agreed. Jaymee said and signed, *No. It's good. I need a break from those people.*

Francis took over and led them to a grave site by the fence. When they arrived, he made the sign of the cross, knelt, and placed the flowers against her gravestone. After a word of prayer, he took some old flowers from a wire sconce in the grass and placed the new flowers in their stead.

"How did your wife die, Mr. Bugg?" Jaymee asked.

"Cancer," he said.

"I'm sorry," she said.

"It was ovarian," he told her, still on his knees.

"How old was Eric when she passed?"

"Eleven," Francis said. "Eleven years old." After he spoke he dropped his head and drifted into prayer or meditation. He didn't speak, so it was unclear. Behind him Jaymee and Eric began to sign.

I want to leave this place, she said.

I thought you wanted to come here for him, Eric answered.

Not here, she signed. *Anadarko.*

Where would you go? he asked.

I don't know. West.

Okay, Eric signed, with a sadness in his eyes.

Jaymee touched his face with her hand and signed, *Not alone. I want you to come, too.*

Eric looked at his dad, his shoulders rounded, his hands now in front of him, on the edge of the gravestone. When he looked back at Jaymee, his eyes were welling up.

We could go anywhere, she said.

When they looked again at Francis, a bird had landed on the stone. Francis lifted his head and provided a finger for the bird to perch on; when it saw the two of them, the bird leapt into the air and flew away.

Birds really like him, Eric signed.

Francis stepped in close, took Jaymee and his son by their arms, and turned to Jaymee. "Don't you ever let him say she's not here," he said, his eyes round with fury.

Francis found Eric asleep on the couch, with his implant microphones unclipped and sitting on the coffee table. A Netflix message was on the television, asking if he was still watching. Francis turned everything off, but before switching off the set, he watched his son. His hands were shoved between his knees and his mouth was wide open. He touched the boy lightly on the side of his face, but backed away when Eric swatted at his hand. Francis wondered, as he often did, how the boy could have ever been so small that the two of them could fit in a twin bed with room to spare. Francis wanted to burrow into the couch to sleep with his nose in the boy's hair, like they used to.

When his wife first became sick, Francis would sleep with Eric, leaving his wife the whole bed because her nights were wracked with pain, and the chemo drugs made her susceptible to germs and disease. Eventually neither of them could fall asleep alone. When his wife had moved to the hospital, they kept the habit, finding ways to push together chairs and ottomans into something passable. She told Francis that sometimes she would wake to see them entwined, which made her worry less about how things would go between them when she was gone.

It was easier for everyone to sleep when she was finally moved to hospice. The thing about being a deaf kid is he could sleep anywhere. Noise didn't keep him up. The hospice center was mostly quiet, except for the machine they kept in the room to monitor her pulse and breathing. She was in a lot of pain. The morphine took her down to where she could talk but left her so incoherent she couldn't say or understand much. Francis mostly just held her hand, careful not to bump the IV.

On the last night, her breathing changed and the beep-beep-beep of her heartbeat slowed. She called for Francis in a weak voice.

He left the boy, went to her, and leaned in. "It's me. I'm here. Should I get Father Andrew?"

"No," she said. "I need to talk to you about Eric.

"Don't worry about Eric," he said. "He's a good boy."

"He's not," she said.

"Now don't say that," Francis told her.

"I've only got one child, don't let this world take him."

"I won't. I swear," he said.

She coughed and drifted off to sleep. Francis was worried that she was gone, but he could sense the life still inside her. He could see that she was slowing but still there. He looked over at the boy who slept, too, under an orange Oklahoma State Cowboys fleece blanket with a white fringe. He scooted the chair closer to his wife and took her hand.

Her eyes remained shut, and she squeezed his hand back. "Francis," she said, "if a rock goes off a cliff, it keeps falling until it hits the bottom."

"I know," he said, trying to keep calm.

"Don't be angry. Be there to catch him. Promise me."

"I will," he said.

She became still, and her grip loosened slightly. Her breathing became even more shallow, and something beeped on the monitor. Her heart rate slowed. He could hear it in the beep, see it in the numbers. He pushed her hair aside, and she moaned a little. For a moment he thought he would call someone and started to rise from his seat, but he stopped and sat again. Her body relaxed, and in a few minutes, in the deep quiet of the room, she stopped breathing altogether. The monitor beeps changed to a single long tone. He could see in her face that her spirit had fled.

He closed his eyes, and a strange thought came to him. From this point on, it would get easier for all of them.

The hospice nurse came in and silenced the machines. "Did she pass?" she asked.

Francis nodded.

Bugg looked over at his son, who slept through the noise, oblivious. Francis didn't wake him. There would be time for him to face this loss, but for now, sleep was best. As he watched the boy's chest rise and fall and listened to the wetness of his breathing, he realized that for the first time in his life, the child's deafness was a blessing.

Francis wanted to reach down and touch Eric without waking him, but he didn't. He was too old now. He hadn't touched him in years. Francis knew this was the way of things, but it deepened his sadness from the memory of that night in hospice all the way to the morning of today. Eric had proven Karen correct. For the last eight years, he'd been in almost constant trouble of one kind or another. Things got better once the life insurance came in, and Francis took Eric to see if cochlear implants might help. He was astounded by the sounds of things, and for a while started doing well in school. When he learned that playing football was off the table, he caved and ended up in the juvenile courts for stealing cars. He didn't keep them or try to sell them, he just drove them around and left them when he was done, keys still in the ignition.

Francis was just about to wake Eric, when his son's phone buzzed and a message banner popped up on the screen.

Robert Earl Cripps: *On my way. Take a shower.*

Francis took the phone and stuck it on Eric's thumb as he slept. Once it was unlocked, he looked back through the text chain with Robert Earl.

TODAY 12:07 AM: *Hey, Robert Earl.*

TODAY 12:09 AM: *What are you texting me for?*

TODAY 12:09 AM: *I remember you talking about an idea you had with your pool business. Can I still get in?*

TODAY 12:37 AM: *????*

TODAY 1:22 AM: *You were going to use The Pool Shark to do something with chemicals. You said you might need a driver.*

Robert Earl sent a picture of himself lying in bed with a tiny pig under the covers. He was flipping off the camera. The caption: *Mr. Big says UR nuts.*

TODAY 4:03 AM: *Use the other number next time.*

TODAY 7:13 AM: *On my way. Take a shower.*

Francis set his son's phone back on the coffee table. The clock on the microwave said it was 7:14. Francis went into the kitchen and started making himself a pot of coffee, splitting his attention between the front door window, the coffee maker, and his kid sprawled on the couch. While the coffee maker heated up, Francis emptied the dishwasher and wiped down the counters.

Outside a massive truck rumbled through the trailer park and pulled in next to Bugg's place. Francis heard it and went to the window, stood to the side, and looked out. The black truck had a white sticker on the door of a grinning shark. The word POOL was written across the place where the gills should be. A kid named Robert Earl Cripps was inside, his hair bleached, mulletted, and wet. He wore the kind of huge plastic sunglasses Francis remembered ladies wearing in the seventies. He was talking on a cell phone while a little black-and-white potbellied pig nuzzled his face.

Eric's phone buzzed again, which made Francis take another cautious step back from the window.

The coffee machine started hissing, which drew Bugg's attention. He took a pillow from his recliner and threw it at the boy, which made him shoot up into a sitting position. When he had Eric's attention, Bugg put a finger to his lips and, with the other hand, pointed to the phone on the coffee table.

Check your phone, he signed.

Eric unlocked the screen and thumbed through the messages. After a couple of swipes, a horrified look leapt across his face. He parted the cheap blinds with a finger and saw Robert Earl out there, sitting in his truck, staring right at him. Eric dropped the metal slat and turned right toward his father with a false look that said, "What's he doing here?"

While the Buggs took turns shrugging at each other, Robert Earl blew the horn four or five times. It agitated Francis so much he shot a look outside and growled, "That's enough." He stormed into his room and came back with a 9mm pistol, which he stuck awkwardly behind his back in the belt of his bathrobe.

He motioned for Eric to keep down, and then he went outside. Eric thought about protesting, but resigned himself to his father's plans.

Francis said, "Hey, mister. I thought I told you to steer clear of this place."

"I'm here to pick up Eric. Tell him to get cracking."

"I'm here to pick up Eric, what?"

"You aren't gonna hear me calling you 'sir,' so quit trying."

This made Bugg ratchet himself straight and square his shoulders. "I might have to call your daddy, Robert Earl. He'll want a report on how his boy backtalks veterans and leans on his horn like some third-world cab driver."

"You're all bark."

Francis stepped back through the door and reached for the old gray phone sitting on the edge of the kitchen counter. It took a couple seconds to sell the bluff.

"I'm here to pick up Eric, sir." Robert Earl said, sighing loudly.

"That's better. While we're at it, Dumbo, I'd like to point out that you were honking for a deaf guy."

Robert Earl stuck a disgusted look on his face and rolled his eyes like a teenager. "Deaf? He's got those bionic speakers in his hair. He probably can hear me talkin' right now." The potbellied pig ran across the bench seat and snuffled along the edge of the open window.

"What the heck is that?" Francis asked.

"It's a pig."

"I can tell it's a pig. Why is it riding in your truck?"

"His name is Mr. Big," Robert Earl said.

"Mr. Pig?" he asked. "Robert Earl, it ain't a name if you just call it mister plus the kind of thing it is."

"Not Pig. It's Big. Mr. Big, like the band. I'm not gonna argue with you. Where's Eric?"

Francis folded his arms.

"Where's Eric, sir?" Robert Earl said reluctantly, then mumbled something Bugg couldn't hear.

"That's a tiny little critter. Calling him Mr. Big don't make sense." Francis turned around and went back into the house, making sure Robert Earl could see the pistol he'd stuck in the belt of his robe. Eric was dressed, sort of, in a black Adidas T-shirt, his orange Oklahoma State shorts, and basketball shoes without socks. His implants were in place, but his hair was crazy.

"What's that no-account doing here?" Bugg said, fiercely.

"Leave us alone, Dad," Eric said. I'm gonna do some work for him."

"Oh, really? You've got a job?"

"I'm going to talk to him about one. Dad, he's got a pool business. Pool chemicals. He's expanding, so he needs a driver. You're always telling me to get a job. Nobody wants to hire a deaffie, but Robert Earl doesn't care."

"Don't call yourself that. I hate it."

"It's what deaf people say."

"Sounds like you've got no pride."

"I've got to go."

"You better not be lying to me, boy."

"I'm not."

"Because if you're lying to me . . ."

"I'm not lying. This is for real."

"Because if you're lying, I'll never hear the end of it." Francis froze when he said those words. The shock of what he said seemed overplayed, but it was legitimate.

Eric met his father's eyes and wouldn't look away. It was his turn to stand taller. Francis slouched and raised his hand to block his son's gaze.

"You didn't hear that," Francis said. "Just. Go."

She doesn't talk to you, Dad. Eric said, speaking and signing together. He swung his hands through the empty air. *She's gone.*

"You don't know anything about it," Bugg said, still cowering.

I know she's dead, and talking is one of the main things dead people can't do. He walked past his dad, jumped down the stairs, and jogged around to Robert Earl's truck. He climbed in and purposely did not look back.

"I been honking," Robert Earl said. "Can you hear me now?" He laughed at his own joke and put the truck in gear.

"Good one. I never heard that one before."

"Really?" Robert Earl asked.

"Never heard it because I'm deaf. Get it?"

"Lame," Robert Earl said.

"Let's get out of here," Eric said. "I need to get something to eat.

As they drove off, the pig climbed into Eric's lap and looked out the window with his beady black eyes.

The diner was half full. Robert Earl and Eric had a booth with a window so he could keep an eye on Mr. Big. "You think he can squeeze out of there?" Robert Earl asked.

Eric looked outside and shook his head. "Not with those hoofs."

"It's toes, man," Robert Earl said. "He's got four on each leg. Two up front and two in back."

"Gross," Eric said.

"Actually, a pig foot is tasty."

The waitress freshened up their coffee, took their order, and grabbed the menus. She looked tired. When she left, Robert Earl glanced around. Everybody in the place seemed like they should be there. A group of contractors at one table. A handful of people eating on their own. Everyone else normal to the eye. When Robert Earl was satisfied, he laced his fingers together and leaned forward on his elbows. "We ain't having this conversation, okay?"

Eric rolled his eyes. "For real?" he asked.

"If anyone asks—"

"Who would ask?"

"I don't know. If somebody in here asked."

"If they ask if I was having a conversation with you, I tell them no?"

"That's right?"

"But they can see that we're talking."

Robert Earl furrowed his brow and growled.

"Fine. We're not having this conversation."

Robert Earl leaned further in. "You seen *Breaking Bad,* right?"

"Some of it. By the way, you're the *most* suspicious-looking person in here."

"Shut up. *Breaking Bad* ain't like how it is. Most of the time people cooking meth don't have some chicken guy bankrolling them. They scrape together some kind of recipe they got off the internet and get stuff from the Home Zone. A lot of 'em blow themselves up." Robert Earl got a cocky look and drank some of his coffee

"Okay?" Eric said, leaning in a little to match Robert Earl.

"Once the cops figured out how these idiots cooked, they started putting everything behind the counter. You gotta show your driver's license for cold pills, right? So the cooks move on to other stuff. Stuff that isn't hot. So, when people started cooking, they used this stuff called P2P."

"Pee two, what?"

"Phenyl-2-propanone, numb nuts. People use it to clean pools. It was, like, the thing until the cops caught wind and started watching for people who were buying it but didn't have a pool, or . . ."

"A pool-cleaning business, like you?" Eric said, brightening.

"*Exactamente*, like me," Robert Earl said. He dumped two packets of sugar into his coffee without tasting it. "People quit using P2P like ten years ago and moved on. Now Johnny Law isn't watching P2P anymore, the Pool Shark's been selling it for maybe a year, no cops, no DEA, no paperwork, nothing."

"You're the Pool Shark, right?"

"It's an LLC, man. Corporations are people."

Eric looked confused for a moment. "Okay. So, what do you need me to do?"

"I just need you to deliver it. If anybody sees me making deliveries to places with no pools, with my Pool Shark logo, et cetera, I'm toast. I can fake the paperwork and make it look like it's all legit. You take the P2P to the cooks, small amounts for each drop. I take stuff to my pool clients like normal. Nobody looks at anything but the amount they gotta pay."

"What if I get pulled over?"

"You got some pool cleaner in the back. Just a little. It's still America, right?"

When Eric didn't say anything for a long time, Robert Earl said, "Did you hear me? Dammit. I never know if you can even hear me?"

"I heard you," Eric said. "I'm thinking, okay?"

"How do you talk, anyway?" Robert Earl asked.

"With my mouth," Eric said.

"That was a for reals question, bro. I've known you since we were little, but I never thought about it."

Eric gestured to his ears. "Cochlear implants. I went to a speech therapist, like, forever."

"But you sign, too."

"People can speak two languages, dork. Not you, but some people can."

"Weird," Robert Earl said. "How come your dad hates me?"

"He hates everybody."

"That ain't an answer. How come he's got it out for me?"

"He blames you for getting me in trouble in high school."

"Me?" Robert Earl said, touching his chest indignantly. "He blames me?"

Eric nodded. "That's what he thinks."

"That's backwards, man. You probably told him."

Eric shrugged, drank some coffee, then some water. "When's our food getting here?"

Robert Earl ignored him. "You tell your piece of crap old man if he's gonna get a gat out when I'm there, I ain't playing."

"Everybody knows you ain't playing, Robert Earl."

"Well, I ain't."

"You never do."

"That's right."

"My dad is nuts, but nobody wants to shoot anybody."

"Is that what Jaymee's dad thought?"

"Come on," Eric said. "That's uncool."

"Uncool, maybe. But not untrue," Robert Earl said.

The waitress brought their food. Two eggs, sausage, and ham, plus a short stack for Robert Earl. Biscuits and gravy for Eric. Both of them covered their food with hot sauce before they started. Nobody talked until they were each about halfway through.

"Let's talk money," Eric said.

"What? And ruin the mood?"

"When we talked before, you said it was good money. How good?"

"Seven hundred per delivery."

Eric tried not to flinch or smile. He just nodded. "How many deliveries per week?"

"Depends. Probably not more than three."

Eric nodded again. "I need to get my own vehicle?"

"That's right, and not that whiny orange thing you drive. It's too loud. Everyone will know it's you. You need to be low-key. Can you handle that?"

Eric nodded. "I'll make it work."

"I will leave the P2P in different places, then tell you where to get it and when. Drop it off. Tell me you did it. You're done."

"Sounds easy enough." Eric said. "By the way, I've told you a million times. Don't talk to deaf people with your mouth full. It's nasty."

Robert Earl ignored Eric, and when the waitress left the check, he slid it over to Eric and went to the bathroom. "Don't let her take my plate. Some of that's for Mr. Big."

ERIC PICKED UP JAYMEE, AND they went to Kim's Country Store for gum and caffeine. Since breakfast the sky had gone completely dark. The underside of the clouds looked like a hundred tiny gray bellies, dark gray with a little bit of yellow. On the way, Eric told her that he'd lined up good work with Robert Earl.

"Can't be good work if it's for him," she said and signed, sitting cross-legged in the passenger's seat of Eric's orange racer. She knew it was dangerous to sign with someone who was driving, but she did it anyway.

"It's good money," Eric said. "I can get maybe nine grand in a month."

"Doing what?" she asked.

"I'm not gonna say," he said.

"It's gonna be you and Robert Earl both in jail," she said, turning to look out the window.

"I'm not going to jail," Eric said.

"Nobody starts out thinking they are."

"I know how it works, Jaymee."

They pulled into the parking lot of Kim's and got out. "We can't leave town on what you have left after the funeral."

"Shut up," she said, walking ahead of him into the convenience store. Eric trotted behind to keep up. A guy in a John Deere T-shirt with the sleeves cut off started to come out, slowing him down. The John Deere guy was halfway out when he stopped and checked his receipt, made a noise, and then kept going. By the time Eric got into the store, Jaymee was already in the back getting her iced coffee. Eric grabbed two Rockstar Revolts and a bag of pickle-flavored sunflower seeds. Jaymee had moved over to the candy aisle, and she bent over getting some red licorice. She stood and looked at him like Princess Leia, and then suddenly looked outside.

Look, she signed, then pointed.

Eric saw a flash and felt a percussive blast in his belly a couple seconds later. Then the sky opened up. Rain fell all at once as if from a trapdoor.

The cars outside were shrouded in a mist of rebounding rain. His implants didn't pick up any intricacies of the storm, and the sudden claps of thunder overwhelmed them. He stood next to Jaymee and watched. Everyone in the convenience store drifted to the front windows and watched. Eric took Jaymee's drink and candy and paid for it all with a ten.

"Ain't it something?" the cashier said.

"I grew up here. I should be used to it," Eric said.

"Don't know how you could. Doesn't seem like a storm's got any rules."

"There's probably rules the storm doesn't know about."

The cashier laughed at that. "That's more likely." He got a serious look on his face, started to say something, then quit, thought for a second, and said, "Tell Jaymee I'm sorry about her folks."

"That's nice of you to say"—Eric looked down at the guy's name tag—"Tyson," he said. "I'll tell her you said so." Eric gathered all the things together, and tried to size up if he could carry it all.

Tyson got him a bag and held it open while Eric filled it.

When Eric got to Jaymee, she was right by the front window watching the downpour with a short overweight lady wearing a baby-blue Dollywood T-shirt and pink leggings. She had a carton of Pall Malls under one arm and a little gray dog under the other. The two of them were talking, but Eric couldn't hear what they were saying. The rain and the thunder and everyone talking right up by the hard surface of the glass made it difficult to focus. He handed Jaymee her stuff and opened one of his Rockstars. The woman talking to Jaymee seemed to know her. Eric cupped his hand over one ear and turned his head to the woman.

In the clamor, he could hear the woman say, "You come from good people, Jaymee. Your Aunt Kathy is a saint as far as I'm concerned, which balances everything out." He didn't hear what Jaymee said back. He was nervous about the possibilities. When provoked, Jaymee could strike like a snake. A huge clap of thunder made his implants short out for a couple of seconds. When he could hear again, the woman was saying, "Makes me wonder if I shouldn't carry a gun." She lifted the dog first, then the cigarettes. "Not sure where it would go." She squeezed the dog so its muzzle stuck into the side of her boob. "Probably right in there with my phone." Jayme reached around and took Eric's hand, she locked down on it like a pair of Vise-Grips.

As they continued to talk, the rain turned to hail. Within half a minute it went from small, white peppercorns to gum balls. Eric tugged on the back of Jaymee's shirt. "I want to move the car," he said. Jaymee didn't respond right away, so he put his hand on her back and he could hear the vibration of her voice. The other woman's eyes got wide, and the little dog barked. "Come on," he said. "Let's go. I don't have insurance on this car anymore." He grabbed Jaymee and pulled her past all the onlookers toward the door, then like people psyching themselves to jump into a lake, he counted: "Three, two, one, go," and they burst through the doors into the chaos.

The stones stung. As they ran, their shoes became immediately soaked. Hair, faces, shoulders, too. Eric scanned the area as they ran to the car. All the space by the pumps was taken. Someone was in the carwash. He looked past the Daylight Donuts next door, and across the street was an old drive-in restaurant that wasn't a drive-in anymore. "There," he shouted, and pointed with his Rockstar. They yanked open the doors and plopped in simultaneously. Jaymee slotted her drink in the cup holder and took Eric's stuff. He fired up the car, backed it up dangerously fast, and lurched through the storm across the two connected parking lots. It was nearly impossible to see, but Eric gripped the wheel and shot across the street and into the open canopy of the drive-in.

Through the implants, the hail sounded like explosions from an old video game. He let the windshield wipers sweep across the glass a couple of times then shut them off. Outside the hail had grown to the size of ping-pong balls.

"That was crazy," Eric said, looking over at Jaymee, who was hugging her knees and tipping her head against the glass. "Are you okay?" he asked.

It doesn't matter, Jaymee signed, knowing that all the noise would make hearing difficult for Eric.

Did that lady say something? he asked.

No.

B.S., he signed.

It doesn't matter, she repeated. *It's the same stuff everybody always says. I hate it here.*

I do, too.

I just want to tell my own story, she said. *You can't do that around here.*

Outside it seemed like the storm was easing up, but it was temporary. A few seconds later, it doubled down. They were both glad to have this shelter. They shared some of the licorice. Eric checked the digital car thermometer, and the outside temperature had dropped ten degrees since they got in. He rolled down both windows, which made Jaymee jump and Eric apologize.

How much money can you get from Robert Earl? she asked.

A lot, he answered.

Is it safe? she asked.

Eric shrugged.

I don't like it, she said.

I hate what happened to you in there worse, he said.

Jaymee looked at Eric and smiled weakly but with real affection. She reached for his face and pulled him toward her. She kissed him once and then stroked her thumb across the corner of his lips. "I don't deserve you," she whispered.

"Huh?" Eric said, which made her sit back on her side.

I love you, she signed.

Francis was watching television when the rain turned to hail. The moment he heard the metallic ping, ping, ping on the roof of his trailer, he went to the window and checked his truck. He leaned against the door and watched for a while trying to decide a course of action. He checked the clouds, which were dark as far as he could see to the west and south. The trees were in an uproar of hail and rain, green leaves tearing loose and disappearing into the wind.

He decided it wasn't going to get better, and when he noticed the size of the hailstones growing, he scratched his head for a moment then went to his bedroom and pulled the comforter and sheets from the bed in a single motion, like a magician. He rushed outside with the bundle in his arms and threw it over the roof of his truck. He used the doors to secure the blankets. As he ran back inside, the hailstones started to sting as they pelted him. He rushed to Eric's room and pulled his bedclothes off as well. His move was less deft, and he pulled the mattress a few inches off the box springs, which knocked over a lamp, phone charger, and other things on Eric's nightstand. Francis ignored it and hurried back outside where the hail had become as big around as golf balls. A great blue fork of lightning split the sky into three sections for an instant. The thunderclap that followed made Francis duck, even though he knew it was coming. He tucked the bedspread into the bumper and into the wheel wells. Not a perfect solution but good enough, he hoped.

The hail was becoming painful, and Francis was soaked right through. He shook off as he came through the door and then turned to see if his plan worked. Hail was still hitting the bed, but the bed liner would take care of that. The blankets looked like they were doing their job, if they didn't blow away. Francis got a towel, dried off, and changed clothes. He then went into Eric's room and put everything back together. When he shoved the mattress back into place, the motion pushed a notebook out of the crack. Francis pulled it out all the way. On the top, in marker, it said, *Letters 2 Mom*. Francis took the notebook and began thumbing through it. The first letter was in kid handwriting.

Dear Mom,

Dad said you died while I was asleep, so I didn't get to say goodbye. I am happy that you're not sick anymore, but I am sad that you're gone. Dad says we can go to a doctor about my hearing. He says maybe I could hear again, sort of. I'll write another letter and tell you if I can. Dad says you're not really gone. It's not true, but I don't tell him that. I know it will just make him sad. I'm going to keep my promise and be a good boy, but it's hard to.

Love,
Eric

There was no date, but Francis figured it must have been from when Eric was eleven, right after Karen passed. He closed the notebook, and breathed until his urge to cry tapered. Eric had hidden this notebook from him all these years. When they moved out of the house. When they lived all over the East Coast when he was starting with the railroad. He opened the notebook again and thumbed through the pages. There were letters about school and missing her. Letters about living in all kinds of different places. Eric wrote to her about not wanting another mom and about how Francis could not cook very well even though he tried. He didn't write regularly, it seemed, sometimes only once or twice a year. Sometimes more. Somewhere in the middle was a letter about getting the cochlear implants.

Dear Mom,

I had the surgery, and it worked. I have cochlear implants now, and I can hear other people and things again. It's not like I remember. Everything sounds fake and far away. That is hard. It's also hard to pay attention at recess or in the lunchroom with all the noises, but I don't need an interpreter at school anymore. But I have to learn how to not hear stuff. I don't feel like the weird kid anymore. I haven't had to beat up anyone for being a jerk to me in a long time. Maybe a month. I still talk like a deaffie, though, but it's getting better. Listening to basketball on TV sounds cool.

Dad says we're moving back to Oklahoma. I don't want to go there. He says it is a promotion, but I don't care. All my friends are here now.

I also found out that the money for my implants came because you died. I would rather have you still here with us, but I guess I should say thanks. This is the first good thing for a long time.

Love,
Eric

Francis walked with the notebook into the front room, flipping more pages. They showed a side of Eric he always guessed at, but never knew. Francis wondered how you could ever know anyone in the end. *People are mysteries*, he thought. *Everything important is.*

He skimmed a few more pages, then stopped at a letter where the handwriting seemed different, more rushed and angled, less like a kid's writing.

Dear Mom,

They just told me I can't play basketball, even with my implants. My shooting is good, but they say since I can't hear it will be dangerous. It's not true, I can hear enough to play. I'm better than they are. It's really true.

Dad talks to you. I am pretty sure you don't know that because, you're gone. That's obvious. He could just write letters like I do, but he walks around the house talking to you. He used to stop when I was around, now he just keeps going. It's really weird.

If he is actually talking to you, could you tell him to stop. I'm worried they are going to think he's crazy and put me in a foster home, like they did with Andy Carlson when both his parents went to jail. I could live alone if I had to. When Dad is on the train run, I am here by myself for like three days. I could do it. When I'm old enough to get a job, I'll have my own money, and then it won't matter if he's crazy. Don't worry about us. We'll be fine.

Love,
Eric

Francis grew furious. He stormed through the house and threw the notebook on the coffee table. He looked out at the hail, which was beginning to taper off. He got a beer from the fridge and sat down in his chair. When he looked up, his wife was sitting on the far side of the sofa.

"You shouldn't be reading those letters, Francis. It's private," she said.

"He can have privacy when he's living on his own," Francis said. He sipped his beer and watched her eyes. They didn't blink. He looked away and then back.

"He's going to act the way you treat him," she said.

He tried to stare her down again, but it didn't work.

"Francis, those letters are to me. I don't care if you see them, but he wrote those things to me, and not you, for a reason," she said. "If he finds out you've been—"

"He isn't going to find out."

She smiled and shook her head.

"We went to see you yesterday," Francis said.

"You know that just upsets him."

"He's told me," Francis said.

"You ignore him, sweetie. You need to stop doing that, or pretty soon he's going to quit talking to you all together."

"He needs to grow up."

"Not that way," she said.

"You baby him."

"You just set him loose like a baby alligator."

"How's he gonna learn anything?"

"You'll teach him."

"Bah," Francis said, and swigged his beer again.

"Is parenting a humbug, then?"

"I'm not the bad guy, Karen."

"But you're the role model, right?" she said. When Francis didn't respond, she said, "Right?" again with more vigor.

He turned away from her to look out the window at the ebbing storm.

"You know they call it a handicap for a reason. Every morning when that boy gets up, he's already two steps behind. He doesn't get to make excuses."

"A good father can make up the difference," she said.

"I'm not always going to be around," Francis said.

"Who is?" she said, folding her arms.

"I'm sorry," Francis said.

"Francis," she said, leaning toward him, elbows on her knees. "Your time with him is limited."

"I know. I know."

"You promised to protect our baby."

"I know I did."

"Then protect him. You are my eyes and ears now, Francis. My hands."

"I'm trying to do that."

"You have to take care of yourself first. How come you haven't gone to see someone about the accident?"

"Some stockbroker stepping in front of my train has got nothing to do with me."

"You still think about him all the time. His calm face, his closed eyes. That red hair. The pair of shoes he left behind on the platform. There's a reason they put you on administrative leave, Francis. You can't kill someone and go back to work like nothing happened, even if it's an accident."

"They put me on leave because that guy is high-profile, and nobody wants the press."

"They put you on leave because you talk to me," she said. "You started talking to me while the police were interviewing you."

Francis was furious. He drank the rest of his beer and then pressed the palms of his hands into his eye sockets. Outside the storm had cooled off. It was back to a light rain, which tapped on the roof of the trailer in the loveliest way imaginable.

"I can only worry about one of you at a time," she said. Francis walked over to the chair and bent down to kiss the ghost of his wife.

The door swung open and Eric walked in. Jaymee was right behind.

"Dad?" Eric shouted. "What are you doing?"

Francis stopped abruptly, but didn't turn. He pointed back at his son without looking and said, "It's none of your business, boy."

Jaymee tried to stop Eric by coming around in front of him and placing her hands on his chest. "Don't," she said. "Seriously, don't."

"What's that?" Eric asked, pointing to his notebook. "How'd you get that? Why are my sheets on your truck?" Eric pushed past Jaymee and grabbed the notebook. "This is mine!" Eric screamed.

"I told you," Karen said, which distracted Francis.

"Don't listen to her. Talk to me," Eric said.

"Now you've done it," she said.

Eric took his notebook and disappeared into his room. Francis scratched the back of his head and looked at Jaymee. "I'm sorry," he said.

"Don't be," she said.

"I'm not sorry about talking to my wife. I'm sorry it upsets Eric. I'm sorry it's upsetting you."

"If I could talk to my parents, Mr. Bugg, I would."

"I'm not crazy."

"I didn't say you were."

"Nobody starts their life thinking it'll end up this way," Francis said. "If you did, you'd never have the courage to finish."

"I had a teacher once who always said, 'We're never as unhappy as we think we are,'" Jaymee said.

"I didn't go looking for that notebook," Francis said. "I didn't even know it was there."

"What was it?" Jaymee asked.

"Letters to his mother," Francis said.

Jaymee looked around the room, then said, "Maybe he wishes he could talk to her, too."

Jaymee woke Eric by placing his buzzing phone against his cheek. It was Robert Earl. He didn't have his hearing aids in place, so he swiped the phone and texted Robert Earl, *Can't hear right now. Text me.*

He rolled over and spooned in behind Jaymee. She reached around and stroked his forearm. They were in his room, with its low ceilings and fake wood paneling. A band of cotton-candy pink spread across the sky to the east. He was still angry with his father, but not furious.

The text from Robert Earl came in: *I had to pull over, dumbass.* After a few seconds, another one came, *You're working for me today. 9 a.m. at my shed.*

Eric rolled over on his stomach so he could type. *Where?*

You remember. By that place.

What are you talking about?

Moron! He sent the policeman emoji, and after another few seconds wrote, *It's by that place those cheerleaders drank our Jäger and then made out with each other. There's a key under the can by the back door.*

Eric smiled and hid the phone from Jaymee.

Roger, he typed.

When Eric shut off his phone, he saw that it was seven thirty. He knew if he went back to sleep, he'd blow everything. He snuggled up to Jaymee and put his face in her hair. He tried to reach around her, but she pushed his hands away and sat up so they could sign. She was braless in his Oklahoma State T-shirt, and her eyes said this was not a time for monkey business.

That was Robert Earl, she signed.

Eric sat up and signed, *Yes.*

Is this job going to get you killed?

No. It's just deliveries. I'm working for Pool Shark, taking chemicals around.

She folded her arms and thought. As she did, a curtain of hair fell across half her face making her the most beautiful girl in the world. When she saw him staring at her, she hooked her hair behind each ear, which returned her face to misalignment. Most of the time Eric didn't notice the deformity, but when he did, it made him hate himself.

If this job you're doing is dangerous, I'll kill you.

Eric got out of bed, slid on his shorts, and found his sandals with his feet. He pointed to his shirt, and wiggled two fingers to indicate he needed it back. Jaymee pulled it over her head and threw it at Eric's face. By the time he caught it, she was safely back under the covers. He put the shirt on, noting her smell.

Can you help me hook these up? he asked, handing her his hearing aids. He sat on the edge of the bed with his back facing her, and she slipped the sound processors behind his ears and connected them to the clear wires, then clipped the coils into his hair. "Thank you," he said.

"I'm serious," she told him. "After Chuck Vogel, Robert Earl might be the very worst person I know."

He kissed her on the forehead, got his keys, wallet, and phone, and left. He drove into town and stopped at McDonald's for a Number 2 with a Coke. He ate it on the way to Robert Earl's shed. When he got there, he didn't see Robert Earl's truck, which surprised him a little, but that's probably why he mentioned the key.

He went around back and saw an empty wedge-shaped ham can. There was a key under it, but it didn't go to the back door, so Eric went back around front and tried it on the padlock. It worked. Inside there were all kinds of pool chemicals on pallets. There was a piece of yellow paper taped to eight or nine big plastic buckets of P2P. It said, #1 MON. Since today was Monday, Eric felt sure that was his load. He sized it up and quickly realized it wasn't all going to fit in the back of his Civic.

He got out his phone and texted Robert Earl: *Didn't think there'd be this much.*

In a few seconds, Robert Earl replied with zipper-mouthed face emoji, immediately followed by: *You'll need a truck. I told you that.*

Eric closed the shed and drove home, swearing to himself and drinking his flat Coke. When he got to the trailer, his dad was out front tending to his flowers. The hail had taken most of them out, and he was trying to tie them to thin sticks. Finches flew back and forth past his head. His dad always had a thing for birds, like some cartoon princess. They would land on his fingers and take seeds out of his lips. It was cool and weird, mostly weird. When he got out, his dad turned around immediately, and motioned for him to come over.

"She left."

"Jaymee?"

"Correct. Is she eighteen?"

"Almost. Don't matter. Sixteen is the cutoff."

"You looked into it?"

Eric nodded.

"I'm sorry I got into your notebook yesterday. I washed everything and put your room back together. You probably noticed. Your mother—" Francis stopped himself. "I see that I wasn't treating you like an adult."

Eric looked at his father and could see that he was remorseful. His shoulders were soft, and he ducked his eyes. "I appreciate that. Doesn't look like the hail got your truck," he said.

"Did in my flowers, though."

Eric nodded and took a couple of breaths. "I got a favor to ask."

"Okay."

"You can say no, but I hope you don't."

"Sure."

"Can I borrow your truck for the day? I'll bring it back with a full tank."

Eric could tell his dad wanted to say no. The look moved across his face fast, like a cloud across the sun.

"It's for work," Eric said. "I swear. It's a real job. The one I told you about for Robert Earl's business."

Francis looked past Eric and saw his wife standing at the top of the stairs. Her arms were folded. He watched her out of the corner of his eye, so he wouldn't appear to be looking at her.

"You know I just paid it off," Francis said.

"Francis Leslie Bugg," she warned.

"The keys are on my dresser," he said.

"You're a lifesaver," Eric said as he ran up the steps and through the front door.

While Eric was driving back to the shed, Robert Earl texted him:

Meet me at the 66. We'll go over your instructions.

Eric loaded the buckets of P2P in the back of his dad's truck and put a strap around them so they wouldn't tip over and spill. He noticed other pallets with more P2P with other numbers and dates written on them. There were a couple of cases of Dr Pepper and a big tub of Red Vines next to an office door in back. Everything in the shed was organized, which blew Eric's mind a little. It gave him a bit of confidence that maybe Robert Earl wasn't going to screw any of this up.

He locked up and put the key back under the can and drove to the 66. Robert Earl's truck was parked along the south side of the building. Robert Earl was inside, sitting at a table by the window wearing those stupid women's sunglasses.

"Locked and loaded," Eric said as he slipped into the booth.

"This 66 is good because it has a place to sit," Robert Earl said.

Eric looked around. "Um. Yeah. Is this some kind of spy code I don't remember?" he asked.

"It's not spy code. It's called small talk, dill weed." Robert Earl slid an envelope across the table and took a bite of his breakfast burrito. "Don't open it here." Robert Earl looked out the window and said, "Just put it in your pocket. There's a paper inside with three addresses on it. Under each address there are two numbers. One is the number of buckets they get. The other is how much money they owe me. They should give you a plain envelope full of cash."

"Should I count it while I'm there?" Eric asked.

"This isn't Kenny Rogers. Yes. Count it," Robert Earl snapped. "If the money looks good, roll on."

"What if the money doesn't look right?" Eric asked.

"Shoot 'em."

Eric's eyes got wide.

Robert Earl laughed a little. "I'm kidding. Don't do anything. They're tweakers, man. They're already two seconds away from flipping out anyway. I just want them to know that you know that they shorted me."

"Whatever, man. I don't want to get shot."

"Why would they shoot you? You're the golden goose, bro. They kill you, they aren't cooking meth anymore."

Eric looked around at the other customers in the 66. He crinkled up his face and said, "I don't want to sound lame, but maybe we could try some spy code. Seems like anyone listening could figure out what we're up to."

Robert Earl rolled his eyes. "These addresses are all over the place. It's going to take you a while to get it done. Text me when you're finished."

"What should I say?"

"You mean *spy code*?" Robert Earl said.

Eric nodded. "Shut up."

"What's something you'd never say to me normally?" Robert Earl said, thinking. "How about you say, 'Go Sooners.'"

"No."

"You'd never say it."

"You're right. I never would."

"Go Sooners. That's perfect." Robert Earl folded the last of his burrito into the foil and put it into his jacket pocket.

"You got that pig with you?" Eric asked.

"Of course I do. He's in the truck."

"That pig has you wrapped around its finger."

Robert Earl slid out of the booth and stood. "You're just jealous. Go Sooners," he said, and then he left the building.

Eric put the first address on the list into his phone. It said it was forty-six minutes away. He plugged his phone into the truck's radio using a port his father didn't know existed and started his Tool playlist. At regular intervals, the phone told him which way to turn. There was a freedom in these commands. Choosing things was exhausting, and he hated worrying about how a decision would turn out. The playlist picked the next song. The list told him where to deliver the chemicals. The map told him where to turn. He felt like he could just ride above it all like crowd surfing in a concert. It's all in the moment. You go where you're going to go. It just happens and you take what comes.

Jaymee was a planner. She liked to have a whole alphabet of plans, with every scenario worked out in advance. These plans were like complicated math problems that took pages and pages to work through.

The two of them together were a cliché of opposites. Eric didn't think Jaymee was crazy to plan. He understood at some subconscious level that his flow was often underwritten by Jaymee's designs. Eric hoped but was never certain if Jaymee reciprocated, knowing in some deep way that their tensions created balance.

What Eric knew for sure was the rightness of being with her. Their connection was deep and immediate. She could sign, and she was smoking hot, but there was always more. Her birth defect seemed like a way of keeping idiots from thinking she was an option. It didn't keep them away, kids at school were cruel. They called her "Wedge" because of the shape of her face. Once Eric heard a Spanish teacher at the high school call her that. He didn't hear it exactly, but he could read his lips a little, one of the benefits of having bad ears. Eric saw this and then saw the teacher point to Jaymee. At this point the teacher could have said anything else, but Eric was already halfway across the lunchroom.

The teacher didn't know what hit him, Eric ducked one shoulder and reached in between the man's legs. In one move, Eric hauled him onto his shoulders and spun.

"You don't call her that," he shouted over and over, then he heaved the teacher onto a lunch table.

Jaymee watched from a table where she ate with a friend. She met Eric's eyes across the crowded space. She turned her face to the three-quarter photogenic position. *That was stupid,* she signed, smiling. Then she looked around to see if anyone was watching. Nobody was. *My hero,* she signed, and blew him a kiss.

Eric was suspended, and they were preparing to expel him from school. The teacher wanted to press charges. Jaymee sent a letter of complaint to the school district saying the teacher in question commonly spoke about her in a derogatory manner, calling her "Wedge" and worse. She sent a yearbook picture, which showed her straight on, and described how she struggled to succeed and felt that with faculty joining in the ridicule she would not have an equal advantage and opportunity to excel. She wrote that the only student, faculty, or staff member of the school who had ever come to her aid was Eric Bugg. Though his approach was unsophisticated, it was much better than the nothing she'd received over the past three and a half years.

Wow, what a girlfriend, Eric thought. When she told him she wanted to leave Anadarko for good, and that she wanted him to come with her, he was all in.

The phone told him to exit and continue right. He drove past a convenience store and a man wearing a black Punisher hoodie and gray plaid shorts, pushing a baby stroller full of empty aluminum cans. He drove a mile or two farther into the country, and the phone said, "The destination is on your right."

The ramshackle house had a yard full of weeds and uncut grass going to straw. There was a BEWARE OF DOG sign on the chain-link front fence but no dog as far as Eric could tell. He unfolded the paper. This address was getting four buckets of P2P, and he was supposed to collect fifteen-hundred dollars. It seemed like a lot, but Eric figured not going to jail for buying this stuff directly is probably worth more than he could calculate. Eric folded the paper back up and hauled out the buckets one by one and set them on the curb.

"Hey," a voice called from a window in the house. "Not right here, dumbass." He looked at the window and saw the glint of two round lenses pressed up against the screen. "What's on your head?"

Eric patted the top of his head. "What are you talking about?"

"On your ears," the voice said. "You a cop?"

"I'm not a cop."

"Then what's on your head?"

"I'm deaf."

"If you're so deaf. How can you hear me?"

"The implants help me hear."

"Implants, huh? Implanted into what?"

"Um, how 'bout we just do this thing?"

"Implanted into what?" the voice insisted.

"Into my cochleas."

"Cochleas? Is that your brain?"

"It's my ears, man. Look. I've got two more deliveries to make today."

"You're saying you've got wires going into your head?"

"Robert Earl said you'd have an envelope for me."

"I wouldn't let nobody put wires in my head. It all goes up into a watchtower satellite."

"What does?"

"All your ideas, man. Everything. Cops know what you're going to do before you do."

"All right, I'm going to load up this stuff and take off. You can call Robert Earl and work it out." Eric hoisted one of the buckets back to the side of the truck.

"Hang on, hang on, hang on," the voice said. "Cash is in the mailbox. Put that back down."

Eric put the bucket back down on the curb and went to the mailbox.

"Open it," the voice said.

"How do I know you don't have a bomb in there?" Eric asked.

"Why would I blow up my own mailbox?"

"Because. I don't know," Eric said, then opened the mailbox. There was a white envelope in there and the wrapper from a grape Tootsie Pop. Eric opened the envelope and counted the money.

"It's all there," the voice said.

"This ain't Kenny Rogers," Eric repeated. It could have been fifteen one-hundred-dollar bills, but of course it wasn't. It was a few hundreds, mostly twenties, some tens, and the rest ones, minus five bucks. Eric looked at the window, made a face, and put the money back in the envelope.

"This is five bucks short," Eric said.

"No, it's not." The voice said.

"Okay. I'll tell Robert Earl."

"Dammit," he said. "Come here."

Eric looked around and figured why not. He went to the gate. "What about the dog?"

"Ain't no dog," the voice said.

Eric came through and went to the door. Before he could knock, the door opened. He still couldn't see anyone inside.

"Hold out your hands." Eric thought he meant so this guy could check them. "No, make a cup. Make a cup." Eric did, and the guy dumped a bunch of change into his hands. Eric looked through the open door into the dark interior of the house and saw the man. He was probably only in his twenties but he looked twice that. He was gaunt, pale, unshaven, wearing welding goggles up on his forehead. The smell of the place made him wince. "That's all we've got, man. Clear out."

Eric carried the change back to the truck and counted it in there. He'd given him another three dollars and seventy-seven cents. He wrote that number on the sheet, put the next address into his phone, and pulled out. He turned around at the next street and drove past the house. At the stop, he checked the rearview mirror and saw the guy he was talking to getting into a yellow Ford pickup, and another guy hauling buckets back to the house.

On his way back to the highway, Eric stopped at the convenience store he passed on the way in. While he was pumping gas, the yellow Ford from before barreled into the parking lot and parked in front. The guy got out and went inside. Eric turned slightly so he could watch him getting cigarettes. When he came back out, Eric turned away as the guy lit a smoke, hung his arm out the window, and drove off. He told himself not to be paranoid. It's not ridiculous for this guy to drive around his own neck of the woods. He shook it off and went inside to take a pee and get a Rockstar.

When he was back on the road, Eric put in the next address and played some Nine Inch Nails. As he got his instructions, he thought about cars and money and how everything in his life would change when he could drive off with cash in his pocket. Problems took a different shape altogether when you could just leave them in the dust. He tried to talk to Jaymee about that feeling. She thought it was leaving a mess behind. She thought it was a sign of weakness. He told her you've got to live to fight another day. Retreat can be an offense. Sometimes the world tries to lure you in. If you don't retreat, it's just a trap, like that fish guy from *Star Wars* said.

Jaymee had always wanted to leave Oklahoma, though. Ever since he'd known her. She wasn't crappy about it, she just wanted to be somewhere else and never thought she could because of the mess it would leave behind. He'd tell her you don't have to hold something together if it wants to fly apart. Even when she told him he was right, he could tell she wasn't convinced enough to leave her family in the lurch. Now there was nothing holding her back.

The phone had him merge onto a bigger road and keep right.

Sometimes his friends would play a game where they would pick teams, sometimes for a heist, or a superhero league, or sometimes they'd pick who'd be the best team of five to be trapped with inside a farmhouse, fighting off zombies. Every single time his first choice was Jaymee, but he'd never say it out loud. He didn't want to put her in front of those guys. Eric just knew she could turn any group of schmucks into a functioning team. She could smooth out attitudes. If there was something she didn't know, she could learn it. If you were wrong, she would find out. If you were right, she'd tell everyone why.

He imagined what her relatives would do if she took off. Pretty much just fall apart, he thought. They were already in shambles as far as families go, so maybe with her gone they'd just disintegrate. With her parents gone, it was two less people to go to smithereens. Lexi was the only one left, and she had nine lives. In the end, everything that happened lately was what Jaymee needed so she could walk away guilt-free.

Eric thought about how pieces move into place sometimes, and you should be watching for it because they'll move back out of place just as quick. It's like in basketball, when someone is guarding you and a second later they're not. You must decide to drive sometimes a half second before you actually can. It's guts and guessing. Always both, never one.

The phone gave him three quick turns and he was there, parked in front of a house that looked the same as every other house in the neighborhood. Same shape, color, windows, roof. He thought all these meth kitchens would be dumps. Who would mess up a place that was worth something? Maybe these McNugget houses were as disposable as they looked.

Robert Earl's paper said six buckets went here, and they owed two thousand two hundred and fifty bucks. He didn't know how much the P2P cost Robert Earl per bucket, but any way you shook it out, this seemed like good money.

Just as he was about to open the truck door, a guy in a sweaty cowboy hat knocked on the glass and cranked his hand around so he'd lower the window. When there was an inch of space, the man slipped a folded piece of paper through and walked away. It said, *Follow the car in front of you*. The cowboy gave one sharp whistle, and a beat-up, blue Skylark turned on and drove off. When Eric didn't immediately follow, the cowboy came back to bang on the hood of the truck twice and yell at him. Eric followed.

His pulse rate shot up, and to calm himself he felt for the pistol his dad kept in a holster underneath the driver's seat. It was there. He wasn't sure what he'd do with it if something went down, but he was glad to have it.

Really, who'd be more paranoid than a bunch of meth cooks? Eric tried to think it through from their way of thinking. There's probably cops everywhere, sniffing out their business. Probably other tweakers, too. Being safe in this game probably meant not letting your guard down, and that is exhausting. He was tired already after part of a morning in this line of work. They must be freaked out to eleven all day long. He'd have to keep that in mind while he was delivering.

He wished he could get Jaymee's input, but if he told her one-tenth of what had gone down already, she would pull the plug on the whole deal.

The car threaded itself back and forth through the neighborhoods and headed out of town. In a few minutes, they broke over a small rise into open fields, and on the other side they came to a stop next to a telephone pole.

A short guy and a woman got out. The woman was driving. She had on red-and-blue cowboy boots, a shift dress with a black T-shirt over the top. The T-shirt design was an American flag with fake jewels for stars. The man was a full six inches shorter than the woman. He wore black jeans, black Velcro sneakers, and a camo-print shirt. His hair was slicked back and he wore a mustache and beard, pointy like General Custer's. The little dude pointed two fingers at his eyes and then moved them to the ground. Eric figured this meant for him to pull forward. It didn't. The man put his hands up, palms out, and yelled at him. The woman was smoking. He stopped the truck and threw his hands in the air to show he didn't know what they were asking him to do. The man repeated the motion and then mimed carrying buckets in each hand. He looked like that cartoon of brooms carrying water. It made Eric laugh, until he realized how serious this was.

Eric got out and pulled two buckets out of the back. He hauled them up to the other car and set them down. "There's six of these. You want to help."

"We're good," the woman said.

From up close, Eric could tell that she'd been pretty once. She wore enough makeup for two people but still looked like a vampire had halfway finished her off.

"Step on it," the little dude said.

Eric really wanted to punch him in the face. He also sort of wished that gun of his dad's weren't still in the truck. Then again, there was probably no way a gun would ratchet things down.

He brought the next two buckets and set them down. The couple had put the first two in the trunk and started right away on the next ones. When he got back with buckets five and six, he stood and waited for the money. The couple put the other two in the back seat, and Eric said, "Hey! Those aren't free, you know."

The little dude stopped and said, "Take a check?"

Eric was so flustered he didn't answer and didn't see him crack a smile.

The woman said, "Robert Earl don't have to worry about his money." She hauled an envelope out of the car and brought it up to him. Eric took it and thumbed through it.

The woman made some crack and then cursed. "Who the hell is that?" she said straining to look up the road from where they came. The little dude stood on his toes to see. When Eric finally turned around, all he saw was a flicker of yellow and some taillights drop behind the rise.

"Who the hell *was* that?" the woman said again.

"I don't know," Eric said.

"Cops?" the little dude asked.

"Not cops if they're turning around. Maybe the handsome stranger here had some backup muscle in case of emergency."

"Wasn't me," Eric said.

"You'd never say so if it was," the little dude said.

"Let's get out of here."

Eric watched the car in front make a sloppy U-turn and whiz past him. He wasn't sure what would happen if they wrecked with that stuff in the car. Wouldn't be easy to clean up.

He thought the situation through for a minute, then decided he better call Robert Earl. He took out his phone and dialed.

"What?" he said.

"I think somebody's following me."

Robert Earl hung up immediately. Eric stared at the phone for a minute and then looked out at the field, which went back for a hundred yards to a line of trees. Above it storm clouds piled on top of each other until they reached a quarter of the way into the sky. While he was watching the clouds to keep from freaking out, his phone buzzed with a message from a number he didn't recognize.

Use this number.

And then a second message: *Who's following you?*

Eric replied: *I can't tell. Maybe a guy from the first house.*

Not cops?

Like I said. I can't tell. Should I skip the last delivery and come find you?

The dots in the next message bounced then went still. Then bounced again and went still. Eric became really worried. A truck came from the opposite direction, slowed, and rolled down its window. "Everything all right?" the driver asked.

"Yes, sir," Eric said. "I'm just texting my lady. Don't want to crash or nothing."

"I wish everyone would think like you," the man said, and he drove off. Eric waved and then his phone buzzed.

Don't find me. Whatever else, make the last delivery.

Eric walked back and forth in the road, staring at his phone. He felt cold and a little sick to his stomach. When no more messages came, he considered sending one of his own, but thought better of it. The rest of the load for today was going to take him the farthest out. It was ten buckets for thirty-seven fifty. Robert Earl was going to take in over seven grand today. Eric's cut was twenty percent. Fifteen hundred bucks to drive around. The people were freaks, but so was everyone. His total face-to-face freak time so far was under ten minutes. So, in the end it would work out fine. Why would anyone want to shoot him? Dead people bring the heat. So, maybe it was time to chill and get rid of the rest of these buckets, grab Jaymee, and get some tacos.

The next address was not an address at all but coordinates: 35.291400, -99.293860, not even any north or south. He typed it all into his phone, worried about messing up one of those sixteen numbers. The map spit back a crossroads near Canute, ninety minutes away. He hit "start route" and got in the car.

He could barely think at all on this part of the drive. He constantly checked the gun and the two envelopes of cash in the glove box. He kept one eye on the rearview for the yellow Ford, but he didn't see it. One thing off his mind. With all this open road, he thought about calling Jaymee but didn't. He wondered what his dad was going to think with three hundred more miles on the odometer. He listened to Led Zeppelin, Beastie Boys, and

Kendrick Lamar until he got to the crossroads, which were in the middle of nowhere. He stopped and put the truck into park.

There was no time set for the delivery, and nobody was there. This time he reached under the seat for his dad's gun. It was a silver .357 magnum with a two-and-a-half-inch barrel, not a movie gun but a plain old-fashioned killer. He flipped open the cylinder, which took eight rounds. Just as he snapped it shut, he heard a high-pitched whine and saw a drone drop from the sky into his field of view. He set the gun on the floor of the truck and watched the drone hover there. It dipped low in front of the truck and then swooped up quickly and hovered above the bed of the truck. There was a camera mounted in the belly of the thing and a speaker. After it gave Eric the once-over, a voice said, "Unload the buckets onto the shoulder."

Eric got out and set each bucket, one by one, in the red dirt. After the first couple of buckets, he stopped and watched the drone for a second and then he looked up and down the road.

"I sense your apprehension," the drone said. "There is no one coming from any direction. You may proceed."

The drone buzzed around as he unloaded the rest of the buckets.

"May I inquire about your tech?" the drone asked.

Eric stopped and looked at the drone. "What?"

"Your tech. The implants there. I apologize if this comes off as insensitive."

"So you can hear me?"

"Of course. There is a mic and radio transmitter on the drone. It's an encrypted channel."

"Dude?"

"I have read about the procedure and the devices, but I have not had the chance to speak with anyone firsthand. Do the implants mimic sound or do they create a new phenomenon?"

"I don't know what you're asking me."

The drone buzzed to one side and hovered. "Is there fidelity to the original sound, or do you hear some new approximation of true sounds?"

Eric put the last two buckets down and wiped the sweat off his forehead. "Do you mean do I hear what's there or something else?"

"Yes," the drone said.

"You know how crazy this is talking to a little helicopter."

"In this business, one needs any advantage one can gain."

"I'm sure you do."

"So what do you hear?"

"It's the same vibrations, but it doesn't sound like sounds."

"Say more."

"It sounds like how a cherry Popsicle tastes like cherries."

The drone raced around in a circle, and the man on the other end laughed. "Oh, well played, my friend."

"I don't want to be a jerk, but I'm feeling a little bit exposed here. Is the money going to pop out of that thing?"

The drone shot up straight into the air until Eric could barely see it, then it came right back down. "I will be there in six minutes." Eric took out his phone and started a stopwatch.

In exactly five minutes and forty seconds a car appeared in a cloud of dust. It was a nondescript Chevy pickup with fake wood paneling on the side. The license plates were caked in mud. The man pulled in alongside Eric and rolled down the window. He was wearing a ski mask with glasses over it. He handed Eric the envelope.

"My apologies for the strangeness of my inquiries. I have a deep interest in the cybernetic human."

Eric took the envelope and stared at the man.

"I meant no offense. Truly. You better go."

Eric got in the truck and pulled out. He left the gun on the floor until he'd gone at least half a mile, then he put it back and kept driving. He threw Robert Earl's instructions out the window and realized that he was starving.

FRANCIS HAD BEEN DREAMING THAT he was under a bridge and there were horses or something clopping across the top. He was down in the riverbed with water to his knees. It seemed like he'd been chased here, but he didn't know for sure. He waited for the clopping to stop once whatever it was up there got to the other side of the bridge, but that didn't happen. He felt himself rising out of sleep into the harsh afternoon light. When he realized the clopping was really the sound of someone knocking on his front door, he jumped out of bed, pulled a shirt from the hamper and walked into the front room.

His wife was standing in the kitchen pointing at the two police officers standing side by side at the door. "Make sure they have a warrant," she said.

"Not now. Really. Not now."

Francis opened the door and rubbed his hair with the other hand.

"Sorry to bother you, sir. Are you Francis Bugg?"

His first thought was to say "Who's asking?" but it was obvious. His second thought was to start worrying. He knew this conversation wasn't going to go in any good direction. He looked back at the kitchen, and his wife shrugged.

"Is there somebody else here?" the other officer asked.

Francis looked back at them. "No. Just me. I was taking a nap. I'm sorry. It takes me a while to come out of that."

"We understand," the first cop said. "Do you own a white Ford F-250, sir?"

"I do."

"Is it somewhere on the property?" the officer asked, tracing a circle in the air with the tip of his pen. We didn't notice it out front."

"I loaned it to my son," he said, and immediately regretted it. "He's using it for work, for his new job. A guy named Robert Earl Cripps. They went to high school together."

"Is that Cripps with two *p*'s?" one cop asked.

The other one said, "One *p* makes it 'cripes.'"

The first cop silenced the second with a sharp stare, then he took a note on his pad.

"Is something wrong, officer? Was he in an accident? Is he okay?"

"Your son was not in an accident."

"So far as we know," the second cop said, which got him a second stare.

"When did you loan him the vehicle?"

"This morning. He said he needed it for work. He makes deliveries. Pool stuff. Chemicals. Skimmers."

"People around here have a lot of swimming pools?" the cop asked. "Wouldn't think so from the looks of it."

Francis was sick to his stomach. "Plenty of people do. It's hot as hell around here, but you know that."

"You need to quit telling them stuff," his wife said from the kitchen. He wanted to look back but didn't. She kept talking. "They are opening you up like a can of soup."

"You didn't say what's going on? I am his father."

"How old is the boy?"

"Nineteen."

"I'm afraid he's of age, sir. We can't say."

The other cop added, "This is all part of an ongoing investigation, so we'll ask the questions."

Francis gestured to the second cop. "This must make you 'good cop,' right?" The first officer tilted his head and looked at him with a complete lack of amusement. "Can you at least tell me if he's dead or not?"

"When was the last time you saw your son?" Francis did not answer the question, prompting the officer to change tactics. He held up a picture of Robert Earl. "Is this Mr. Cripps?"

"That's Robert Earl, why?"

"No reason. He's the boss. Correct?"

"Well, he owns the pool company. Pool Shark, I think it's called."

The first cop wrote something down on his notepad. He said the two words "Pool" and "Shark" aloud as he did. "Is your son armed?" the first cop asked.

"There's a gun in the truck. I don't know if he's got into it or not. I'd say probably not."

"But there is a weapon?"

"Yes."

Francis's wife whistled through her teeth. This time Francis had to look back. She lifted her eyebrows and shook her head.

"Mr. Bugg?" the second cop said. Francis dragged one finger across his throat to get her to be quiet. "Mr. Bugg," the cop said again, louder. "Can we have you turn around, please. And keep your hands where we can see them?"

"I was just having a nap. I'm on medical leave," Francis said. "Some guy in Connecticut stepped in front of my train. They give us time after that, you know, before we can go back on the line."

"Are you currently in treatment or taking any medications?"

"They give me some Valium to help me sleep, but I don't need it. Can you tell me what's going on?"

"If your son comes home with your truck, we need to talk to him," the first cop said, handing Francis a card.

"If he comes home *at all*, we need to talk to him," the other cop said.

"I'll tell him," Francis said.

"Maybe you just call us, okay?" the first cop said. "We'll come back out."

After Francis agreed, the two officers left, and he watched them return to their car, looking at things and snapping pictures with their phones. When they finally drove off, his wife said, "You told them too much."

"The hell I did," he answered.

Eric pulled into a Taco Bell and locked the cash in the glove compartment of the truck. He made sure the pistol was back in its holster, safety on, the thumb break snapped in place. He sat in the truck for a minute, breathing, trying to keep his freak-out under control. He admitted to himself that everything that went down today was weird but probably not out of the ordinary for criminals. He told himself that television never really showed people that this was a business, like selling phones or furniture. When he felt calm, he got out and looked at the empty truck bed, thought about all the money, smiled, and went inside for something to eat. He hadn't been this hungry in a long time, and he figured the stress of everything had been grinding him up on the inside.

He ordered more than he needed and sat there, wolfing down his food, with one eye on his phone. At this point, he figured, there would be nobody who knew what he'd been doing, no record. He was moving about on his own. He thought about texting Jaymee, but stopped himself. He wanted to make sure there was no trail, nothing to say he'd been out in the western part of the state. Except he'd bought gas with his credit card. But that was closer to home. He'd paid cash for this food, so he was okay. He'd have to throw out the receipt. He stood up and did that right away. He had the call from Robert Earl, and the texts, but those were also closer in. He closed his eyes and thought everything through. When he felt okay, he ate a seven-layer burrito from start to finish without stopping, like a chain-smoker, and washed it down with Mountain Dew Baja Blast.

When he was done with everything else, he crumpled all the papers up and threw them out. He went to the bathroom, washed his hands and face, and got back in the truck. He drove in silence back to Robert Earl's shed, which took more than an hour. Robert Earl's black Dodge was out front, but the door was locked. Eric got out the cash, went around back, and saw that the ham tin hiding the key was kicked over to the side. No key. And the key didn't matter because the back door was open, but just barely. All the lights were on. He went back to the truck for the .357.

"Robert Earl," he called out as he pushed the door open the rest of the way. "Hey, bro. You taking a nap or something?" When there was no response, he said, "I delivered all of it. It all worked out." From of the corner of his eye, he saw something scurry out from under a table and dart across the office. He fired the gun at it but missed, which was good because it was Mr. Big, who kept running through the door and into the warehouse space. Eric followed and watched him zip behind some large white bags of potassium pellets.

He cursed at the pig and then asked him where Robert Earl was. That's when he noticed a line of small red rosettes painting an undulating line across the boxes and buckets of pool chemicals six inches above the floor. He followed the sinuous path across the room, past an empty pallet where he'd taken some but not all of the P2P this morning.

"Hey, Robert Earl," he said. "Mr. Big is loose. Looks like he got into something, maybe got hurt."

By this time Eric was petrified. He was starting to piece it all together but wouldn't allow himself to think things all the way through until he saw the broad dull black pool of blood and Robert Earl facedown on the cement floor, his head twisted unnaturally away from him and his lady sunglasses flung to the side. His face, neck, and hands were purple, like a birthmark. Both his legs were spread amphibiously in a way no living person could have endured. Mr. Big climbed through the bags and boxes and jumped onto Robert Earl's body and started licking a slick, nearly invisible spot on the back of his head where the bullet went in.

Eric held his head and backed away. He immediately wondered if the people who shot him were still here, but based on the growing stench, he figured they were long gone. He stuck the pistol in the back of his pants and tried to step around the blood and grab the little pig. Mr. Big didn't want any part of being picked up, so he zigzagged across Robert Earl's back as Eric grabbed for him. When the pig saw an opening, it bolted for the back door. Eric turned, pressing his right foot into the blood, and as he ran, he left a single, fading arc of footprints on the floor.

He eventually caught the pig outside. It squealed and squirmed, and Eric tried to soothe the thing like it was a cat, which only seemed to aggravate it. Eventually the animal bucked and corkscrewed so much that it flew from Eric's arms and disappeared immediately into the brush.

"All right," he said. "You're on your own."

FRANCIS COULDN'T PACK EVERYTHING, BUT he managed to get most of what she told him to gather into a military duffel he brought home from the army. She thought of things he wouldn't have: save the underwear for last so it'll be on the top, make sure he has a towel and a coat. He won't need everything, it might not be permanent, maybe just a few months.

Francis told her she was probably right. She said to make sure the shower shoes go in there. "He's prone to foot fungus."

"I know," he said. "But it's gotten better." Francis put some medicine, toothpaste, and a toothbrush in a Ziploc bag with a comb and the batteries for his implants. Francis took everything and brought it to the front room.

"He won't have much time," she said.

"If he makes it here at all."

"Don't start talking like that," she said.

"I don't know what Robert Earl has him messed up with, but they aren't little kids anymore, so I'll bet it's not vandalism."

"What about the notebook?" she said.

"What about it?"

"He should take it. You don't want it here. Really, you don't."

"I don't," he said. "But I want him to come back at some point."

"That's manipulative," she said.

"Yes, but it's also true."

"We both know truth hasn't been anyone's top priority lately," she said, lifting one eyebrow.

After everything was packed, Francis sat in his chair without talking. He didn't feel like sitting up and he didn't feel like kicking out the recliner, so he slumped forward with his elbows on his knees and his head in his hands. He watched the clock and he checked his phone. More than once he started to dial Eric's phone number, but he'd seen enough *Law & Order* to know that the police would check his phone records, and he didn't want to mess the boy up that way. When he'd glance over at the couch, sometimes his wife would be there sitting with her legs crossed at the knee, sometimes she would be pulling some thread through her needlework, sometimes she would have her hands folded in her lap, sometimes that spot in the couch would be empty.

He couldn't remember time ever moving so slowly. Except when that stockbroker stepped in front of his train in Connecticut. That moment had frozen so he could see it now like a photograph: his red hair, gray suit, bare feet. He was squinting, and his arms were straight, hands balled into fists. Then he was gone. The man's name was Barclay, he discovered later. He'd been part of the legal mess those television people Barbara Stein and Chuck Vogel were in. It didn't seem that serious on the news, but the man's suicide suggested something worse. Now that Eric was in some trouble of his own, all Francis wanted was to keep his son from the desperation he saw on that man in that fraction of a second.

Francis heard the truck, finally, and the sound of the engine brought tears to his eyes. He lifted his head to the blank spot in the couch and she was there, smiling.

"Do you remember what happened when the prodigal son came home?" she asked.

Francis wiped his tears and nodded.

"Good, then you'll know what to do when he comes through that door."

Francis stayed sitting, his heart racing, as he heard Eric come up the steps. When the boy came in the room, he saw the olive duffel bag on the floor, the notebook on top. He had three envelopes in one hand and the truck keys in the other. He looked at Francis, and he seemed like a very tall and broad-shouldered little boy.

"You're okay?" Francis asked.

"What's going on?" Eric said.

"The police were here."

"Crap."

"That pretty much sums it up."

"They were asking about Robert Earl?"

"How long ago?"

"Couple of hours."

"What happened to Robert Earl?"

Eric shook his head.

"You're in some trouble, boy."

Eric nodded.

"You need to disappear." Francis opened his wallet and took out all the cash he had. It was eighty bucks. "Take it," he said.

Eric stepped forward and handed his dad his keys and took the money without protest. He looked at it for a moment and stuffed it into one of the envelopes. Eric walked past him, into his room and came back with his phone charger and the keys for his own car. He carefully took the trailer key off the ring and set it on the kitchen table.

Francis was standing already and gestured to the duffel. "It's not everything, but it's enough to get you by. We tried to think it through for you so nothing would slow you down."

Eric noticed the notebook. He picked it up, and the duffel, then tried to hug his father. Francis felt everything start to quiver and melt inside of him, but he stood tall. "We better not talk," he said. "It's best I don't know anything."

Eric took his things to the door and stopped. He held up the notebook. "Tell her thanks," he said, and then he walked out of the trailer.

Francis stood at the door and watched him load everything into his car. Eric looked up once, fired up the car, and drove out of the trailer park with the hoarse growl of the tiny aluminum engine filling the space behind him. Francis turned and went back inside, shutting the door behind him. He looked for his wife on the couch, but she was gone. He walked slowly through the trailer, room to room, ending in Eric's bedroom. He crawled onto the bed, like a little kid, and fell asleep.

ERIC DOWNSHIFTED AS HE CAME off the road and onto the driveway of the relatives' house where Jaymee was staying. Normally he'd text ahead and let Jaymee know he was coming, but under the circumstances, he stayed off his phone. As he was sitting in the car outside, he realized that the police can track phones, so he turned his all the way off. Almost immediately he felt isolated and disconnected, which caused him to worry deeply.

He went up to the door and knocked. Nobody answered. There were shadows moving deeper inside the house, and he didn't feel like he could wait for anything, so he opened the door and went in. He could hear some kind of noise, a fight maybe. In the living room, Lexi was sitting on a chair crying. Jaymee was yelling at her. Lexi looked away from her sister, saw Eric, and pointed.

Eric read her lips. "Um, your boyfriend is here," she said.

Jaymee stopped yelling and went to the door. *What are you doing here?* she signed.

Robert Earl is dead, he signed back.

Jaymee's posture changed. Eric began to shake. He felt his eyes start to burn, but he dumped all that feeling into a bin in the very back of his mind and stood on the lid.

Lexi signed, *You remember I can sign, too, right? Who's Robert Earl?*

Jaymee pulled Eric through another hallway. "Robert Earl? What?"

"Somebody shot him in the back of the head."

"Who would do that?"

"Don't know. Any of these meth cookers he's working with?"

Jaymee dropped her chin and glared at Eric through the top of her eyes.

"There is no time," he said. "Remember how we always said we'd run away together?"

Jaymee could see where this was going and she started shaking her head.

"The police are involved, too. They went to my dad's today, looking for me."

"No," she said. "I am not—"

"I have to leave town right now. I want you to come with me. Before you say anything, I have eight thousand dollars in cash. If we leave now, we can make it to Tucumcari by midnight. Then California the next day."

Jaymee just looked at him, no expression on her face.

"You're not saying no," he said. "This is it; if we're gonna do this, we gotta do it now."

"I can't—"

"Don't say it," he told her.

"Shut up," she said. "I can't leave my sister."

Eric's face fell as he thought about how suddenly impossible everything felt. Jaymee lifted his chin and looked him in the eyes. "If I go, she comes, too."

"Yes," Eric said. "There's room."

Jaymee walked away without saying anything. There was more yelling in the other room, but Eric stayed where he was in the half-darkened space surrounded by boxes and bags and stacks of old and worthless things. He thought about how they'd all be on the road soon, and it felt like a movie. For the first time since he saw Robert Earl shot, he felt like maybe his luck would hold. He didn't want to think about it too much because luck turns on a dime. He'd already seen that enough times to know.

The two of them were packed faster than he thought possible. Part of him thought Jaymee and her sister would be the kind of people who always had a bag packed. They probably had a whole plan worked out ahead of time. Jaymee would have had them run drills.

"She said okay," Jaymee said.

"She rides in the back," Eric answered.

"Screw you guys," Lexi said. "Let's get out of here." She walked past them with a green duffel bag, a pillow between the handles. Lexi had a light-blue backpack covered in embroidered patches and buttons. Right in the middle was Captain America's shield. Jaymee took Eric by the hand and led him through the hallway and the now-empty room. They went out the door and straight to his car. When they were situated, the girls looked at each other for one second, and then Jaymee reached back to squeeze Lexi's hand. Eric looked up at the one lit upstairs window and saw Kathy watching them, one hand on the window, one hand over her mouth.

6

Small World

THE MOJAVE DESERT CONVERGED ON a small knot of on- and off-ramps, gas stations, and fast-food restaurants. It was midday and cloudless, the sun silently incinerating the bleached vault of the sky. A silver Nissan Sentra eased away from the straight flow of east-west traffic on the interstate and drifted down the off-ramp, decelerating, like a boat with its engine cut.

A flashing blinker, then a pause. There were no other cars. The Nissan turned down the frontage road, drove, signaled, then pulled into the nearly empty parking lot of a Burger King. A few seconds later, the car parked on the shady side of the building.

A man and a woman emerged, stretching their limbs. The woman reached both hands above her head, bracelets sliding down her arms. She rocked from one side to the other, wearing a gray racerback tank top and distressed jeans. She extended her fancy boots one at a time and rotated the stiffness from her ankles. In the front seat was a beach basket full of magazines. A bone-white Stetson sat directly on the seat behind.

The man kicked one foot backward, caught it, and leaned forward, balancing himself with the car door. He had on a blue golf shirt with an embroidered logo on the breast, tan khakis, white Reebok running shoes. He looked like someone who had escaped from a trade show.

She looked up at the Burger King sign at the top of its massive iron legs, then folded up her sunglasses and slid them into the neckline of her shirt.

She watched him repeat his stretch with the other leg. He appeared to know exactly what he was doing, wobbly as he was in that pose.

"I'm going in," she said, closing her door.

He dropped his foot, shut his door, and dashed gallantly to the building, but she arrived first and opened the door herself. A handwritten sign taped to the window said *Hiring All Shift's.*

He held the door for himself, which allowed him to sort of appear courteous and kept him from being able to open the inner door. She turned immediately toward the bathroom. He followed.

He was in and out quickly, though he washed his hands for a full thirty seconds. He waited for her near the registers, watching CNN on a wall-mounted flat-screen television. It was talking heads discussing conflict in the Middle East. A woman from Al Jazeera made the point that new settlements in the West Bank indicate that Israel is not ready to come to the table, and as long as Americans support these settlements, it shows that they, too, are not interested in a resolution. During this discussion, the crawl at the bottom of the screen read: *Television personalities Barbara Stein and Charles Vogel will be tried separately for white collar crimes.*

"You didn't have to wait," she said, startling him. Her hair was now up in a ponytail, revealing her large earrings. He noticed that with her hair up and fresh lipstick on she looked a lot younger.

"It's okay," he said. "I'm not in a rush."

She ordered a Whopper combo meal, and as she pulled out a small packet of folded bills, he leaned in and said, "That's okay, I got it."

"Doyle, you don't have to keep paying for me."

"I dragged you into this," he said. "Least I can do is get you all the way home."

"I let myself get dragged into it," she said. "And I think I can handle a cheeseburger."

Doyle stood down and held his hands up in resignation. She paid with a ten-dollar bill. The change was three dollars and thirty-five cents. She folded the singles into her one remaining five and jammed it all into the front pocket of her jeans.

Doyle ordered a salad and paid with a debit card. By the time he was done, she was sitting at a table facing the interstate. He stayed by the counter and looked back at the television, which now showed a commercial for a mutual fund. A slender older couple was riding bikes through a field of tulips, then sea-kayaking in Alaska, then nursing baby pandas. As the name of the mutual fund hovered over the waters of a fjord, Doyle found himself thinking about how long you'd have to work and be married to retire that way. Thirty years? Forty? Could anyone attain that kind of life? Would you tire of it in the end? What if you didn't start until you were halfway done?

After the commercial, a news story came on about Barbara Stein and Chuck Vogel. There was a split screen of the two of them in handcuffs getting into different police cars. The voice-over said the state of Oklahoma would try Chuck Vogel for manslaughter in the shooting death of a local man, then he would be tried for trading violations in federal court.

The slight Asian woman at the register called CJ's order. Doyle feigned interest in the television as CJ walked up, but he watched her walk to the drink dispenser. The back pockets of her jeans had golden wings embroidered on them that seemed to flap a little as she walked.

"Excuse me," the server said impatiently. "Mister, your food." It was obvious that she had seen him distracted, and he felt like he should apologize. The server's eyes were deferential, and so were his. He looked at the tray, which had only the salad in a clear plastic box. He could already tell that he wouldn't like it.

"What kind dressing?" the server asked.

"Ranch, I guess," he said. "And does this come with a drink?"

"Drink is separate," she told him. "You want the combo?"

"I'll just have a drink off the dollar menu, then." He paid her with a twenty, and she gave him the change, which he dumped onto his tray.

When Doyle sat down, he faced the room. There was a heavyset man crammed into a booth by the window. He was typing something into his phone, which seemed to Doyle like someone trying to thread a needle with a bowling pin. A woman with two children sat in the opposite corner. One child was on his knees with his uneaten food spread around him. He was struggling with the package of the toy that came with his meal. The other child was in a high chair, screaming as her mother tried to feed her bits of french fry. She would throw them onto the tray and then try to squirm out of the chair.

CJ was half finished with her burger. Doyle checked his phone. Three weeks ago, the emails asking him where he was had all but stopped, the calls and voice mails, too. The rest of the world had gone on without him.

Doyle thumbed through the messages, shaking his head.

Doyle's boss appeared suddenly in his cubicle with his arms spread so they reached across the entry. A wind blew his hair and tie to one side. He was a tall, imposing person, and with Doyle looking up at him from his chair, he looked twice as tall and extra unhappy. "Look, Doyle," he said. "I'm not sure I even want to ask what happened."

"Well, I hit this lady's dog on the way to California, and—"

"And I'm pretty sure I don't even want to hear anything about it either. Point is, you don't work here anymore. We had to move on. You have to understand our position. We had a project to finish, and you were gone for three months, Doyle. Disappeared without a word."

Doyle felt his boss's voice detach from the room and start falling away. He shrunk the way things do in a rearview mirror. His boss said, "Point is, you don't work here anymore. Point is, Doyle. Point is . . . you don't work here anymore, anymore. Point is . . . we had to move on . . . point is, point is, point is—"

"Doyle?" CJ said. "Are you having a seizure?"

He looked down at his phone and switched it off and opened the stiff, creaking lid of his salad. "No, sorry. I was just . . . I don't know what I was doing. How's your burger?"

"Okay," she said.

"They let you have it your way, so it should always be perfect," he quipped.

"Or it means that something's wrong with the way you want it." After a minute, she said, "Just saying."

Doyle tore the dressing packet open with his teeth and applied it to the salad, thinking about how right she was about what people want. If he'd learned anything about this woman in the last three months, and he was not sure he had, it was that she was not satisfied. So, she'd know about desire.

"You know," he said, avoiding her eyes, "I'm sorry things turned out the way they did." He stabbed a mouthful of salad then crunched it.

"You shouldn't be sorry," she said. "Neither of us knew what was going to happen. You can't have a fling unless you get flung."

"I guess that's the problem. You were having a fling and I was falling for you, or something."

"Doyle." She tried to touch his hand.

"No, it's okay. I'm a big boy. We spent a lot of money, and I burned a lot of bridges. It's just that usually when you break up with someone, you can kind of just walk away. We broke up while we still had an eleven-hour drive in front of us. Well, it's just two hours now."

"Counting the hours, huh?" She smiled.

"Yeah, but it's probably not what you think," Doyle said.

It was exactly like a hospital room, except it was in the house. His stuff was all there. Photographs of horses, bulls, dogs. A lariat thrown over a chair. His daughter was texting, her thick French nails clicking against the screen of her smartphone. One of her brothers was eating a cheeseburger out of the wrapper. He had mayonnaise on his lip, and he was dropping shreds of lettuce onto the carpet. Her other brother was working, focused on the screen of his iPad. CJ thought it was work, but it turned out to be the roster of his fantasy basketball team.

Three of the five children were there. The other two were on their way.

"Is he awake?" the daughter asked without looking up.

CJ said, "No, he's not, but he's breathing."

The brother who was eating crumpled up his paper and wiped his mouth with it. He chewed a couple of times and then he leaned over to his sister and whispered something into her ear that made her eyes flick up at CJ. She stared, without blinking, for a moment. While her brother talked on, her mouth tightened slightly, nothing at all like a sneer but worse somehow for all its brevity.

The sister nodded three times and then said "I know" loudly enough to make it clear that she was sending a message.

CJ unlaced her fingers from Doc's hand and placed it back onto his belly, just under the other one that had an IV running into it. She stood and smoothed her dress, took a quick look at the LCD display that showed the old man's vitals.

The mayonnaise-faced brother stuffed his wrapper into the bag and wadded it up. As CJ crossed the room to the door, he handed the bag to her. She looked down at him and said, "I'm not your father's maid, I'm his wife." Then she left the room.

Doyle dropped his fork into the salad container and stood. He had a smear of ranch dressing on his chin and CJ thought of saying something about it but didn't.

"I'm going to get more Coke," he said. "You should, too. Looks like you're about ready to pass out."

"I look what?" she asked. She glanced at her reflection in the window. She saw it on herself: fatigue. She let her eyes shift focus to the parking lot and then back to herself. She took the lid off her drink and slid it over to Doyle. "Diet Dr Pepper," she said.

"You know, artificial sweeteners are probably worse for you," he said. "I saw a thing on the Discovery Channel about it."

"The other stuff's too sweet."

Doyle nodded, but it didn't look quite like agreement. She watched him walk stiffly to the soda machine, and she sighed. When he showed up at Doc's house in Congress, she was at something a lot like rock bottom. It was her forty-fifth birthday. She was alone in the childhood home of a man she married so he could exact vengeance on his children. When she left with Doyle there was a grinding in her stomach, a feeling of someone has who just read the nutrition label on a now-empty pint of Ben & Jerry's. Taking off with him seemed like the right thing to do for only about ten minutes, which was enough. Trouble is always easier to get into than out of. They were just getting settled in the car when the wrongness of it all took shape. She set that feeling aside in favor of the one that said the universe had brought him here. She told herself to see where this would go. What she got out of it was days piling up on each other, turning into week-long stays in cheap motels all over California, each stop getting worse as the money ran out. Sometimes they'd get a paper and look for jobs, get bored of it, and sleep in. Eventually, they stopped talking to each other except to figure out whose turn it was to go to the laundromat. Months ago, she was desperate, and Doyle just happened along. It seemed like a lucky break, except she didn't believe in luck. Two things held her in that house: the dog, and having a car she couldn't afford to fix. The dog died, and Doyle was willing to run away.

Doyle set CJ's drink down and then slid into the booth. He stared at his food, sucked on his straw, and fidgeted.

"I'm sorry," she said. "I really am. You're a really nice person, you know, but it's obvious this isn't working out."

"That is one perspective," Doyle said without looking up.

"You know we both have to agree on the perspective for there to be a relationship, Doyle."

He plunged his straw up and down and made a smashed-up shape with his mouth. She watched to see if he was actually going to speak. He didn't.

"You are really nice."

"You said that."

She sighed. "But I'm not looking for nice."

"What are you looking for?"

"I wouldn't be good for anyone right now. I'm a little bit broken."

"If you're broken, why'd you cook me all that food? Why'd you strip naked in your kitchen? We've been doing this for eighty-seven days."

"You've been counting?"

Doyle was embarrassed by the question. "When people do what we did, it's supposed to mean something," he said.

"Not always. Sometimes it is just the thing. Just the thing and that's it."

"But you came with—"

"That's not always what it is either."

"You came to the wedding," Doyle said. "And then we lived in all those places. Why would you come if it didn't mean something?"

"'Living' doesn't seem like the right word." When she said it she could see that Doyle was legitimately hurt, that she had hurt him. Usually in situations like these, you grab your bra and panties and dress in the entryway. You end it with a quick jerk, Band-Aid style. You don't return calls. You ignore texts. You unfriend him. It's kinder that way, in the end. If you linger, if you have breakfast with him, if you have a second dinner or meet for drinks, it gives the lie time to metastasize.

It was her turn to stall, stare at her tray, play with the edge of the waxy paper her burger came in, sip her drink, pinch the tip of her straw. As she did, she gazed out the window at the parking lot.

What did it take to get here, in this particular Burger King on the edge of the Mojave? How does anyone end up anywhere?

She thought about fate and how deep in her memory a story of the fates lay curled up like a pill bug. Her father had read it to her. The fates were sisters, three in total. They arrived at the birth of a child and called its future, set the course. These sisters were so powerful, even the other gods feared them. Sisters. Old women. And the gods minded their p's and q's around them. They were weavers, she remembered. The fabric of the universe was on their loom. Her father told her lots of old stories like that when she was a girl, before he left. Many were hard to remember, but this one stuck. When she thought of how she arrived somewhere, she imagined the loom clattering, mindlessly adding line to line.

SHE WAS WORKING FOR BELL South in Texas, in a huge room full of people processing bills. At lunch a woman burst into tears, crying, "It's over. It's just over." Mostly people ignored her. CJ sat across from her and tried to ask her questions. "He won't leave his wife. I'm just someone he screws on Thursdays."

She patted this woman on the back then walked out of the office and never returned. She saw a future of desperation. When she was a girl she wanted to sing. She was good, too. Other people said so. In two weeks, she moved to Nashville. In four weeks she was in another office, just like the one in San Antonio. She wasn't singing, she was just somewhere else. Every couple of months she took out her guitar and worked on a song.

Eventually, she met a man. They dated for a while and then slept together, always at her place. One day she was having lunch, and she heard the looms of fate, saw the weeping woman in her mind, realized that she had traded places with her. She understood that he was never going to leave his wife, and immediately she felt like something was trying to crawl out of the inside of her belly. She wanted to weep and scanned the room to see if anyone was watching. Everyone was looking at their phones, forking food into their mouths. A week later she was waiting tables in a diner. She got the slow shifts with all the bad tippers, but it was better. A person waiting tables was, at least, out in the world. She got a cheaper apartment. There was a fan next to the bed.

One day she served an old man, who came in alone. He asked her to call him Doc. He didn't flirt, just ate his meal (short stack, bacon, skim milk, cantaloupe) and wrote things down on a small yellow notepad.

They didn't talk. He was there the next day. And the next. Eventually he asked her name. She told him CJ.

He said, "No. Not the letters."

She looked around and saw everyone in the place like they were flowers in pots. Doc's eyes were honest. He was not playing her. She cleared the next table and took the dishes back. When she returned, she said, "Charlene." He nodded, wrote the name on the pad. "And the J?" he asked.

"Joelle," she said.

"Don't hear that name a lot," he said.

"I don't say it a lot," she answered.

He left for two weeks and then came back with a man in a suit. "This is Curtis," he said, and then he motioned for Curtis to talk.

"I handle Doc's business affairs," he said, rising as he spoke. "Doc would like me to discuss an opportunity with you."

"Well, I'm working," she said.

"That might not be important anymore," Curtis said. Doc winked at her and opened his menu.

It had all been planned. Remember: bad shifts. The place was empty, except for the three of them and the cook, who apparently stepped out for a smoke.

Curtis explained that Doc is a very rich man, and has found himself in a situation with his children that caused him to adjust his will.

"Those sometime kids been stealing from me," Doc said.

Curtis explained that they had been written out of the will, and Doc was looking for someone to—and here Curtis lost focus a little—Doc needed someone who could function as a distraction.

Doc leaned across the table. "Charlene. I'm wondering if you'd marry me."

"Doc, I don't hardly even know you," she said, unflapped.

"That's right. Curtis tell her."

"Tell me what?"

"Hey! Oh man, that's my car!" Doyle shouted, pointing out the window. "Somebody just ran into my car."

Outside, a Day-Glo orange Honda Civic hunkered behind Doyle's Nissan, the passenger's-side fender splintered. There was no hissing water line or smoke, just the stillness of the two vehicles and the white blown-out light of midday. The windshield of the orange car was an overwhelming smear of pure white. CJ had to look away to save her eyes.

Doyle was on his feet, tossing his napkin down in a gesture that seemed, for a moment, like a heroic act. "Who does this?" he shrieked. He looked like he was going to rush outside, but he waited there for CJ to make some response, which never came.

Outside, the driver's door opened and a tall guy got out. He wore stupid oversized sunglasses and a white tank top. His shoulders and biceps were sculpted and deeply tanned. He hoisted his orange Oklahoma State shorts and ducked down to look at his passengers. He made three gestures with his hands. The girl in the passenger's seat watched closely, then nodded. The second girl did nothing. From his squatting position, the tall guy looked around the parking lot.

He rose and shut the door.

CJ finally looked at Doyle, who was huffing.

"He better not hit me and run," he said.

"He shut the door. Doesn't look like he's gonna run."

"This is going to affect my rates," Doyle complained.

"You didn't do anything," she said.

"They're always looking for some way to squeeze you."

"Are you going to go talk to him?"

"I guess I'll have to."

Doyle glanced out the window and blew air into his cheeks. As he thought, he pumped the air from one side to the other and then looked at his watch. He lurched from his position and headed out the door. As he walked away, CJ heard him mutter, "With my luck he'll be uninsured."

Doyle ran through the Burger King with one hand on his phone, which was holstered on his belt. Every tenth step or so, he would slow and walk quickly in an attempt to avoid attracting attention. All this did was make him look like someone who could see himself in a security camera. The woman who took their orders looked up and watched Doyle with disapproval. As he moved across the lobby, she followed him with her eyes. Outside, the passenger's-side window came down and a young woman leaned out. She was yelling, but the man ignored her. He crossed around to Doyle's car and inspected the bumper. Doyle appeared outside. The older of the two girls noticed him, but the kid did not. Doyle stopped and placed his fists on his hips and stood his ground. CJ grabbed her drink and took two deep drafts. Doyle appeared to be speaking, and the man didn't notice him. Doyle made some small motions, and then looked back through the window at CJ. The younger of the two girls took pictures with her phone.

Initially, Doyle went right for the damaged section of his car, but the man's presence deflected him so that the orange street racer was between them. The tall guy pulled on a shattered section of his front fender, and Doyle was having trouble seeing any damage to his vehicle. He thought he might begin with accusations, but he thought it would be stupid to start in without any information. The guy ignored him completely, turning instead to the girl who was with him. She was drop-dead gorgeous, with a figure that seemed photoshopped. She wore tight, urban camo cutoffs with a woven belt. She was squeezed into an American flag halter top that came down far enough to show the world that her belly button had been pierced, twice. Her hair was wild and sun-bleached, ponytailed on the side. The other girl was clearly her sister. She wore slouchy thrift store clothes, and blew tiny pink bubbles with her gum.

She looked right at the man and spoke to him: "Eric, there's nothing wrong with his car."

He signed something back to her, and she said, "I know, but he's here. Behind you."

She looked up at Doyle, and from the front, she seemed completely different. Her face was perfect in profile, but deformed from the front: squeezed and asymmetrical. Her left eye was half an inch higher than the other. Doyle couldn't look away. It was so strange to see such a lovely woman damaged like that.

The woman tilted her head and leaned toward Doyle, "What are you looking at?" she sneered.

"I'm sorry," Doyle said, unsticking his eyes. "You know, your boyfriend hit my car."

"There's nothing wrong with it," she said, walking back. Doyle found himself distracted from this angle as well. She scraped at the paint with her thumbnail and then said, "Come look."

Her boyfriend was pacing behind the two cars, gesturing to himself.

Doyle squatted down and edged in underneath the woman as she bent over. "Nothing? You're not gonna take that dent out with a hair dryer, ma'am."

"That could be months old."

"There's orange paint everywhere."

She looked over at her boyfriend's car, then stood. She reached into her bra and took out her phone, checked it once, and then sighed. "We're not from around here," she said.

"Of course you're not," Doyle said. "Oklahoma plates."

"Y'all're from Texas?" she asked, noting his plates.

"Plano," Doyle said.

"You're gonna want to do insurance cards or something, right?" she asked.

"We'll have to," Doyle said.

"Baby, we gotta go," the boyfriend said in a loud, flat voice.

When Doyle heard this he freaked out and started shouting that leaving would make this a hit-and-run, which is a felony.

What is he saying? the boyfriend signed.

Nothing, the girl signed. *He's crazy.*

The boyfriend got into the car and turned it on. He looked ready to go.

Doyle pulled out his phone and ran to the front of the car and tried to take a picture of the license plate, but the front plate said OKLAHOMA CITY THUNDER. The car lurched backward and screeched to a halt as the boyfriend yelled for the girl to get in.

Doyle ran around behind him and snapped a photo of the rear plate, saying, "I got it. You run now and it's game over."

All through this the girlfriend held the sides of her face and frantically told her boyfriend to stop. "Eric!" she screamed as she got in the car. "Eric, this is a bad plan."

Doyle held his phone up to the windshield and said, slowly, that he was going to call the cops. The girlfriend's face went white, and she banged on the roof of the car.

"That's right. I am so calling 911."

The girlfriend looked at her boyfriend and got back out of the car. She was clearly scared out of her wits as she walked toward Doyle. "Don't, mister. Please don't do that," she said.

The boyfriend got out of the car but stood at the door. She paused for a second and then shifted her face to a three-quarter reveal, which instantly transformed her from sideshow freak to knockout. Doyle realized that, like a pool shark, she must constantly be aware of the angles required to make her next move. "My boyfriend and I just can't get tangled up with the cops right now."

"What about my car?" Doyle asked.

"There's barely anything wrong with it," she said.

"It's the principle of the thing."

"Mister, do you believe in love?" She looked over at her boyfriend, who looked exactly like the kind of person who should be modeling for a men's magazine. She signed to him, then blew him a kiss. "Do you?"

Doyle looked back at the window of the Burger King, the glare of the sun threw the image of the parking lot back at him, but he knew CJ was inside, staring out. He thought about their trip and how they had shown up at the wedding dinner already a little bit drunk, their fingers interlaced, Doyle thinking about the newness of CJ, the foreignness of her smell. He thought about how he hid inside the giddiness of this new relationship, ignoring his father and his bride, a woman he knew only a fraction longer than the woman who was doing things to him with her feet under the table.

Was that love? Possibly, but probably not. The sad truth of Doyle's life since he arose this morning was that whatever had happened between him and CJ was at best an impersonation of love. He had gone out to the motel pool at dawn and slipped into the water in a pair of red and silver trunks, he floated, faceup, staring at the rusted edges of the neon palms. He thought about where they would go from here. The sex had already tapered off, and they were beginning to lapse into normal activities. The night before, they had done laundry together in a coin-op laundromat. He tended the massive booming dryer and folded the clothes while she went for tacos. In front of him had been a stack of her things and a stack of his. He was tempted to blend them, but didn't. Carefully he packed his things into his bag, and scavenged a Walmart sack for hers. As the pool water lapped around his face, he thought about that moment. What did it mean to see himself and her as two separate things, two distinct entities? *Don't you always see the separation first,* he thought. *Even if you say, "I love you," you are basically admitting that above everything else, you recognize that you are not me and I am not you. Goo goo g'joob, and all that. We're different, and if we weren't, there wouldn't be any us.*

Doyle floated there, trying to remember all the lyrics to that Beatles song, until CJ dove into the water next to him.

"HEY, MISTER, I ASKED YOU a question," the girlfriend said again.

"Goo goo g'joob," Doyle said.

"What's wrong with you?" she said in the meanest way possible.

"Nothing," Doyle answered. He stared at the girlfriend, looked her right in the eye. "I was just thinking about your question. It's a good one," Doyle answered. "I haven't been in love in a long time." Saying it hurt worse than anything else he could remember.

"I asked if you believed in love. You don't have to be in love to believe in it."

Doyle's lips pulsed involuntarily. He looked away from the girl and back. As he did this, he became aware of exactly how suspicious his expression must have seemed. He tried to make himself look benign, but in the end, he realized that it just made it look like he was hiding something. He realized in the middle of it that he used to like a song that asked this question. He fought the urge to sing it in his head. "Yes," he said finally. "There's probably something like love out there, for some people. Not for everyone."

"You sound like my little sister," the girl said.

"No, he doesn't," Lexi said, typing into her phone.

"Whatever it is, it's not what most people think it is."

During the discussion CJ came out. She had an overhand grip on her soft drink, the straw sticking up between her ringed fingers. "Is everything okay?" she asked.

Doyle turned when he heard her voice.

The girl said, "Everything's fine, ma'am."

CJ's eyes went to the tattered flap of fender hanging from the front of the other car. She got Doyle's attention and said, "I'm gonna get something out of the car and then lay low, unless I can actually help. Better to be out of the way."

Doyle was infuriated, but there really wasn't anything she could do, especially since they weren't together. Doyle would have to take care of the details, and he would, just as soon she vanished. It didn't stop him from being irritated that she was so nonchalant.

"No, whatever," Doyle said.

CJ ducked into the Nissan and came back with a few magazines and took a sip from her drink. "Come get me," she said, and then walked slowly back to the Burger King, watching the conversation resume in the reflections of the glass. She knew Doyle would be upset by what she was doing, and she was a little glad her strategy seemed to be working. She was impressed by the idea that not much had changed since middle school. You couldn't just sit down with a person and say, "You know what, this isn't working out for me." You had to devise a stratagem, create a plan to make the other person break up with you. In this way, every teenager learns that to be successful, one must become a con artist. A commitment to the truth is like being under house arrest.

"Let's go inside, sit down, and figure this out," Doyle suggested.

Months ago, they had wrapped themselves in sheets and blankets and done the dishes in Doc's kitchen. Eventually, it became so difficult to keep the blanket sarong around his waist that Doyle let it drop to the floor. He continued to wash the dishes, and CJ also abandoned her sheet and began putting things away.

"It's like the Garden of Eden," Doyle said.

CJ lifted a stack of plates into the cupboard. Her reaching pulled the shape of her breast into near perfection. "What?" she asked.

"The two of us, doing this. It's like Adam and Eve."

"That didn't end well," she said.

"Never mind," Doyle said and returned to the suds, careful now of where he positioned himself. In a few seconds, he shook his hands dry and left the room. He returned wearing pants. CJ noticed and covered her breasts with a forearm and walked past Doyle. She returned in a bathrobe.

"I don't normally do housework naked," she said.

"Me neither," Doyle said. "You are beautiful, though. I think you're really pretty."

CJ pushed some hair behind her ear and started putting other things away.

"I'll be ready to try it again in a little bit," he said.

CJ pulled out a chair and sat. "Why don't we try it again in California?" she said.

Doyle looked surprised.

"Take me to this wedding. You said you didn't have a date. Take me."

Doyle scratched his chest and then looked at the clock on the wall. It was one thirty in the morning. If he left within the hour, he could still make it. "What about your job?"

"I'm not working."

"I guess you don't have to take care of the dog."

CJ looked up.

"Sorry," Doyle said.

"Look, I'd love to get out of here with you. I'm just stuck in this dead guy's house. That dog was the last thing holding me here. I'd love to go to LA."

"Santa Barbara."

"Sure, whatever. You seem like a really careful person, Doyle. Let's break the rules a little."

"We could," he said, smiling a little. "We could bend 'em."

"Or just get a hammer and start swinging."

"If we're going to go, we need to go."

In twenty minutes, they had the whole place cleaned up. Doyle was dressed. CJ had stuffed some things into a bag. When she came back through the kitchen, she saw Doyle on his hands and knees next to the hot water heater.

She bent over and looked at him. "What are you doing?" she asked.

"Setting the thermostat to vacation. It'll save energy and make it less likely to leak."

She stood looking at him for a very long time, and then said, "Okay, do it."

Then they were on the road, heading west.

"That is a lot of stars," Doyle said.

"It's clear and dry out here. We're a million miles away from anything."

AT THE TABLE INSIDE BURGER King, the girl surprised everyone by taking out a stack of cash and pulling off a rubber band. She counted out ten one-hundred-dollar bills and fanned the money out on the table. She re-banded the stack and returned it to the bag, which was full of similar stacks.

Doyle could see that CJ noticed this and it made her eyebrows furrow. The boyfriend stood behind her with his arms folded. His physique was remarkable.

"This is complicated. We have insurance," she said. "We just can't use it right now. We've got people looking for us."

"Cops?" Doyle asked.

"It doesn't matter who it is."

"Course it does."

"Look, we didn't kill anybody."

Doyle slipped CJ a look, but she wasn't responding.

"You're probably star-crossed lovers, right?" Doyle said. CJ looked up at him for a moment, and a look moved upon her face that Doyle might have noticed if they were close. She breathed out more deeply than normal and held it. "Your parents are probably feuding. You got together against their wishes, and now they've got private detectives on your trail."

"You don't have to be disrespectful right now, sir," the girlfriend said. "I'm trying to give you a thousand dollars."

"Hush money?"

"Jeez, mister. There's like nothing wrong with your car. Can't you just walk away from this? Can't you just let us go? If you call the cops or your insurance people or anything like that, then it's over for me and him, and for my little sister. She'll end up in the system, and she didn't do anything to deserve that. I wish I could just tell you what's going on, but I can't."

"Then I'm not going to sign off on this."

"Doyle, can I talk to you for a minute?" CJ leaned over the table and scooped up the money, tapped it square, and handed it to the girl. "Come with me, please," CJ said, her voice tight and slightly uncertain. Again, this was not something Doyle picked up.

CJ CROSSED THE RESTAURANT AND sat down with Doyle at an uncomfortable table underneath a television. The server had her eye on the both of them.

"What was that all about?" CJ asked.

"They smashed into my car."

"This has nothing to do with your car. I understand that you're mad at me about everything. You know what, you should be. But if you're mad at me, don't take it out on them."

Doyle hung his head.

"I really do wish I could be in love with you, Doyle. After the last few years of my life, I could stand a little consistency. I'm glad I could help you make a scene at your dad's wedding. I'm glad we could spend a few months living day to day. I think I needed this fling as much as you did, but these kids need your help. They're honest. You can see it in their eyes. They're really in love, and they are really scared. I don't think you want bad karma around your neck right now. This is your chance to change something in the universe."

"Why do you *wish* you could be in love with me?"

"Because I'm a mess and you're not. I never told you this, but that Doc guy, the one who's buried in the backyard of that house, I married him so he could stick it to his kids. He arranged to pay me a million and a half dollars to marry him and jam up his estate. I met with his lawyer, and they worked everything out. He would change his will to lock them out and include me. The kids would contest the will, the probate proceedings would take forever, and if I'd just wait (he'd make sure I had some place to live) then I'd be paid through some offshore account, and I could ride off into the sunset."

"But?" Doyle asked.

"But there hasn't been any money. Everything's frozen. All I've got is a couple of bucks. I'm sure when I get back, the utilities will be off at the house. I've got nothing, Doyle. Nothing."

"So, I was better than nothing," Doyle said, resigned.

"You were a lot better than nothing," CJ answered. "But I don't want you to think this is something it isn't. It's not fair to you."

Doyle sighed and looked into the distance. "Well, after all this, I've got nothing, too."

THEIR ARRIVAL AT THE WEDDING had been a shock. As Doyle replayed it, he could see with absolute clarity how it would have seemed to everybody that he'd brought a prostitute as a date to his father's wedding. He knew nothing about her. She had to introduce herself. As his relatives asked him questions, he found himself making up answers and CJ would reply with distinctly different ones. By the end of the rehearsal dinner, Doyle was drunk and toasting his dead mother and his father's two other wives. CJ and his cousin had to drive him to the motel and put him to sleep on a layer of towels. As the room spun, Doyle thought he saw his cousin kissing CJ. He tried to throw the alarm clock at them, but the cord stopped the missile short, and it dropped to the ground. And then he passed out.

DOYLE BRACED HIMSELF AGAINST THE table and rose. "You're right," he said, then he walked off without saying anything else. He went straight to where the boyfriend and girlfriend were talking. He leaned over the table and said, "Give me the money."

The girl looked bewildered and slid it over to him. Doyle picked up the cash and sat down. "Here's what we're going to do. I don't know who's after you two, but if you try to go anywhere in that car, you're nailed. The color of the paint alone is going to make it so they can spot you from space with a good set of binoculars. So, we're going to trade cars."

"What?" the boyfriend asked.

"Trade. You get your title, I'll get mine. We'll write up a bill of sale. You give me a buck. I give you a buck, and then you head to Mexico or wherever you're going in my car. I head east in yours. It's not going to fool them, but it'll get you enough time to get across the border. You both have passports?"

They shook their heads.

"Then, hell, I don't know. Go to Idaho."

The girlfriend looked her boyfriend in the eye and said that she thought this was a good idea.

"But I love that car," he said.

"But if you love me, you'll disappear," she told him. "I left everything to do this with you. We just need an edge, and this could be it. How long do you think your dad can keep the police off your back? How long before they piece all of this together? We might have the rest of today and that's it."

The boyfriend agreed, and they proceeded to swap cars and titles. It took a little less than twenty minutes, and the other two were driving off in Doyle's Nissan. As they disappeared up the frontage road, Doyle tensed to keep himself from sobbing. When CJ touched him on the shoulder, he pulled away and went to the other car. He checked through it and pulled his suitcase from the trunk, put a few things from the console and glove box into the suitcase, and zipped it closed. He pulled the handle into place and wheeled up to CJ and handed her the keys.

"What are you doing?" she asked.

"I took two hundred of that cash. The other eight hundred is in the glove box." He jingled the keys. "Here, the car is yours. I put your name on the bill of sale."

"My name?" she asked.

"Charlene Joelle Banks," he said.

"How did you? I never told you my full name."

"I know. That night in Ojai, I got into your purse."

CJ was furious, but she kept quiet.

"The money's yours. The car is yours. I never want to see you again. Good luck."

CJ tried to say something, but her voice was dry. Her legs were paralyzed. Doyle took his suitcase and pulled a blue baseball cap onto his head, and he walked across the parking lot with his suitcase wheeling behind. As Doyle grew smaller, CJ felt her heart shrink. She felt that in one version of this movie, she'd run after him and they'd embrace, with the cars zinging past on the interstate above them. In another version, she'd drive two hours back to the house and discover that Doc's lawyers had come through. With a million and a half dollars, plus eight hundred, she could buy a car, drive it to Texas, and leave it in front of Doyle's place with a note inside thanking him for everything. In yet another version, she'd drive off in the orange Honda, and a state trooper would pull her over because her vehicle matched the description of a vehicle used in a crime in Oklahoma. She would be detained and questioned and held overnight. The car would be impounded, and she would be back to nothing.

By the time CJ had run these scenarios, Doyle was out of sight.

CJ crouched on the sidewalk and wept. The white sunlight spun and pulsed as she did so. Across the parking lot, two crows landed on the rim of a dumpster. One of them seemed to be watching CJ, while the other shook a paper bag until it ripped and spilled open. Together, they gorged themselves on the spoils.

Without knowing how or why, CJ thought about a scripture she learned years ago at Bible camp. It said to behold the fowls of the air. They do not sow or reap, or gather into barns. How much better are ye than they?

She stood, looked around in every direction, counted her money, then pocketed it. She pulled her bag out of the orange monstrosity those kids left behind and went back into the Burger King to see about the job.

ACKNOWLEDGMENTS

Thanks to Nat Sobel, Jack Shoemaker, and Megan Fishmann for helping bring this book to life. I also can't say enough about Nicole Caputo's design work, which is out of this world. Thanks also to Siobhan McBride, Adia Wright, Jenny Alton, Wah-Ming Chang, Jordan Koluch, Dallin Jay Bundy, Mary Einfeldt, and everyone else in the back line for their invisible work.

I could not have written huge sections of this book without the help of Amber McConnell, who walked me through the mysterious chemistry of old meth recipes. We should all be glad she's not evil. Thanks to Karston Reed, my good friend and realtor, without whom I would know nothing about foreclosure auctions and how real estate "really works." And finally, thanks to Kyle Bishop for making me stay on target. He's a zombie literature scholar, so he knows how to keep going.

Please allow me to offer my sincerest apologies to Alisa Mitchell Petersen. She will never get the chance to just read this book without spoilers, because I always drag her into these projects from the start, talking her ear off. You should thank her for all the times she said, "No. Do not do that, Todd. It will be stupid."

Finally, I want to thank Zoë, Ike, and Max, the three little ones who grew up alongside this book. They are the coolest people I know.

TODD ROBERT PETERSEN lives in Cedar City, Utah, with his wife and three children. He is a professor of English and the director of Southern Utah University's project-based learning program. His recent academic work focuses on film and television.